A
FIRM
STATE OF
HEART

**CALUMET
EDITIONS**
Minneapolis

First Calumet Edition March 2024
A Firm State of Heart © 2024 by Bob Gilbert.
All rights reserved.

This is a work of fiction. All of the characters, names, incidents, organizations, and dialogue are either the products of the author's imagination or are used fictitiously.

10 9 8 7 6 5 4 3 2 1

ISBN: 978-1-962834-08-7

Cover and book design by Gary Lindberg

A FIRM STATE OF HEART

BOB GILBERT

**CALUMET
EDITIONS**

Minneapolis

For four brothers:

Bruce Mark Ackerman
John Britton
Habib "Carlos" Kuncar
James Earl Copley

CHAPTER 1

In Washington, DC, humiliation is a predicament of equal opportunity. It doles itself out in a democratic fashion to big and small, to each and all. Tonight, it was my turn.

We turned off the music a half hour ago. The lights were dimmed, the doors were locked and the stools were on top of the bar. The waiters, bartenders, cooks, dishwashers and busboys were out the door. Apart from Ron Robbins, the manager doing bookwork in the backroom office, only I remained.

It was 11:15 in the evening. I was waiting for the two-top sitting at table 54, a very private booth gilded in mahogany, to pay their tab and leave.

But the couple wasn't going anywhere. The venom spewing between them was now entering its fourth hour. Lost in their own quarrel, they were oblivious to the fact that they were the only customers remaining. And I was in limbo, waiting for them to realize it.

Everything was good when I dressed in my black tie, white jacket, and apron and prepared for dinner service. After working months of lunches, I finally earned my right to work the more lucrative nights at Tadich Grill. The pace was slower, the check average higher, and the tips were better. Tonight was my first dinner shift.

Located at Tenth and Pennsylvania Avenue Northwest, Tadich Grill is an elegant place of green glass, inlaid tile floors and dark wooden panels. It is an offshoot of Tadich Grill in San Francisco, the third-oldest restaurant in America. It recently opened this DC branch.

Located midway between the US Capitol Building and the White House, people liked to call this section of Pennsylvania Avenue "America's Main Street." It's the city's number one parade route where civic holidays are celebrated and the loyal opposition demonstrated. On a smaller grid, Tadich is located on what some of the staff referred to as "the evil vortex." It's smack-dab between two DC institutions that currently hate each other.

The J. Edgar Hoover Building of the Federal Bureau of Investigation is situated next door. Catty-corner and across the street is the Trump International Hotel. If you drew a line from the center of the FBI building and connected it to the center of the Old Post Office Building (which is now the hotel with the president's name on it), the line would go right through our dining room.

FBI and justice department officials are regulars. So is the president's cabinet. Arriving in DC to work for the executive branch, many of them reside at this hotel while searching for homes of their own.

Tadich is well managed by Robbins, a Bronx Jew in his early sixties whose accent sounded just like my father's. As an older man, I considered him a good role model. Tall, dignified, and bespectacled, he took me under his wing and coached me into being a better waiter. I had to up my game because, age-wise, most of the staff were in their forties, fifties, and even sixties, while I was the youngest waiter there, still in my twenties. They'd been lifers in the restaurant business, and many knew one another from working together at other DC dinner houses.

As the FNG ("the fucking new guy"), I was still navigating the subtle points of service. Dinner was a bit more complicated than lunch. I had to ask for help from fellow staffers when ringing in special orders on the computer and seek their recommendations regarding the wine list.

At tonight's pre-shift meeting, there were five waiters. Besides me, there was a sixty-one-year-old Iranian waiter named Khalid. He was a real hustler, smart, energetic, and professional. He was probably the hardest worker there.

When I was hired, Robbins told me to use Khalid as my role model. Tall, lean, and handsome with silver hair, he was called "the General" since his father had once been an Iranian general in Shah Mohammed Reza Pahlavi's army before he was overthrown by zealots of Ayatollah Khomeini, forcing Khalid's family into exile back in the 1970s.

Chico Gardner, fifty-five, was from Chile. His grandfather emigrated there from England. Even though he was born and raised in Santiago, the heavy-set, bespectacled man spoke perfect English and looked and acted more like a Londoner than a South American.

Harold Lamb was a forty-four-year-old former University of Florida wide receiver. He was tall and thick with a shaved head. He, like the others, was a former restaurant manager who gave up the long hours and responsibility in order to run around the restaurant, make the big money and dash out the door.

Leon McFadden was a fifty-six-year-old African American from South Carolina. His charm was the result of his good looks, bigheartedness and sense of humor. He had a wife and six kids. He drank vodka on the job but never got caught because he held his liquor so well.

Leon and I worked a lunch banquet together in the private dining when I first started. It was at a five-thousand-dollar-per-person fundraiser for a US senator from Missouri. He was great to partner with since he knew the wine list by heart and recommended expensive vintages to the banquet host. Later, when he offered me a ride home, I accepted.

"Here," he said, handing me a brown paper bag, "stick this in your backpack for me and meet me out front. I'll go get the car from the parking garage."

I didn't think much of it. But when I swung my backpack onto my shoulder, I realized the bag contained two bottles of Napa Valley cabernet left over from the banquet that the host paid for, and I helped him steal.

At tonight's pre-shift meeting, Leon greeted me with the line, "Hey, look, the kid finally made the big leagues."

"Kid? Who you calling kid, old man?"

"Sonny boy, we were waiting tables when the better part of you was dripping down your daddy's leg," he said. Khalid, Harold, and Chico laughed.

"Yeah, but that was some strong-ass sperm," I said, "and the two legs he bequeathed me can run circles around you."

Certainly, at twenty-nine, I was the youngest waiter there. But despite my junior status in the company of these seasoned pros, there were lunch shifts where my sales and speed surpassed theirs, especially on those sunny days when the outdoor patio tables were seated on Pennsylvania Avenue.

Chef Sarah Smith, a tall, thin blonde with an Ivy League education, showed us tonight's special. It was sautéed rockfish with a lemon caper sauce. "We're charging twenty-four dollars and ninety-five cents for the fish," she said. "There's an add-on button programmed on the computer. For an extra eight dollars, you can get it with lump crab meat." She handed out six forks and returned to the kitchen. We all got to taste it.

Ron warned us about the early evening rush that would happen at 6:30. Some of the guests were attending a concert at the nearby Warner Theater at 8:00 p.m. He wanted to make sure they all finished dinner with enough time to make the performance. "Tonight is Samuel's first dinner shift on the floor," he said. "I need all you guys to keep an eye on him to make sure he doesn't run into any problems."

"We got his back," said the General.

"Samuel, do yourself a favor," Harold said. "Try not to stare at your female customers when they're wearing low-cut dresses. It's unprofessional."

Leon laughed out loud. "Oh, you must mean table 22 last night when he was training. You saw those boobs, and you froze like a deer in the headlights."

"Was it that obvious?" I asked.

"Totally, dude."

"When was the last time you got laid?" asked Harold. I dismissed his question with a wave of my left hand.

"She caught me off guard."

"Next time, try not to swoon," Harold said.

"Women don't dress like that at lunch," I said.

"That's true," said Ron.

"I was running food for the table. I walked up from behind her, and when I finally got a look at her from the front… well, it startled me."

"I heard you gasp from across the dining room," Chico said. "However, in your defense, I got the feeling that those breasts were brand-new, and last night was their coming-out party."

"Her husband was uncomfortable with how much she was revealing," Harold said. "But, Samuel, your response didn't help things."

"Hey, I'm sorry, Harold. I didn't mean any disrespect. But holy cow, that was provocative."

"He wasn't the only one," said the General. "The whole restaurant was watching."

"What should I have done instead?" I asked. "I mean no disrespect to you guys, but I'm still young, and my libido overpowers me at times. What's the correct response to something like that?"

"You don't want to embarrass her or yourself. Show some self-control and pretend they're not there," said the General.

5

Leon disagreed. "If a woman didn't want you to look, she wouldn't be showing off. It's not your fault you're standing, and she's sitting."

"Oh, Sam, they're just girls," Chico said.

"No, man, they're way more than that," I said.

"How can women complain about 'Me Too' issues and then dress like that?" asked the General. "If women want men to behave better, they shouldn't be provoking lust like that."

"Like everything else, women don't speak with one voice," I said.

"Look, kid, nothing's ever going to replace the inevitable battle of the sexes," Leon said. "Men are still men, and women are still women. That's never going away regardless of what political correctness currently dictates."

Robbins had the last word. "Let's all try to avoid that situation. Keep your heads up. If you get caught staring, my advice is to raise your head, make eye contact and smile."

"That makes sense. Thanks," I said.

With that, the small group went to their sections to prepare for dinner. I polished the silverware and the wineglasses. The silverware must align in perfect form. The wineglass is just above the spoon. It's an expensive restaurant to eat at, so management sets high standards right down to the minutest detail.

Since political big shots come in regularly, I get to meet and interact with individuals of consequence in the nation's capital, including congressmen, senators, media personalities, cabinet members, and lobbyists.

Waiters are privy to the private lives of public figures. Part of our professionalism is about discretion and a dignified response to these players while eavesdropping on their private conversations. For it is at salons like Tadich, away from the prying eyes of reporters, that much of the work of government is done. Especially now, in the contentious era of Donald Trump.

Capitol Hill lawmakers sit in our private booths and craft legislation on yellow legal pads while their Secret Service escorts watch their backs from nearby tables.

There's a word in ancient Greek literature that sums up this culture. The word is *kleos*. It refers to the pursuit of fame, renown, and personal glory.

There's nothing wrong with seeking merit. It's the city's cottage industry on both sides of the political aisle. Men and women arrive in DC to rise above their stations, to leapfrog their dismal rural, small-town, suburban and inner-city existences in pursuit of the same glory as the heroic men personified in stone and bronze stationed in the city's public spaces.

On the floors above the restaurant are the offices of the Carlyle Group, the largest private equity firm in the world. Over the years, their board of directors included CIA directors, cabinet members, and former presidents like George H. W. Bush.

The hedge fund invests in the defense industry and profits from war. It's alleged that Osama bin Laden's brother was meeting upstairs with Carlyle executives on September 11, 2001.

David Rubenstein, one of DC's richest men, is a founding partner. He dines at Tadich for lunch. Since my great-grandfather was also a Rubenstein, I thought to mention that fact to him. But he is a gruff individual, and during the times I've waited on him, the opportunity never presented itself. To his credit, the plutocrat donated ten million dollars to repair the Washington Monument after a DC earthquake damaged it in 2011.

Most often, however, it's the tourists from around the world taking a break from their sightseeing that I enjoy most. Their candid opinions of the city and its culture are honest, spontaneous and unfiltered.

I was a reporter for my Minnesota hometown newspaper before moving to DC. As such, I tend to ask a lot of questions and still myself in order to listen to their replies. Quite often, their answers stay with me. By opening my mind and my heart, I glean new ideas, opinions, impressions and thoughts from what I am told. It goes a long way in informing my emerging worldview. In opening myself like this, human truths are confirmed, altered and repealed. That's why, in addition to being physical, waiting tables is also an intellectual endeavor.

My first four tables of the night were all on their way to the Warner Theater, and I had them on pace to be at the show on time. The second wave at 8:00 p.m. put Shayla Reeve, the news anchor on the local NBC affiliate, in my section, and my night descended into chaos.

She laughed and batted her eyelashes when I went to the table to get a drink order. She seemed as delightful as she was on TV. It was fun to chat her up while she waited for her dinner companion.

She was fair with blue eyes, big white teeth, a creamy complexion and long blond hair that hung upon her shoulders. She was in her forties. Sitting in that booth, she possessed the same emotional presence as she did on TV.

She wore a black skirt and a pale blue Mexican-style top that matched her eyes. The elastic in its sleeves could easily be pushed down the shoulder to show more cleavage when the occasion called for it.

It wasn't her first time at Tadich Grill, but it was her first time in my section. She asked about the Cioppino, our signature fish dish, and ordered a glass of cabernet while she waited. "Can you bring me some of your sourdough bread while I wait?"

"Certainly," I said.

Shayla's date arrived a few minutes later. He sat facing her, directly across the table, eye to eye in the large booth separated from the others by walls that almost reached the ceiling. Like her, he was in his forties. He was tall and professional-looking, with stylish eyewear, an expensive suit and a fresh haircut. After consuming her second glass of wine, something unexpected happened: Shayla showed her shadow.

The broadcaster, so pretty, so self-assured on the six o'clock news, started an argument. I wasn't sure if he was her boyfriend, her agent or her lawyer. He might have been all three. I brought her another glass of wine and him a Tito's and soda.

In the first salvo shot across the tabletop, she hollered, "One word from me, and you do as you goddamn please."

"What are you talking about?" he protested.

"You know very well what I'm talking about. You stood by and let him talk to me that way, and you did nothing. Nothing! You're not a man. You're a mouse."

There, in the midst of a crowded restaurant among dozens of patrons eating, drinking, feasting, laughing, seducing, and pontificating, her malcontent voice rang out. In the course of the evening, every imbroglio, peccadillo, wrong move, wrong word he ever uttered was thrown in his face. My muscles tensed up every time I went to the table as fresh complaints poured from her lips. It was as great a dressing down as I'd ever seen one man take.

Was he so deeply in love with her that this was the price he paid? Was he under contract so that such a tongue-lashing was part of his job description? With the exception of a few chirps of innocence, he took all of it.

A young woman dining with her husband flagged me down. "Excuse me. It's our fifth wedding anniversary. We don't want to listen to this. Can we please move to another table?"

"Yes, ma'am, I'll return with the hostess immediately," I said. They were given another table far away from my station. The booth was so private that Reeve and her companion thought no one could hear. But everyone could hear. A second party asked to move a few minutes later.

She was ruining my debut, and I started to hate her for it. But that's what happens when you're a waiter. You accept your woe and wait it out. Especially here in DC, where so many customers are stressed out, Type-A personalities with big jobs and anxiety issues.

Harold, who had the station nearest to mine, warned me. "She has two hundred thousand Twitter followers. Stay on her good side, or she might write bad shit about you online and get you fired."

"You're kidding, right?"

"No. It's happened before."

Shayla spit flashes of fire about Stacey, his secretary, possibly his lover, the toilet seat he never put down and the papers from his open briefcase that were strewn all over the living room. "Were it not for men like you, women like me would be running things and doing a hell of a lot better job of it, too!"

She was the big breadwinner and the important one in the relationship, the one in front of the camera who bore up to the pressure and the limelight. Her continued success was what mattered most. She made sure he understood that.

The booth was on the restroom route. Customers walking by stole quick glances, curious to see who it was. With smirks and snickers, each came away with wide-open eyes and expressions of astonishment for the insider gossip that was now theirs.

A pretty woman in her thirties and out for the night with her husband and another couple walked by the table and recognized Shayla. From her expression, I believe her first impulse was to ask for her autograph. But when she realized a battle was raging, a mischievous smile came to her face. She returned to her friends. Bending down, she whispered into the other woman's ear. The message was conveyed perfectly. Her friend grabbed her smartphone and started for the table. I think she wanted a snapshot of Reeve with her fangs out.

I figured out their intentions and intercepted them. "Please don't do that," I implored. "I could lose my job over this, please."

They remembered themselves and sheepishly retreated. Had they snapped that picture of Shayla and put it on the internet, it would have gone viral. And they'd have been stars for capturing such a rich, scandalous moment.

But the last thing I needed was an anchor from a local news affiliate holding a grudge against Tadich Grill and perhaps me, personally. I had this terrible notion that next week she might do an on-air feature story about bad waiters and hold me up as its poster child.

No TV makeup artist could hide the redness of her complexion. Reeve, so welcome into the homes of hundreds of thousands of Washingtonians who listened attentively to her measured words, was not acting now. This was the real her. The harangue continued while I refilled her water glass. "You just better realize the dynamics of this situation, or you're done," she said.

With a sudden jerk of his hand, her date accidentally knocked over his water glass. It spilled in her direction. It might have been a deliberate slip, an effort to water down her fire. "Clumsy oaf!" she shouted.

I picked up the glass and refilled it. "I'll get a napkin to soak it up."

"Don't bother," she said and threw her own on top of the puddle.

Her wineglass was nearly empty. She just finished her third. There was no way she was getting a fourth. I never did have a poker face. When she noticed my disapproval, she snapped at me. "What's your problem?"

"I'm not used to having my customers make public spectacles of themselves," I said.

"Would you rather have me do this at home where he can beat me up?"

"Wait a minute," he protested.

"Oh, so now you're going to deny it?" Staring at me, she abruptly brushed her sleeve off her shoulder. Her bra strap followed the motion, and her breast popped out of its C cup. It lay there in plain sight. "Look at this," she shrieked. Above the breast was a blue bruise. "Well, what do you think of that?"

It was a deliberate provocation. She seemed intent on humiliating him and using me as her foil. I gave it a good, hard look. I raised my head and looked her in the eye. "It's big," I said. But I didn't smile.

His fork was in his left hand, and the bruise was on her left shoulder. If it was a left hook, it just missed her chin.

"For God's sake, cover up!" he shouted.

She did and then grabbed his wrist, sinking her fingernails into it. He jerked it away.

"Oh, look at you," he said. "The terrible tyrant of office politics who stirs up all kinds of mischief but ultimately can't shoulder the stress of the nonsense she herself creates."

Furious, I went to Robbins to inform him about what was going on. "You need to throw them out."

He was circumspect. "I need you to stay professional here."

"Me stay professional? What about her?"

"Stay on her track, not yours. Don't make it about you," Robbins said. "We won't be sitting anyone else in your section tonight. Go home early. Come back fresh. I'll make it up to you tomorrow."

Dejected, knowing that my first dinner shift was a disaster, I walked away.

I cleared the dinner plates from my other table. They were a gay couple, two African American women in their thirties. Their hands were touching. Their conversation was whispered. How calm, how centered, how trusting, how in love they seemed and oblivious to the discord just feet away. "Of course, we want to look at the dessert menu," they said in unison.

I think they enjoyed the spectacle of the privileged White couple engaged in an internecine campaign to ruin each other. It made their own love real, and they adored it. More than once, I watched them wince at the unkind words issuing from Shayla's lips and giggle at their own good luck with love.

Whenever Reeve got too loud, I went over to refill her water glass, hoping that my presence would distract her. But it didn't. "It's hot as hell in here," she shouted. "Turn up the damn air conditioning."

Harold, who thought the spectacle was comical, was now angry because his table asked for the check before they ordered dinner, claiming that Shayla ruined their appetite.

"What the hell is going on?" he shouted.

"Feel free to go over there and reprimand her," I answered.

"Those fucking assholes. Is this the kind of energy you bring to the dining room, Sam?"

The man finished his steak. He looked at Shayla's uneaten entrée. "For God's sake, shut the hell up and eat your dinner already."

When she started to fire back, he held up his steak knife as if he were going to cut her. I was standing right in his line of vision, and spontaneously, I grabbed a knife off Harold's empty table and took two steps forward. The guy saw me, hesitated and lowered the serrated edge.

I thought to myself, *Sam, what are you, an idiot? Are you really going to threaten him with a butter knife?*

Now it was the man's turn to shout. I didn't want to hear a word of it. Humiliated by the fact that I was sinking down to their level, I walked away.

Standing at the bar, with a martini in front of him, was one of my favorite customers, a Lithuanian diplomat named Johan Gimbutus. He had a suave Old World European charm I recognized from old movies. I waited on him a few weeks ago with two of his young aides, Mara and Lukas. We had a fabulous conversation.

My paternal grandfather, a Lithuanian Jew, lived in Vilnius in 1939. He escaped the murderous arms of the Nazis by escaping to the forest. He became one of the Vilnius partisans, a Jewish guerilla band who fought back. When I told Gimbutus my grandfather's story, he took an interest in me.

It was flattering to have an older, distinguished man commenting on my family's history. Because table 54 was still arguing and I was no longer being seated, I welcomed the conversation.

"Back when your grandfather was a Litvak, which means a Lithuanian Jew, Vilnius was a wonderful, multicultural city," Gimbutus said. "It had Lithuanians, Jews, Germans, Russians, Poles and ten percent of the city was Italian."

"I once heard him call it the Jerusalem of the North."

"The Jews once had a large presence in Vilnius, our cosmopolitan capital," he said. "It was a center of great learning filled with yeshivas, synagogues, and Jewish cemeteries. Then the Nazis came in and decimated the entire culture. Currently, our government is going to great lengths to recognize the historical presence of the Litvaks of Lithuania, including the renovation of the great synagogue of Vilnius."

"I'd like to visit it one day."

"You'd love it. I'd compare the Baltic states to America's New England area. It's educated, historical and enlightened."

"Are there any museums commemorating Jewish culture there?"

"I'm afraid not. The Nazis destroyed all the traces of it. Later, when the Soviets took over, they never mentioned the Holocaust. All their references were about the collective victims of fascism."

"That's unfortunate."

"Yes, regrettably, the KGB still impacts the Lithuanian consciousness," he said. "There's a self-censorship that Lithuanian intellectuals are still trying to rise above."

"I've never heard that expression used before. What do you mean, 'self-censorship'?"

"Since censorship is so abundant in Eastern Europe, people are hesitant to even explore their own personal truths. They shutter their minds because if they speak out, they might get in trouble."

"In a digital age, I find that surprising."

"Unfortunately, it's true. I'm old-school and a product of that same small-minded environment," Gimbutus said. "I suppose that's why my young staff was so impressed by you when you served us last week. They marveled at your wide knowledge and conviction."

"My grandfather thought a strong intellect was the true measure of a man," I said.

"In Eastern Europe, cynicism is the true measure of a man."

"That can't be good."

"It is what it is," he said.

"You know, I've never been satisfied with that response. Of course, 'it is what it is,' but it's incumbent upon a man to search for the meaning of it all. Otherwise, it's just an expression of intellectual laziness."

He considered my words, nodded his head, and changed the subject. "I'd imagine that working here, you must see a lot."

"I pick up information now and then," I said. "I'm like a sponge, unassuming in my duties but able to soak up twice my weight."

"What kind of things do you see?"

"Last week, I saw an angry FBI agent rail to his peers about the new attorney general who shut down his eight-month investigation after the alleged corporate felon gave a million-dollar donation to the president's reelection campaign."

"That's just like Eastern Europe," he said.

"Plus, I knew the president wouldn't be able to repeal the Affordable Care Act two days before the Senate roll call because I heard the majority leader say he didn't have the votes."

"Perhaps you'll make a great spy one day," he said.

"I'm not good at keeping secrets."

He laughed. "Let me buy you lunch sometime. I'd like to pick your millennial brain about what young people your age think about this world."

"I'd like that," I said.

"Next time we meet, we'll set up a date," he said. "Now, you'll have to excuse me. I have a date at the hotel across the street."

"Say hello to Lukas for me," I said. "I enjoyed meeting him last week when he came in for dinner with you."

"I will." We shook hands, and he left the restaurant. Gimbutus got me thinking about how, of all the diplomats stationed in Washington, DC, American and foreign, few are as skillful as the city's waiters, who must gracefully navigate awkward situations to earn their tip.

Within the social hierarchy, I was pretty low on the food chain. But considering the required grace and decorum of a DC waiter, I felt as if I, too, was a member of the diplomatic corps.

My remaining tables were gone by 9:30. Until Reeve ran out of venom, I was her hostage. Robbins checked my impulse to tell them to leave. "We're in the hospitality business," he said. "That's why you're called a waiter. You have to wait."

"It's not fair," I said.

"It's just another DC meltdown played out publicly," he said. "It happens all the time. I remember when I was managing the restaurant at the Jefferson Hotel a few years ago. The wife of a congressman surprised her husband and his mistress in the dining room. They were eating bone-in rib eyes. The wife grabbed the rib eye by the bone and started beating the mistress with it. Au jus was all over everything. When the mistress finally wrestled her meat back, the wife started ripping off her clothes."

"What did you do?" I asked.

"I had two of my female servers drag the wife away to the bar. We gave her a few shots of vodka to calm her down."

"Did you call the cops?" I asked.

"Are you out of your mind?"

"No, I suppose you couldn't do that, could you?"

"The mistress begged me not to. I think the wife wanted us to call the cops just to cause her husband a scandal. But of course, we didn't."

"Okay, I get it, Ron."

"I'm sorry, Sam. You just got to wait this out."

So, I waited. There's nothing worse than a waiter stuck in neutral. During a busy dining room rush, all my energy is renewed. My imaginative strength, range, dignity of thought and feeling are supercharged by the physical demands put upon my body. Performance in the midst of great stress is everything.

And there's a karma involved, which you constantly work to master. For instance, if I'm in a bad mood, chances are the people who find their way into my section that night will also be in a bad mood. Like attracts like. Keeping my demons at bay is part of my formula for success. I wasn't interested in that steel-eyed, square-jawed, self-important DC look. A smile was good enough for me. It singled me out as normal. Plus, I make better tips when I'm happy.

I cleaned the espresso machine and folded one hundred napkins. But I couldn't run my report because their unpaid check was sitting at the edge of the table in a black book. It was waiting for a credit card. In the stillness of the dining room, her voice, while losing some of its intensity, still had things to say.

I walked to the host stand to see if their reservation was on the computer. There it was, table 54, reserved for two under the name Phillip Talbot. I reached for my cell phone and googled him. He was a partner in a big-shot DC law firm. He had to be rich since he'd been there for fifteen years. His area of expertise was corporate mergers.

His phone number was listed on the reservation. I got this idea that maybe I should send him a text. "Hey, sad sack, the restaurant's been closed for an hour. Take the shrew home. Sincerely, your waiter."

Robbins wouldn't like it. It would probably get me fired. I refrained.

With nothing to do but wait, I found a lit place in the darkened bar, removed my white jacket and the apron around my waist, and folded them on the stool beside me.

I grabbed a notebook out of my backpack and a pen from my pocket, wanting to make the most of my time. I changed gears and decided to write. And then, I considered what to put down inside the red-covered composition book that cost three bucks at the drugstore.

What I printed out first, of course, was this:

> In Washington, DC
> Humiliation is a predicament
> Of equal opportunity.
> It doles itself out in a democratic fashion
> To big and small, to each and all.
> Tonight, it was my turn.

Now, I didn't care how long their fight lasted. I was sublimating my anger into words and putting them onto the page.

The essence of my life can be summed up best with two letters of the alphabet, *A* and *R*. Those two letters are the second digit of an almost identical word: *waiter* and *writer*. Within those words are the component parts of my day.

In the course of my waiter's shift, I exercise, socialize and serve beautiful food. It demands that I engage the world: hosts, managers, cooks, waiters, dishwashers, busboys, bartenders, certainly my customers and everyone else who enters the restaurant.

Here, imagination is a liability, a distraction from the hand-eye-coordinated tasks that the job requires. Your speech, attention and body demand your full focus. It's not unusual to have ten thousand steps in the course of a single shift.

Contrary to that is the letter *R*. It stands for writer where I am solitary and cerebral. It's an introvert's world where I stoke my imagination and write out what it reveals. It's how I order, clarify, and deconstruct the spontaneous episodes at Tadich Grill.

I'm currently engaged in a literary project. It's a long poem entitled, *A Firm State of Heart*. The poem is slowly piecing itself together on the page. Solving the riddle of what's happening to America and articulating a new American myth are its goals. One relevant for the digital age, promoting an inclusive manifest destiny of multiculturalism, globalization and civil liberties.

In cultivating this poetic vision, I stand clear of any affiliation with a political party, religion, leader, nationality, clan, ethnic group, school of thought or economic theory. My sole allegiance is to my own imagination and the unseen forces guiding it. I let divinity reach for me unencumbered as I reach for it.

I had no interest in writing about politics. I wanted to write about the creation of literature, its processes, its expression, its meaning and the way to bring the American body politic into a better alignment.

My literary practice is not unlike the culinary practice of Chef Sarah. Pull a piece of pasta from a boiling pot. Throw it against the wall. If it sticks, it's good.

When interesting insights and ideas stick to me, I work them into my worldview. Just like those pasta strands. The undercooked pieces fall to the floor where the dishwasher, Manuel Ortiz, sweeps them up at the end of his shift and tosses them in the garbage.

How gracefully the two pursuits—waiter and writer—dovetail. After each shift, everything is written down. There's something about literary confession that makes life meaningful for me. I chronicle it and then let it go. For my personal agenda is not anchored to the DC macrocosm; it's moored to the microcosm of my literary life.

In my poem, you won't find the expression of an alienated soul searching for some inner meaning in a ruined world. Nor will you find me railing fire and brimstone against the times. I don't see the apocalypse. Nor am I looking for a higher innocence. I'm from too good a family to write tragedies or dirges with any convincing weight. Instead, I like to rub shoulders with the masses and open myself to their ways.

At Tadich Grill
I'm given an opportunity
To fuse realpolitik
With personal understanding
And place it in the context
Of something deeper
Than the shallow stream
Most individuals barefoot through

Poets, said Percy Shelley, are the hierophants of unapprehended inspiration. Thus, they are the unacknowledged legislators of the world. Okay, maybe not in the digital age. But Shelley dreamed it all in the early 1800s. Now, the dream must be renewed. I've taken it upon myself to do so.

I find my best material right here at Tadich, where my eyes witness DC drama firsthand, unfiltered by cameras, journalists or newscasters. I'm looking for the cosmic factors that move society and their relationship to emerging cultural expressions. And I am a valiant witness who listens carefully and is hawkeyed and intuitive regarding what deeper meaning might be gleaned from random incidents.

Looking up from my journal, I saw Shayla Reeve standing at the top of the three steps leading down to the bar. She was staring at me, didn't know for how long. Tonight, she made everybody around her miserable. Finished with Talbot, was she now coming for me?

The expression on her face was hard to figure. It was a combination of humiliation, rage, and exhaustion. She seemed to be seeking some sort of feedback.

What the hell! I had no idea what to make of her outburst. If she was looking for some sympathy, she wasn't going to get it from me. But there she was, unwilling to break eye contact until she got some sort of response. Finally, she wore me down. I raised my eyebrows and shrugged my shoulders.

An empty wineglass was clutched in her hand. I hadn't been to the table in twenty minutes, and she wanted more. Finally, she realized that they were the last customers in the restaurant. She laid the glass on a ledge and walked to the ladies' room.

Finally, I had enough. I planned my words and tone carefully, lest I catch the same hell as her beau. With Robbins's permission, I said, "Excuse me, folks, the restaurant is closed, and you are the last people here. I hate to rush you, but I'm afraid I'm going to miss the last train home. Can I trouble you to pay the check?"

They finally noticed the black book at the edge of the table. "Well, don't just sit there. Pay the man," she said.

Talbot threw down his gold card. I ran it at the computer station and returned it to the table. Standing inside their personal space, I waited for him to sign it. He left a big tip to placate the humiliation we both endured.

"Damn it," she said. "My phone battery is out of juice. Walk out to Pennsylvania Avenue and hail me a cab."

I looked her straight in the eye. "No."

After running my report, I brought it to the office. Out of sympathy, Robbins released me. "You can go," he said. "I'll reset the table."

"Thanks, boss." I shook his hand in gratitude and dashed out the door.

Crossing Pennsylvania Avenue, I looked at the clock tower atop the Trump Hotel. The last train pulled out of Federal Triangle Metro Station at 11:49 p.m. I had two minutes and ran the whole way.

CHAPTER 2

An automated voice called, "Doors closing," as I dashed onto the Metro train, and the two converging doors met in the middle behind me. I found an empty seat on the Blue Line train moving east.

I was really steaming and sat there reliving the indignity I suffered at the hands of the famous broadcaster and her hapless boyfriend. "Fuck! That was awful." Several people heard me say it.

Reeve's face was on billboards around DC, promoting her journalistic integrity. She was an oracle of informed opinion with high name recognition and a sunny disposition. No one saw the beast I suffered tonight.

I was on my way to a bar to meet my housemates. They were always eager to hear who I had seen and what was said in the course of my restaurant shift. Tonight, I had a horror story to tell.

Though the hour was late, the train was crowded. There were old people and young people. A diversity of Asians, Caucasians, African Americans, Arabs and Hispanics sat in close quarters. There were tourists too. One can always tell. They wear apparel advertising home. The two Kansas folks sitting behind me wore blue Jayhawk T-shirts. Metal train wheels over metal train tracks provided the soundtrack while our temporary community of commuters sat silent. There was no interaction, no acknowledged

23

sense of place, no laughter, no conversation in the brightly lit car. Almost everyone on board had one thing in common: their eyes were glued to their smartphones. Their attention was in cyberspace: Facebook, *The Washington Post*, Instagram, Tinder—anywhere but here in this train car whose last stop was Largo Town Center in Maryland.

A few years ago, to help sagging ridership, the Metro installed free internet service throughout its system. As a result, the back-and-forth between strangers was replaced by a library-like hush, lest you interrupt the digital focus of the men and women in transit. Had these commuters been paying attention, they'd have noticed the dark-haired woman across the aisle, facing me, in the seat beside the door.

If asked, I'd guess she was Italian, Greek, Indian, African, Hispanic or perhaps an American combination of all five since her skin color was cinnamon.

She was in her twenties and wore a small, shiny blue cocktail dress that stopped at her thighs. Black high-heeled shoes were on her feet. Her long black hair was up in a bun on this warm night. A gold chain hung around her neck with a red stone, perhaps a ruby. In some cultures, it symbolizes a love of God. She must have attended a formal event and was now on her way home, alone.

The dress had a plunging neckline, revealing an alluring line of cleavage. I've always been a sucker for vertical lines, especially on a woman's body. Doesn't matter if they're found on top or bottom, front or back. Those narrow canyons all lead to erotic places.

Her horizontal lines were as impressive. They manifest themselves in the shape of her lips spread across her face. Their width and length suggested a smile that was a natural event even when unintended. Two thick, coiffed eyebrows were beneath her hairline, which was parted on the side. Her wide-set, big brown eyes rested upon round cheekbones. There was a green tattoo on her wrist. She sat too far away from me to identify it.

I, too, was accustomed to coming home late at night by myself. Over the years, I've frequently worked nights in restaurants. While the majority of Washingtonians were at work doing their nine-to-five, I was home. At night, when they played, I worked. It cast a pall over my social life. How many times have I traveled home alone on a Friday night longing for company just like hers?

While I'm no stranger to Tinder hookups, sexual adventures would be more fun if I didn't have to do it with DC women. I prefer women from Minneapolis, my hometown. They are pretty, warm and sensuous. The majority of women I meet here in DC are ambitious, status-driven and focused on their careers. There's nothing wrong with that, except I'd rather not date them. It's a personal preference.

When our eyes met, I was startled. Perhaps she mistook the look on my face for passion. No, honey, it's anger. I'm pissed off at Shayla Reeve. She was still a bug up my ass, and I just wanted to push on it a while longer. It took me several minutes to recognize that this gal was way more captivating. And then I noticed something about her eyes: they were glistening. Was she holding back tears?

Afraid that she might cross her arms or legs and close herself off, I moved a bit left in my seat for an angle that put her reflection before my eyes in the glass window beside me. As the train sped through the dark subway tunnel, I admired her without showing my hand.

No enthusiasm rises higher than the prospect of love. Suddenly, I was enthralled by its potential. Our tacit romance consisted of a coy exchange of smiles. She seemed gratified that someone noticed her clad in her Friday night best. I sat watching as her head bobbed during a rough patch of track and then, as if she were on to me, she turned and caught sight of me staring at her mirrored image.

The windows in the well-lit car were like mirrors. Turning to her own window, she realized that her eye makeup was smudged. That was when she reached into her bag and pulled out a water bottle, a cell phone and her wallet, placing them on the seat beside her while searching for a box of tissues that was at the bottom. Finding them, she dabbed her eyes.

Then she reached up and undid her bun. Giving her head a strong shake, her thick black hair fell to her shoulders; another shake sent the strands down her back. And for just a second, the corners of her mouth turned down, revealing a look of vulnerability that punctured her imitation of Venus.

Here, in the nation's capital, where human hearts often wither, desire is still the greatest adventure. If it seemed as if we were the only two live souls on the train, it was because we were consumed with each other's persona and uninterested in the netherworld of our smartphones.

I'm not going to lie; I was smitten. Her face had an exquisite symmetry. I could have gone full-fledged troubadour, waxing poetic about the desire she inspired in me like some Provençal singer from the Middle Ages. I was no stranger to such moony longings. Not only did I know the landscape of idealized love, I knew the zip code too.

Perhaps she remembered herself as an object of desire. She rubbed her thighs back and forth with two hands. Slowly, she closed her eyes, lowered her gaze and tucked down her chin. She was like that for about five seconds. Then she raised her head, opened her brown eyes and stared right at me. Though the gesture seemed practiced, it was disarming. It was as if she had emerged from beneath the water's surface to the light of day as a different person, someone baptized, someone cleansed, someone confessedly as lonely as me.

Adjusting herself in the seat, she pointed her knees in my direction. Cupid was offering a romantic diversion following the exhausting interlude at table 54.

I always try to be obedient to what love tells me. Now, she had my full attention. The more I stared at her reflection, the less I cared about Shayla Reeve.

Her hair, her complexion, her face, her breasts, her skin color, her legs and her smile were wonderful. You could build a religion around such beauty. Codify it, and I'd be one of the faithful.

In Washington, DC, such women are a wonder, a relief from the terrestrial demands of living in this capital of pitched polemics where the vanity of human merit is well-hung and always on display. To stand outside of that DC storm and stress even for a few minutes, like right now, right here on this Metro car, in the sight of a woman noticing me and letting me notice her, was like the coming of dawn.

There's always a parade of beautiful women on a Metro train. They're there to be admired for their faces, their figures, and their physical grace. Some dress up just to ride, something they wouldn't do if they chose to walk down the sidewalk.

As I stared at her window reflection, I sent out a thin, green stalk from the left side of my chest and watched it inch its way toward her in a smooth motion. It looked like a beanstalk as it slid through space, unsupported by legs, defying gravity. It went over the seat in front of me and twisted itself once around the horizontal pole above me that people held on to when the car was packed. Then it reached down and attached itself to her fourth chakra. She let the psychic cord enter her. We were now pinned. I watched her chest expand and contract with each breath, and I synchronized mine with hers.

What it revealed was that she was pretty on the outside and pretty on the inside, too. Young and talented, perhaps she'd be the kind of woman who would avoid Shayla's contentious path.

We considered each other in a tacit, surreptitious manner, visually through the window's image and psychically via the thin green cord connecting us. I felt her heartbeat. It was expansive and looking for love. I sensed her sexuality, which was brimming. And though she was in search of love, she feared her desire might expose her to something baleful, so she was cautious.

"To the gentle heart, love always makes repair," wrote Dante. As the train rolled east toward Maryland, I felt as if there was no one else on that train but the two of us. Now I went searching my mind for that alchemy of the word, that magic abracadabra that might open her eyes, her mind, her heart, her mouth, her legs to what desire planted inside me.

A valiant voice from inside spoke, "Go talk to her. Find out her name and where she lives. Tell her about yourself and all your dreams."

I fantasized about bravely standing, sitting myself beside her on the seat and her welcoming my advance. It would have to be a brilliant presentation lest she recoil in embarrassment. For certainly, other passengers would be watching. How do you explain yourself to a stranger?

Here's what I might say, "Hello, my name is Samuel Taylor Meckler. I'm a twenty-nine-year-old single, straight male living on Capitol Hill…" No, no, no, that sounds like speed dating. Like most men my age, I feel more comfortable delivering such sentiments via email rather than in person.

Should I confess that my literary urges are so demanding that my other activities are often completed in a half-assed fashion? That so much time and attention is devoted to literature that the full expanse of my personality is often distracted? Probably not. But it's true that there's always a little bit of myself that holds back, a detachment that keeps my mind's eye aloof in order to focus on the demands of my poem.

Sometimes, it seems that I am pricing myself out of the local romantic market with literary values that do not conform to the DC mainstream's desire for career, power, income, and status. With me, imagination, not ambition, comes first.

My own uncertainty about courtship in America is indicative of the shaky ground between men and women in this "Me Too" age. Old rules no longer apply. Many of the men I admired in politics and the media were recently taken down over sexual abuse charges. The macho stance that men practiced and women once admired now seems like a pantomime perpetrated by cavemen. At present, the right way to address courtship and the inevitable battle of the sexes is lined with mushy boundaries.

I was reminded of the current ambiguity by the advertisement above her seat. It was a small billboard that pictured an attractive woman riding the train alone. It read, "If it's unwanted, it's harassment."

When the train stopped at Eastern Market station, she stood and waited for the door to open. That was when I noticed the arc of her spine. Her shoulders were wider than her hips. I got a closer look at her tattoo. It was a heart, solid green in color. On cold winter days, in warm clothes, it was situated beside her sleeve.

She stood waiting for the door to open. The green cord between us snapped when she left the car. Was she going to walk out without offering me a second glance? Was she going to deny the tacit connection we'd been sharing for the past five minutes?

I thought to bang on the window to get her attention. But as she passed my window, walking to the escalator, I caught her eye. She smiled as if to say, "Good night," and I smiled in return.

Looking back at her seat, I saw that she left her water bottle behind. The vessel was glass encased in thick pink plastic and was still half full. I walked to her seat, picked it up and shoved it in the outside webbing of my backpack.

CHAPTER 3

I've detailed how the letter *A*, as in waiter, appears in my life. Now I'll tell you a little bit more about the letter *R*, for writer.

In my home state of Minnesota, I began as a cub reporter writing feature articles for a small, twice-monthly Twin Cities newspaper called the *Highland Villager*. The neighborhoods it served hugged both banks of the Mississippi River—the Highland Park neighborhood in Saint Paul to the east and the Longfellow neighborhood of Minneapolis to the west.

It was a good start for a young graduate of the University of Minnesota with literary dreams. The *Villager* was a forty-page community newspaper, and it held fast to those values. I had two editors, older men, John and Dale, who lived in the neighborhood, attended church there and sent their children to its public schools. They liked me and coached me into a competent newspaper reporter.

The *Villager* avoided hyperbole, scandal and uproar in an effort to bring out the best in the people who lived in its distribution area. It didn't cover national politics, pop culture, murder or nonsense. Those stories were left for the big daily newspapers and the twenty-four-hour cable news networks. But it did promote an inclusive civic responsibility that its citizens respected.

Published every other Wednesday, the free paper appeared in street corner boxes and was stacked at coffee shops, liquor stores and retail outlets. It was delivered to the doors of neighborhood homes. Being that it focused on issues immediately at hand and was around for two-week stretches, people actually read it.

If any new neighborhood business opened, it got a mention. The workings of neighborhood councils and the mayor's office were detailed. The public schools were covered assiduously. Its hallmark was feature articles on its leading citizens. My editors gave me interesting assignments that were all close to home while tempering my youthful inclination to be a young smart-ass.

I brought a certain swag to the job because I spent my early years in New Jersey. Its street values and regional accent were still keen in me. The culture shock of living in the Twin Cities instead of the suburban Jersey town bordering New York City where I spent the first thirteen years of my life was deeply felt.

For me, Midwest folks were missing that taut bottom guitar string that hit the high notes. I vibrated at a higher decibel, perhaps from my East Coast interaction with different ethnic minorities, a higher population density and different weather. I was more intense than the more circumspect, slower-paced Minnesotans.

I was the education reporter at the *Villager* for two years. Then, one day, I got in trouble. When the publisher, Mike McCabe, who liked the positive stories I wrote about the Saint Paul schools, discovered my mother was the Saint Paul school's lobbyist at the state capitol, he was furious.

What made it worse was that he discovered that fact on the same day we had a late-night chance encounter at a Selby Avenue bar called "Fabulous Fern's." It was my third stop of the evening. McCabe had been drinking there all night.

"Hi, Mike. How are you?" I called. He came right at me and caught me off guard.

"You compromised the integrity of my paper by not disclosing your mother's job," he shouted.

"We're a community paper," I answered. "You taught me the ideals of community. Now you're claiming something else?"

"The *Villager* is not a shill for inept administrators and union hacks!" he shouted.

"If people lose faith in the schools, they'll flee the city and move to the suburbs. The city will lose its tax base and go right down the tubes. Is that what you want?"

"That's not the point," he shouted. "There are ethics involved here."

"It is the point."

When McCabe pulled his sweater over his head, he was not preparing for a fistfight. Adrenaline was surging in us both, and being that it was the dead of winter, he just wanted his arms free to express himself and better feel the rush.

By now, a small crowd had gathered. The bartender, not knowing how to react to this public spectacle, broke in when McCabe laid his sweater on the stool and said, "Mike, can I get you another beer?"

"Yes," McCabe shouted back, "and get him one too." Alcohol stoked our passion, and a spirited back-and-forth went on for another ten minutes. The fact that a local civic debate was emerging spontaneously in the bar diverted the eyes of the patrons, who, just minutes before, were tuned to the Minnesota Timberwolves game on the television.

"You had an ethical obligation to inform your editors that you had a conflict of interest when writing school stories, and you did not!"

Actually, I did inform my editors of my mother's position. But each time we spoke about how the Saint Paul schools, financed with state money my mother helped procure, were struggling to get the Hmong, Somali, African American and Mexican students acclimated to this new Upper Midwest culture and on their way

33

to citizenship, my editors urged me to go ahead and write it. But I didn't reveal that fact to McCabe because I didn't want to throw Dale and John under the bus.

"Test scores are declining, and the schools are in shambles," he said. "Why should I respect that?"

"That's because you have poor families moving into Saint Paul that can't even feed their kids. The schools have to provide breakfast and lunch, medical assistance, language and counseling services so one day they can grow up and pay for your social security."

"Let them go somewhere else," McCabe said. "Catholic Social Services and the Lutheran Brotherhood shouldn't be resettling these people here in the first place. Send them back to where they belong."

"Mike, the quaint days of Garrison Keillor's 'Lake Wobegone' are over in Minnesota. We're part of a globalized network now. And it's never going back to those halcyon days of innocence. Get used to it."

Had it happened in Jersey, f-bombs and fists might have flown. Despite our keening in on each other, neither of us crossed that line. After all, we were Minnesotans, a state where civility prevails. I believed what I believed, and he believed what he believed, and neither one of us budged.

Of course, he made it plain that as publisher, his money was on the line while my pose was the result of my insufferable idealism. But to me, the Saint Paul schools seemed heroic in their effort to turn Third-World immigrants into Minnesotans.

It was good theater while it lasted. When we ran out of words, the crowd seemed satisfied. I stared at him and shrugged my shoulders; he stared at me and shrugged his shoulders. The next words I expected to hear were, "You're fired!"

Two old men out drinking together were part of the crowd. As the crowd dispersed, one came forth. He wore a wool stocking cap and a cardigan sweater. "Hello, Mike," he said.

McCabe turned, and his eyes lit up. "Governor Nelson, nice to see you, sir."

"How's your mom?"

"She's doing great. She's down in Scottsdale for the winter."

"I envy her for that."

"Me too," said McCabe.

"Can you introduce me to your friend?"

"Samuel Meckler, meet Governor Russell Nelson."

I admit to being star-struck. Nelson was a US senator who, at the end of his second term, opted to return to Minnesota, where he won two terms as governor. During that time, he also published three volumes of poetry, two of which were reviewed in the *New York Times Book Review.*

When he reached out his hand, I shook it. "Nice to meet you, sir."

"I'd just like to say how much I enjoyed your debate. You comported yourself very well for a young man."

"Thank you," I said.

Turning to McCabe, he said, "Mike, in case you didn't know, I am living on Summit Avenue now. I have a new book that some big outfit in New York is publishing next month and I'd be grateful for a feature article about it in your paper since I now live in the distribution area. I'd like this young man to write it."

"I'll talk to my editors," McCabe said.

I barely slept that night. When I arrived at work the next morning, expecting it to be my last, McCabe and his editors were in the conference room. I could hear them through the glass door. They confessed to Mike that they knew about my mother's job at the Saint Paul schools. It earned them a good tongue-lashing. To my relief, I was not fired. However, from that time on, I was never allowed to write about the schools again.

It turned out to be a blessing. Beginning with that feature article I wrote about Nelson, I inherited a column called *On the Town*, which heralded coming cultural events.

If a local artist published a book, wrote or starred in a play, cut a musical album or had an art opening at a Twin Cities gallery,

I wrote a feature story promoting it. In doing so, I got to pick the minds of individual artists about how their creative process worked.

Some of the plays, music, books and art were not inspired or well conceptualized. It didn't matter. I found that I had a talent for zeroing in on what motivated the work. Over the course of several months, I not only got good at portraying their artistic method but also learned how to integrate their insights into my own oeuvre. It changed the way I wanted to be a writer.

When Nelson published his memoirs a year later, I was sent to his Summit Avenue home again to write about it. Born in 1934, Nelson's narrative brought images to the page of his military service in Korea. Rough and tumble eyewitness accounts of the Democratic-Farmer-Labor Party in its early years, complete with stories about Iron Range Communists like Gus Hall and mainstream politicos like Hubert Humphrey, Walter Mondale and Warren Burger, chief justice of the Supreme Court, were documented.

He loved to wax poetic about Minnesota politics in the old days when the Swedes ran the place. His personal accounts about famous people and events he witnessed in DC were told with great orchestration.

We became friends. He was happy to find a follower, two generations removed from his own. He was a lonely old man whose wife, friends and time had passed.

"The greatest part of my life, the part I am proudest of," said Nelson, "is that I got to express my passion in its entirety. Not only in the public, political affairs of men but in the private world of literature as well."

I was impressed by how deftly Nelson embraced higher truths and made use of them in his career. When the article about his memoir was published, I walked a copy to his house so he could read it. He loved Saint Paul and no longer cared about the rest of the world. He was famous in his hometown, which was now his whole life.

When he was diagnosed with cancer, he sunk into a lonely depression. Seeing him so vulnerable made me sad. He was undergoing chemotherapy. It weakened him. My visits became less frequent. He lost his hair, his weight and his resolve. That was when I got an idea of how to alleviate some of the ill effects of his treatment.

"I brought you something that might help."

"A new intestine?" he asked.

"No, a joint." I pulled it out of my pocket, lit it and took a hit.

"Haven't tried this stuff in a long time," he said. I handed it to him; he inhaled it and blew out a large lungful. It was a thick joint, and the smoking of it lasted several minutes. By the time it burned down to the size of a roach, he was blowing smoke rings through pursed lips and smiling. Ten minutes later, he said, "You know, I got some Oreos in the cupboard. Go get them. I'm hungry."

The weed renewed his interest in food and living. Over the weeks, he actually gained weight. Soon, despite his age, he was in remission. Our friendship grew with his newfound strength.

Whenever we'd share a joint, suddenly, as if inspired by a muse, he would wax poetic on seemingly divergent tangents that he somehow always tied together into some meaningful conclusion.

"When your father has lived an unfulfilled life, a diligent son works to heal that," he said. "I realized it years ago. My dad was a Swedish immigrant and an alcoholic. When I was growing up, he lost a half-dozen jobs because of it. And yet he was at all of my inaugurations. The last time, at my second gubernatorial ceremony in Saint Paul, I told him, 'You know, I did it all for you.' And he looked at me and said, 'I know you did. Thank you.'"

I found it ironic that even though he was in his eighties, memories of his long-dead father meant so much to him, even more than his children.

On the next visit, I brought him a quarter ounce of marijuana and a metal pipe to smoke it out of. But no, he didn't want the pipe.

It was too small. He feared that if he lit it himself, he would burn his nose. He preferred joints. I taught him how to roll one. Even though he suffered from arthritis, he enjoyed the challenge.

When he was done, he offered it up for my inspection. "Damn, Gov, it looks like a pregnant guppy," I said. "Let's see how it smokes."

We lit up. Though it was thick in the middle, it burned evenly and had a good draw. And then, with a carefree glee, he'd start blowing his signature smoke rings across the living room and singing old lyrics from his early years, including Frank Sinatra's "Fly me to the moon and let me play among the stars."

What I loved most about our time together was the conversation, especially when we were stoned. It was what he liked most about our time together, too. Sometimes, I taped them on my smartphone.

"You know, when you get to be my age, there's an inevitable sadness that comes from the pleasures old age takes away," Nelson said.

"How does that work?" I asked.

"When you give up ambition, your urge for money and sex and power, there's just one thing left that matters."

"What's that?"

"The opportunity to inspire young people with the values that motivated your life."

"Well, here I am, Gov."

"Yeah, but it's a tricky thing," he said. "You offer a young person advice, and the minute you say it, you become partially responsible for its outcome."

"What's the problem with that?" I asked.

"It might be the wrong advice!"

"True, but what if it's never uttered, and a guy misses out on his best chance in life?"

"I'm not sure."

"What are you trying to say?"

"Sam, you don't belong here," he said. "The best part of you is not given adequate expression in Minnesota. I'll tell you where you belong—Washington, DC."

"Why DC?"

"Because it's East Coast, and you have an East Coast soul. You can certainly succeed here in Minnesota, but you'll never utilize the best parts of your personality. In DC, you'll be competing with the best and the brightest. I went there straight out of law school, and it was like a finishing school. I met people from all over the world, watched historical events unfold and drank myself silly."

That was the first time I ever considered moving here. As time went by and I got to know Nelson better, much better, usually because when I got him high, he talked nonstop, his DC eyewitness accounts as a young attorney and later as a US senator from the Land of Lakes inspired me.

"Here's what you should do," he said. "Go to Washington and be a witness. Take a good, hard look around and continue your community newspaper journalism. It's what they need there. You'll grow as a writer and as a man."

"You could have been a senator there for life," I said. "Why did you return to Minnesota?"

"I saw the writing on the wall. During my second senate term, the Reagan era was upon us. It flew in the face of everything I believed in. I returned to Minnesota and won two gubernatorial races to keep the New Deal liberalism of my early years alive. Sam, move to DC and write about the end of the Reagan era," he said. "Detail the times and a liberal path forward. It will be important for members of your generation."

"I'll consider it," I said.

"Good. Hey, are you in the mood for Chinese food?"

The idea of returning to the East Coast grew on me. It seemed like a grand adventure, and encouraged by the governor, I did.

Arriving in Washington, inspired by the stories Nelson told me, armed with community values and a fistful of newspaper clips with my byline written upon them, I hoped to move right into a full-time reporting job. Unfortunately, I lacked the right stuff. I didn't recognize it at the time, but tough-minded DC editors did.

An English major? A community newspaper reporter from Minnesota? Those hiring had no time for me. They raised their eyebrows and suggested I was out of my element, a mere rube. I soon realized that perhaps they were right.

The Tea Party was making all the noise in Washington. Their caucus had just won a big election, and they had been sworn into office three months before I arrived. The conservative values they championed were now the rage. Their goal seemed set on one thing: diminish the influence of President Barack Obama, no matter what.

That conflict between the African American president and the Caucasian congress played out in all the emerging news. Perhaps such drama sold more advertising and stimulated audiences to a greater pitch. But as a young Minnesota idealist, I thought Tea Party members were dolts whose ideology all led to nothing.

Granted, I had no experience with their rhetoric, and I confess, I didn't know how to respond. I was raised in a left-wing neighborhood. Minnesota State Senate District 64, located on the south side of Minneapolis near Lake Harriet, was a haven for liberal Democrats.

My state representative was a Jewish man married to the woman rabbi of the largest synagogue in Minnesota. My state senator was openly gay. My congressman was a Black Muslim. My US senator was a former *Saturday Night Live* comedian and my governor was elected on a tax-the-rich platform.

It didn't take me long to figure out that the political culture in which I was raised and the *Highland Villager* newspaper I wrote for was out of sync with the prevailing DC political culture.

And yet, despite my Jersey roots, I realized that Minneapolis was a good place to grow up, and for the first time in my life, I found myself defending it. So, the talk of me being a rube didn't bother me much.

Yes, it's cold there and perhaps the last bastion of culture before the empty two-thousand-mile westward American stretch of prairie, great plains and big mountains separating the Twin Cities from the West Coast. Snow covers the Minneapolis ground with white five months a year. And yes, statistically, Minnesotans are some of the worst drivers in America.

But Minneapolis has twenty-two lakes within the city limits. In summer, the lake's gentle eyes reflect the blue summer sky until its hue becomes what it beholds: the mirror image of a clear, calm, azure heaven. Sometimes, the water reflection was more beautiful than the sky itself because it's surrounded by a deep-green verdure of summer leaves and grass.

Minnesota was a culture based on the eye. The lawns of most yards were immaculate. Their sidewalks were shoveled clear of winter snow with great precision. Minneapolis, its biggest city, was a high-functioning white middle-class society of mostly Scandinavian descent.

Garbage was picked up on time, the streets were plowed of snow immediately and homes were well-kept. Should an alley garage have chipped paint or a sagging roof, Minneapolis building inspectors were there to remind you that it was in violation of the law. If you didn't fix it in thirty days, they would fix it for you and hand you the bill.

That was how diligent they were about maintaining property values and protecting their tax base. Only 14 percent of its homeowners had children in its public schools. Yet school referendums generally passed by a margin of 70 percent. In Minnesota, I was part of a political culture of civic responsibility, engagement and high function.

Of course, it's true that no one there could dance or talk trash. As a Jersey boy who moved there in seventh grade, I recognized that fact early on. New Jersey culture was based on the ear. There was an audible beat to the way people moved. The women could dance, and men were defined by the strength and the rhythm of their speech. They could out-curse everyone, even New Yorkers.

Though I was a half-breed, sharing equal time in the Garden State and the Land of Lakes, my poetic sensibilities mostly came from Jersey. I preferred its audio track and the syncopated measure planted inside me during my formative years.

Arriving in DC, where the community was evenly divided between Whites and Blacks, where people came from all over the country and the world, where local news was national news, expanded my ken.

I loved the city's architecture. It stoked my enthusiasm. The timeless themes of liberty and equality personified in granite, bronze and marble statues all over the city are testaments to the highest sentiments of its great men. Americans embrace these icons as if they are a birthright, and rightfully so. The city is laid out in such a way that's welcoming to all.

But this is a drama-drenched place, too. Learning to tune out its shriller sounds is an acquired skill. I recognized my inability to compete with my fellow journalists pretty fast. My parents raised me to prize community over controversy.

Interpreting the negative Tea Party myths circulating around the Capitol was beyond me. I was dumbfounded that a city of such grandeur was run by so many shallow men. During two different interviews for a reporter's job, I was actually mocked for being naive.

There was one other interview. A writing job cranking out two-hundred-word pieces for the internet. "Bidder Pays One Million for a Pair of Jay-Z's Sneakers." "Florida Woman Fights Off Alligator." They were filler pieces of little consequence and no literary value. And though I was offered the job, I declined.

Somewhere in DC, there was a clearinghouse looking for writers like me. I just knew they were out there. But I never found them. I stopped applying for writing jobs and returned to the restaurant business, which supported me during college. And yet I didn't really give a damn about not making the DC press corps. I found their rhetoric uninspiring. After two years of writing *On the Town* and being coached by Nelson, I decided to be a poet. Yes, a poet. Laugh if you want. Sometimes, that ambition sounds ridiculous, even to me.

But at my deepest core, I knew it was what I wanted to do and who I wanted to be. There was no letting go of it. My goal is to write "A Firm State of Heart" in 1,200 lines.

My poem will be a grand confession about America in this era. I want nothing less than to be a part of a great emerging movement, a consciousness professing peace, prosperity, multiculturalism, globalization and hope. I'm going to sing out American virtue and compete against the nihilistic troublemakers hell-bent on ruining it all. The poem's first two lines offer an ominous warning:

Lies, lies
Darken the skies over America.

Politics and poetry are related to each other on a subliminal plane. I'm looking for the neural pathway that connects the two. Nelson put me on that path. There's something rotten in Washington, DC, and I wanted to see it, articulate it and bring it into the open. What was the etymology of this stain, this lack of morality, honesty and the irksome haze hovering over the city?

I couldn't name it.

All I knew was that there was a disparity between the petty men making noise on local airwaves and the American ideals that inspired me. The literary opportunity to describe the republic in its current state and to push public discourse forward to a healthier, progressive, more American place is my goal.

The problems of this American era are not going to be solved by pundits or politicos. It's beyond their scope. Only poets can reckon with it, and I wanted to be one of those guys. I still haven't grasped the way forward in the manner that Nelson committed me to. He claimed that no man could be a good poet unless he was also a good man. But to be a young poet in search of an authentic voice, a relevant point of view and a sure expression in heroic meter is a worthy, moral undertaking.

From the outset, I knew it was going to be a lonesome endeavor. Yet I'm committed to it. So, I am careful with my time and my desire, lest I fall into a love swoon with a longhaired beauty, the likes of which I corded on the Metro train tonight and get derailed from my quest.

I'm looking for a way forward through this contentious age. One that no longer pits native-born against immigrants, urban against rural, conservatives against liberals, pro-life against pro-choice, Fox News against CNN, African Americans against Caucasians and most importantly, men against women.

> Speak, muse
> Tell me why the American songbook
> Which orchestrated the music of idealism
> No longer desires the dance.
> Lash me to the mast
> And let me listen to the aria.
> Pour divine agency into my humanity
> For a firm state of heart.

"After all, if you don't do it, who will?" asked Nelson. "It's not like young men are lining up for such an assignment. Someone has to defend America."

Nelson considered me his last attempt at greatness—the last spot on his extensive résumé. Inspire a young man to pick up the gauntlet and carry it forward in a fine, liberal Minnesota tradition. That was the direction he pushed me. "Listen, every new generation demands new feelings and new values on the part of its young people in order to fuel progress," he said.

So, going forth, I'm aware that I must shoulder new feelings and conceive new values in order to bring forth a modern narrative. My goal was not to solve the problems of America. My job was to flush out the particulars and put them into a context so politicos and pundits might get a deeper grasp and work their remedial magic.

Currently, my innate perceptions are greater than my power to articulate them. Channeling a poem from the deep is, at best, a part-time job. But I'm patiently writing it out.

In the meantime, a man still has to earn a living. I don't have to worry, though. I am young, focused and, best of all, I know how to carry a tray.

CHAPTER 4

Let me tell you about where I live. It's a Capitol Hill row house on North Carolina Avenue near the Potomac Avenue Metro Station. Our narrow home was built at the start of the twentieth century and reflects the smaller stature of people back in the day before bovine hormones and fast food made modern men and women so large.

Our home has a nickname. We refer to it as "the Fourth Estate." That's because all four of us are involved in some sort of media. I'm a poet, Johnny Zuma is a Knight-Ridder newspaper reporter, Cortez Brown is a cameraman for CNN, and Caleb Hannemann sells and creates advertising for the Christian Broadcasting Network.

It's a three-bedroom house on a tree-lined block occupied by me and my three roommates. There's a two-room garret on the third floor; that's my space. A narrow second-floor staircase leads up to my attic lair. I have a bedroom and something I never had before—a study, high above the street among the treetops.

Summer heat is tempered by window fans in each room. The winter cold is more than the others can bear.

Being that I was raised in Minneapolis, I do not feel the cold the way they do. I have a space heater for those cold winter nights, long underwear and wool blankets for my lap when needed.

I was on my way to meet my housemates at "The Veil," a Pennsylvania Avenue dive bar we often attended to discuss house business. Its walls were bare, it had six tables, couches lined the room in different places, and the bar had twelve stools. I was the first one to arrive. I ordered a beer from the pretty bartender.

"Aren't you one of Johnny Zuma's housemates?" she asked.

"Yes, how did you know?"

"Me and Johnny go way back. I remember someone pointed you out to me last summer when you guys hosted that house party."

"Yes, I had just moved in. My name is Samuel Meckler."

"My name is Vickie."

We shook hands.

"Are you the poet?"

"Yes," I said.

"Johnny speaks highly of your talent. What kind of poems do you write?"

"I'm working on a long poem."

"Why poetry?"

"Because it carries a certain purity that's unsoiled by pop culture and social media."

"Is it a love poem?

"No, it's more of a romance like Walt Whitman might have written about America a hundred and fifty years ago."

"What does it take to become a poet?"

"A mastery of language and a firm state of heart."

"What's your poem about?"

"America in its hour of need."

"What need is that? The economy is good, we're not at war and life is good."

"I'm looking to comment on the entire gestalt."

"Why would you do that?"

"Because the digital age is moving so fast that collectively it's outpaced our ethics, morals and values. I'm trying to establish some new, definitive lines."

"Are you going to bash the president?"

"No, I'm not going to mention his name," I said.

"How do you work on a project like that?"

"You begin at the beginning, write it to the end, then return to the beginning and go to the end again. You do that until you figure out what it's all about."

"And what is it all about?"

"A cosmic vision for the new millennium."

She laughed out loud. "That sounds funny."

"I know, but here's my dirty little secret. The composition of it is really fun."

Like most Minnesotans, I'd rather not talk about myself. I changed the subject. "What do you do when you're not tending bar?"

"I'm in grad school at Georgetown University. I'm getting a master's degree in counseling."

"What are you going to do with it when you're done?"

"Get the hell out of the bar business," she said. "What are you going to do when you finish your poem?"

"I don't know."

She chuckled. "You know, I've been tending bar for ten years, and I never met anyone who copped to being a poet before."

"It's not something you go bragging about."

"Does your poetry rhyme, or is it strictly free verse?"

"Both. I've given it a lot of thought. I decided that it's more interesting if it rhymes because it allows the image to linger a little longer in your mind. But sometimes, when you have something urgent to say, that's not practical."

"I've known three poets in my life," she said. "One was a madman, the other a neurotic. The third claimed to be a genius. Which category do you fall under?"

"I suppose it depends on the outcome. If I never finish it, it will be because I'm too neurotic. If it sucks, people will call me a madman for wasting so much of my time with it. If it's hailed as a great work of art, perhaps they'll call me a genius."

"I never met a real genius before."

"Me neither."

"Which one do you think it will be?"

"To be honest, the way things stand now, a neurotic," I said.

"Well, at least you're honest. Who is going to publish it when it's done?"

"I don't know."

"Who's going to read it?"

"I don't know."

"Well, you certainly sound like an eccentric."

"Perhaps, but there are pleasures to being an eccentric that only an eccentric can appreciate."

"Well, good luck with that," she said.

"Hi, Sam," said Diego, a Veil regular who sat down next to me and ordered a martini. He was a Bolivian native, tall and handsome, with a cocoa complexion. He formerly worked as a waiter at "Joe's Stone Crab," one of the most lucrative restaurant jobs in the city, then he gave it up. Currently, he sells weed under DC's semi-legal marijuana laws. He's making a great living at it.

"Where are your pals tonight?" Diego asked.

"They'll be here soon."

"How are things at the house?"

"We have a new roommate. Caleb's a friend of Cortez's from the army. He's a White boy from a small town in Tennessee. He makes commercials for the Christian Broadcasting Network."

"Is Cortez still a cameraman at CNN?" Vickie asked.

"Yes, he's still hoping to get in front of the camera one of these days," I said.

"Did you see the Facebook video Zuma posted of him?" Diego asked.

"That was funny," I said.

"What was it?" Vickie asked.

"Johnny threw open the bathroom door while Cortez was sitting on the pot. He took out his camera phone and called out, 'Ladies and gentlemen, here is Cortez Brown stinking up the whole second floor with one tremendous crap.' Then in an aside, he said, 'Dude, open a fucking window.'"

"Then Cortez puts down his *Penthouse* magazine, smiles at the camera with those big pink lips and without missing a beat, says, 'I used to take craps that looked like a map of the Philippines. Now, thanks to Zuma's fruits and vegetables, they're looking like Havana cigars.'"

"Then you can hear Zuma prompting him with his station's current ad campaign. Cortez farts out loud, looks squarely into Zuma's camera, says, 'And this is CNN.'"

"It got ninety-three likes," Diego said. "But I heard his ex-wife, Deirdre, saw it. She thought he was in Michigan. When she realized he was actually living in DC, she came after him because he owes her child support."

"Not only that, his boss at CNN saw it," I said.

"Did he get in trouble?" asked Vickie.

"No. Actually, his producer was impressed. He said if Cortez can show that much poise with his pants down, just think how much better he'd be zipped up and standing. They promised him a screen test."

"Isn't that just like Zuma?" said Vickie. "Just when you think he's fucked you over, you end up sitting beside a pot of gold."

"If Cortez gets on camera, it will make Johnny crazy," I said. "When he's covering a Capitol Hill story, he has to go back and spend hours writing it out at his desk while TV broadcasters pick up a microphone, spill the story like it's a rumor and go home."

Caleb called out my name and sat down beside me. The White kid is an Evangelical Christian. He was tall, thin and handsome with a freckled face and strawberry-blonde hair. The tattoo around his wrist was written in Hebrew. Its English translation is, "Jesus Christ is my Lord and Savior."

Admonishing us to adore his vision of divinity sometimes made him tedious company. Thus, I preferred him in small doses. Knowing my progressive sympathies, he liked to bait me with the rhetoric surrounding such issues as immigration, abortion, and law and order. He'd pick an ambiguous point and spin a whole universe out of it with arguments inspired by Fox News. The idea that I might not walk lockstep with liberal ideologues never crossed his mind. He was blind to shades of gray.

And yet, even though our political lodestars orbited in different rotations, Caleb and I were closer spiritually than my other two roommates. Both of us believed in God, intelligent design and that the soul had substance.

But what I felt always seemed at variance with what he felt. His assumptions were not my assumptions. The right relationship to divinity, the world and ourselves was so at odds that we rarely found common ground. He ordered a beer from Vickie.

"What's new in the televised world of Christ, Caleb?"

"It's all about the love, Sam, all about the love."

"Hallelujah."

He looked down at my backpack. The pink water bottle was sticking out of the webbing. "Getting in touch with your feminine side?"

"Something like that," I said.

"Listen, I have a complaint to make, and now is probably a good time to discuss it."

"What's on your mind?"

"Sam, if you want to drink, get stoned, drum on your redskin tom-tom, chant all that nonsense and dance with the devil in your pagan lair upstairs, that's your choice. But my bedroom is right underneath your study, and having to listen to it late at night is degrading."

"I don't experience God the way you do."

"It's that drumbeat that gets me most. Dude, why don't you just masturbate and get that shit out of your system like a normal man."

"That's the twelfth step."

"You have a twelve-step process to all your nonsense?"

"Definitely."

"I always know how awful an evening's going to be by the number of times you go downstairs to refill your scotch glass with ice. The devil is the source of your poetic fire. Especially since you can only raise him when you are in a state of moral degradation."

"I'll try to be more considerate," I said.

"I'll pray for you."

Diego interrupted. "I just started selling this new vape cartridge. Want to come outside and try it?"

"Sure," I said. We left our drinks on the bar and walked out to the sidewalk.

"Thought I'd rescue you," Diego said.

"Thanks, bro. I had a shitty night at work, and the last thing I need is him bitching at me."

"What's with that guy?"

"I don't know?"

Diego handed me the cartridge, a Brass Knuckles brand. I took a big hit.

"I had a long conversation with Caleb last week," Diego said. "He thought I was Mexican and tried to justify the current rhetoric against Hispanics. When I told him that I was Bolivian, he acted like he didn't even know such a country existed. Then he wanted to argue about God."

"He knows more about the Bible than he knows about himself," I said. "He wears the bulky armor of Evangelical Christianity where every human impulse is measured in accordance with scripture. It's a one-size-fits-all dogma. I try never to talk about religion or politics with him."

Suddenly, a DC cop on a bicycle appeared. He slowed his bike and rolled on by giving me and Diego the once-over. "Good evening, officer," I said.

"Hello, gentlemen, have a great night," he said and kept on going. Diego's smile tacitly acknowledged how wonderful it is to live in a city where the police did not prosecute marijuana smokers.

"I don't think I'd enjoy having him for a housemate," Diego said while exhaling a large cloud of smoke. "He invited me to his church and offered to help me convert to his religion."

"What are you two criminals up to?" asked Cortez as he walked up from behind us. Without missing a beat, he grabbed the pen from my hand and took a toke. After exhaling, he asked, "How was your first dinner shift at Tadich?"

"A nightmare."

"Want to talk about it?"

"No, not yet. I'm still processing it. You know me, I never like to discuss things until I've written about it first."

"Is it really lurid?" Cortez asked.

"More than you can imagine."

"Can't wait to hear about it."

Of the three roommates, Cortez was my favorite. We talked better together than the others. There was a melody to his speech. He made you want to match it in tone and tenor because imitating him put you on a positive plane that increased your joy.

He's a big Black man, well over six foot three and weighing about two forty. He has short hair and a hearty laugh. Cortez was a local DC kid who went to Afghanistan with the US Army. Afterward, he did two years of college on the GI Bill. After an internship at CNN, he got a full-time job as a cameraman. Like Caleb, he longed to be in front of the camera.

Unlike my other friends, he was very private about his personal life. Following the *Facebook* video posted of him on the toilet that resulted in Deirdre's wrath, he took down his Facebook, Instagram, and Snapchat accounts. Of course, he kept his Tinder account. He had two children from his marriage. Unfortunately, he came back from war traumatized and was unwilling to play the role of Deirdre's diligent husband.

"What do you think of the cartridge?" Diego asked.

"Pretty good, but I never seem to get a full spectrum high on cartridges the way I do when smoking flower," I said.

"You got to get used to it. The nice part is that you can smoke it anywhere because it has no smell."

"What are you selling it for?"

"Probably about fifty dollars."

"Got any on you now?" I asked.

"Yes."

"I'll buy one and see how I like it."

He handed me a cartridge wrapped in a cardboard package, and I forked over the cash.

When Cortez, Diego and I returned inside, we were high. We grabbed our drinks off the bar and moved to a table. Caleb joined us. Finally, I was able to rise above tonight's drama at Tadich. But Caleb wanted to pick up where he left off, hoping that with Cortez there, he'd have an erstwhile ally. But I gave him a dismissive look.

"I suppose that now you are stoned, this conversation isn't going anywhere," Caleb said.

"That would be my first choice," I said.

"The light that shines upon you is a crescent moon, just like the Muslims," he said. "Revelation can never be found in artistic or occult rituals, only in Christian sacraments."

"My sacraments are mine and earmarked to address my needs, not yours," I answered. "This may come as a surprise to you, Caleb, but when it comes to spirituality, one size does not fit all."

He rolled his eyes. "If you were Adam, you'd have been thrown out of the Garden of Eden even before Eve met the snake."

"Don't act like I haven't thought this through."

"It seems like you used pretzel logic to think it through. It's all twisted. And what the hell is that pagan altar all about?"

"What were you doing in my study?"

"Looking for the TV channel changer."

"Do you ever see me watch television?"

"No, but I ran out of places to look, so I went upstairs."

"Where did you finally find it?"

"Underneath the couch cushion."

"That altar is my connection to divinity. If it offends you, I suggest you stay out of my space."

"You don't know the difference between the gospel and the apocryphal," he said.

"Why do you always try to make me wrong?"

"I'm like Caleb from the Old Testament, my namesake," he said. "He crossed the River Jordan with Joshua and brought down the walls of Jericho. Moses didn't make it to the Promised Land, but Caleb, my namesake, did and I—"

Johnny Zuma arrived and immediately stuck his nose into our conversation. "Dude, Jericho only let you in to use the bathroom. Once you flushed, they sent you back outside," said Johnny.

"Don't make fun of my faith," said Caleb.

"It's a monstrosity proffered by child molesters, philistines, racists and snobs. When are you guys going to throw the money changers out of the temple?"

"Hi, Sam," said Johnny, turning his attention away from Caleb. "How was your first dinner shift?"

"It sucked."

Johnny Zuma and I went to grade school together. We had the same fourth, fifth, and sixth-grade teachers. Then, my family packed its bags and moved to Minneapolis. His parents owned an Italian restaurant in our town. Sometimes, we'd go there after school to eat with the staff between the lunch and dinner shifts.

His dad, Gino, handled the kitchen. His mother, Janine, handled the dining room. I loved hanging out there. Restaurants always suggested family to me, and it's because of Zuma's Italian Paradise.

To honor his family's restaurant tradition, Johnny cooked an elaborate Sunday night dinner monthly that no one was allowed to miss, if only because it was expensive and he needed our cash.

By luck, we resumed our friendship when I came to DC. Though he was a cynic, he was a natural leader. Everybody was more than willing to let him be in charge. He was about six feet high, had thick lips, black hair parted on the side and a beer belly.

In Zuma, I found a friend who was more robust in mind and spirit than me. He was an extrovert, a concrete sequential man who had his finger on the pulse of the world, unlike me, who apprehended it intuitively. We were both writers, while Cortez and Caleb were broadcast guys.

There was another part of him that I liked. He was a Jersey boy. Hanging out with him helped me rediscover the roots I lost after my dad got an administrative position at the Veterans Hospital in Minneapolis and we became members of my mom's Minnesota Catholic family instead of my dad's Jewish family in Jersey.

When we were kids, Johnny was the king of Jersey trash talk. "What are you, serious or delirious?" The loudmouthed preteen would ask. While the challenge was "in your face," it was not necessarily intended to belittle. His true intention was to engage, to call out your manhood, to bring forth a verbal debate that would provoke a dialectical clash of ideas that might bring some deeper insight to an issue. Such confrontations are a Jersey art form. He was great at it. Minnesotans were not talented enough to pull it off.

He had a high-tech beat for his newspaper chain. In it, he explored emerging issues of the digital age. Last week, he published a piece entitled "Who Is Smarter, Alexa or Siri?" In the piece, he described the two models of artificial intelligence each was based upon.

He walked to the end of the bar, called out Vickie's name and gave her a big hug. After some small talk, he returned with a cork tray with five shots of Rumple Minze upon it. He handed out one to each of us, then raised his glass and said, "Here's a toast to the inheritors of unfulfilled renown." We tossed it down.

"Anyone famous come into your section this week, Sam?" Cortez asked.

I wasn't ready to discuss Shayla Reeve. But I did have another story to tell. "I waited on former Speaker of the House, John Boehner, yesterday. God, he hates the Tea Party."

"That's baloney," Caleb said. "I heard him give a testimonial to them at a Christian retreat. He had nothing but praise for the men and women of that caucus."

"How many people were in attendance?" I asked.

"Two hundred."

"Well, when I saw him, he was on his second bottle of merlot with his wife and a friend," I said. "They were sitting in my booth. The only one who could hear him was me, and you know what he said?"

"You can tell me, but I'm not sure I'm going to believe you," Caleb said.

"He said that the Tea Party is just a bunch of anarchists who only want more power so they can create more anarchy."

"A good Republican would never say that," Caleb said.

"Well, he said it, all right. He was sitting in booth 53 at lunch. I heard him as plain as day."

"Caleb, you're a douchebag. How long have you been in this town?" Johnny asked.

"Six months."

"You don't know anything. This town is all about public relations bullshit played out for the benefit of the pseudo-news organizations that you and Cortez work for."

"All I know is that he champions the values of White Christian virtue."

"Dude, let me tell you something about White Christian virtue," Johnny said. "Three of the latest DC museums were created to document the dastardly deeds of White Christian men. The Holocaust Museum, the African American Museum, and the Native American Museum."

"What about the Museum of the Bible?" Caleb countered.

"All right, Johnny, back off," said Cortez. "There's no need to let politics interfere with our household."

"Here's another thing," Zuma said. "The electric bill came today. It's my name on the bill and it was three hundred dollars. I want seventy-five dollars from each one of you fuckers by Monday. You morons need to go naked and stop turning the air-conditioning down to sixty degrees."

"Dude, it's hot," said Cortez.

"Yeah, it's summer. What do you expect?" Then, looking at me, Zuma said, "Can you believe these wimps?"

"The heat doesn't bother me," I said. "I lived in Minnesota for ten winters. I'm still trying to thaw out my chilblains."

"I want the money by Monday," Zuma repeated.

"So, what are you working on, Johnny?" Cortez asked.

"I'm doing a story on porn sites. I mean, they all show sex videos for free. Do you ever wonder how they make their money?"

"As a matter of fact, I do," I said.

"Those sites are the haven of the devil," said Caleb.

"You know you look at them, Caleb. You can lie to your Evangelical brothers if you want to, but don't lie to your housemates," said Johnny.

"What did you find out?" asked Cortez.

"Fuck you, Cortez. I'm not telling you. I've been working on this story for two days. When it's finally published, some shallow douchebag from *CNN* will recite its highlights in front of a camera like girly gossip and steal all my fire."

"Come on, Johnny, you know I'd never pass your story on to my guys. What have you discovered so far? Come on. Throw me a bone."

"There's a thousand different scams they use to make money. You'll go to a site featuring busty Asian women and suddenly your computer freezes up. They give you a number to call, and some schmuck from India takes your credit card number and charges you a hundred bucks to unlock it."

Caleb grew pale. "That happened to me," he said.

"Are you kidding me?" asked Johnny. "Damn, Caleb, all you have to do is turn your computer off and then turn it back on, and you're free of those crooks."

"Oh god, I gave them my money machine card number."

"It's a pretty sophisticated racket preying on the fact that most people don't understand the digital technology they're utilizing and therefore are easy marks," Johnny said.

Caleb, lost in reverie, swallowed hard.

"Check your bank account, bro," said Cortez. "Make sure they didn't clean it out."

Caleb reached for his phone and nervously checked his bank account. Nobody laughed.

"Their biggest marks are naive Evangelicals who visit the sites and then feel so guilty about it that they welcome the opportunity to give their money away to lessen their religious guilt," Johnny said.

Caleb let out a sigh of relief when he saw his bank account hadn't been raped.

"Hey, Johnny, I just thought of a great lead for your story," I said.

"Let's hear it," he said.

"Last week, Caleb Hannemann's computer froze while searching a porn site featuring big-breasted Christian babes. The Capitol Hill millennial—"

"What are you, high?" Caleb shouted. And then, looking at Zuma, he said, "You do that, and I swear I'll sue you for libel."

When everyone at the table started laughing, Caleb stopped mid-sentence, realized it was a joke and put a sour look on his face.

"When's your story going to be published?" Cortez asked.

"Hoping that it will be ready by the middle of next week," Zuma said.

We were there together for about a half-hour with Zuma holding court. All the house business was covered. When two African American women walked into the bar, Zuma turned his attention. One of them with rather large breasts wore a tight T-shirt that read, "Blessed."

Cortez assessed the shirt and agreed. "Damn, that girl certainly is blessed."

"And endowed," said Johnny.

"Uh-oh, Johnny Zuma got his swag out," Diego said.

Caleb reached into his breast pocket and pulled out his glasses for a better look. But the lenses were smudged. Looking around for a napkin, he found none. He pulled out the white of his pants pocket and wiped his lenses clean. However, in the process, about thirty-five cents fell to the floor, which he chose to ignore.

"Are we done here?" Johnny asked.

"I think so," I answered.

"Then excuse me."

"You're going to go and talk to them?" Caleb asked.

"Yes."

"What are you going to say?"

"Son, that's my Tinder date this evening," Johnny said. "Didn't think she'd bring a chaperone."

"Johnny Z's going for the double Ds," said Diego. "That tall one seems like a Christmas stocking full of goodies."

"Sam, are you in?" Johnny asked.

I looked at them both. Being that I've known Zuma since he was nine years old, I knew which one was his. The other one would have been my first choice anyway. But I shrugged my shoulders.

After my evening with Shayla Reeve and the girl on the train, I had my fill of female energy. "Sorry, I got writing to do."

"Prose before 'hos,' Sammy?" asked Cortez.

"Sam would rather romance his muse than that big bitch over there," said Johnny. "Cortez, you want some of this? I need a wingman."

"Swoop, swoop, slide," Cortez called out. "Oh my, Christmas has come early."

"That's right," Johnny said. "And I'm Santa Claus."

"The fallen man seeks passion instead of a fitting bride," said Caleb.

"Don't be a prude, Caleb," I said. "The basic paradigm of godliness is union and penetration."

"That's not in the Bible."

"Well, it should be," I said.

"Listen, Johnny, before you go, here's the first advice I ever got about dating Black women," Diego said. "Never touch her hair."

Cortez laughed; Zuma gave it a moment's thought and acknowledged his words. Caleb looked puzzled. "Why is that?"

"Because it might be a wig," Diego answered.

"Really?" Caleb said.

"If you see a Black girl tapping her head, just know she's not trying to jump start her brain," Cortez said. "Her wig is making her scalp itch, and she can't scratch it."

Johnny and Cortez got up and walked to where the women were sitting. Zuma started. "Good evening, ladies. Welcome to the Veil," he said.

"Are you the Italian stallion?" the blessed one asked.

"Miss, I am so much more than that," he answered. "I am the master of ceremonies, the greeter with the heater, the man with the plan..." It wasn't until five minutes later that he stopped talking. By then, he had established his beachhead.

"I have no idea how Johnny does it," Caleb said, staring at the four of them. "To me, he looks like Jabba the Hut."

"He has something more important than movie star good looks."

"Oh yeah, what's that?"

"Masculine strength."

I looked at the clock on the wall. It was veiled with a purple piece of lace. I momentarily wondered if it might be a fire hazard. No matter, it was time to go.

"I need to go home and write," I said.

"What are you going to write about?" asked Diego.

"Beauty and the beast."

"But you only had one drink," said Caleb.

"Tonight, I was held hostage by a celebrity, corded by a siren and insulted by you. That's enough for one evening."

"I'm going to stay and stare at Vickie," Caleb said.

"See you guys later," I said.

"Enjoy the cartridge," said Diego.

"Sam, please," Caleb begged, "no drumming tonight."

I got up and walked home.

CHAPTER 5

Upstairs in my garret, I cranked open the two quarter-moon windows in each room and opened the doors between them. I was waiting for the late-night breezes to blow through my rooms. When it did, I smelled the fragrance of summer blossoms. The sound of a police car siren fading in the distance competed with a chorus of nearby cicadas. Looking out my window, I saw the familiar sight of Venus, whose summer orbit was in full view throughout the night.

I sat down at my desk, turned on the lamp, pulled out a pen, opened my backpack and pulled out my journal. Pouring myself a scotch and filling my pipe with good sativa weed, I was ready. Deep house music with its tribal beat was in my headphones.

Above my desktop, on a small shelf before me, six crystals were lined up at eye level. Each was no bigger than two inches. The desk lamp shining down upon their occlusions reflected prism light—pink, purple, red, blue and green. They were aligned so that when sitting at the middle of my desk, I saw their luminous splendor in one glance. Staring at them inspired me. The vertical crystals lit up like Christmas trees. The round ones, with their greater depth, cast back the light of rainbows.

To augment the light, I lit a votive candle. The flickering flame swayed in the night breeze rushing through my rooms. For me, it represented the holy spirit, at once alive and present.

Sitting here in my plastic chair, belly up to the desk, was where I took my psychic temperature. I gathered my spiritual forces and put them in motion. Pen in hand, I documented my day in my finest hand, printing out block letters with a ballpoint pen inside a two-hundred-page composition notebook. As a poet, it was here that I found the best part of myself.

In this ritual space, I am spoken to. A whispered, almost inaudible psychic voice, a woman's voice, called out the play-by-play. She was a minor deity, a jinn, a muse, an angel, a holy ghost, a psychic guide belonging to me and me alone. These spirits are good to me, so I try to be diligent with my literary responsibilities in order to earn their endorsement.

Attuning my mind to the utterances of this voice came in baby steps. I had to learn her language and method of conveyance. It took years to master the insights, gnosis and meaning of what she told me. The good channel I've mastered, for me, is the greatest literary gift a young poet could ask for. Sometimes, she dictated ideas and imagery at such a rapid pace that I needed to slow down what passed in and out of my mind with THC and alcohol just to keep abreast of her narrative.

> Life is a man-made fiction
> I know more than I'm able to say.
> Lead me down that gnostic trail
> And keep all distractions at bay.

At my desk, the mysteries of life reveal themselves in a whisper, without commercials, glossy images, credits or context. The ambiguities of my life are written down and considered. Something new always emerges. It isn't programmed; it's experienced. Here, intuition, insight and inspiration bask in the spiritual spotlight. The process is a spontaneous, nonscientific, random, ridiculous, undisciplined, irreverent, stoned, drunken, blasphemous and preposterous truth-telling.

Throwing off the restraints of logic, decorum and propriety, I am more apt to tell the bitter truths buried inside me. The seamy, inappropriate, libidinal and tawdry content of my unconscious is set loose upon the page. Sometimes gems, sometimes embarrassments, come forth. That no one else reads these sheets allows me to be honest. There's a German word I am fond of: *selbstständigkeit*.

It refers to a personal initiative, the ability to think for oneself. I think it's attributed to the German poet Goethe. But the same notion rang out in American literature when Ralph Waldo Emerson coined its equivalent: *self-reliance*.

Following an intense restaurant shift, punctuated by concrete sequential tasks, spontaneous conversation, the art of being charming, displays of physical grace, courage, speed and aplomb, often under enormous stress during a busy rush, I am stirred inside with a physical and emotional duress that stays in my body hours after the shift ends. The idea of returning home and going right to sleep is out of the question.

I'm wired, and the only way to calm down, especially if I have a lunch shift the next morning, is by detailing the public occurrences of Tadich and dressing them up with my personal revelations. Sometimes, you just have to write out the drama to find out where things stand. That's what I do here at my desk in the quiet hours of the night.

For me, it's actualizing my zodiac sign, Aquarius. It's symbolized by a water bearer emptying his jug. Instead of pouring out the waters of life, I spill out written thoughts upon a page. After several hours of composition, my psychic jug is empty, and I'm ready to refill it with the challenges of tomorrow.

I looked up at the drum hanging on the wall. It was from the Blackfeet Indian Reservation in Browning, Montana. I love that drum. It's elk skin stretched over a thick wooden hoop. On it, I painted a green and purple mandala. When I tapped it with the stick, it vibrated out a tone that centered me.

Since Caleb wasn't home yet, I thought to reach for it. But there was no need to drum out revelations on it tonight. So emotionally charged were my feelings that everything was front and center.

The first thing I addressed was Shayla Reeve. Why did she show up at Tadich and ruin my first dinner shift?

I hesitated to speak of it to my friends because I wanted to figure it out first. Something about the juxtaposition of her and the woman on the train, one right after the other, seemed significant. Both women were hurting tonight. Age, beauty and income were no protection against the vicissitudes of their lives.

What did these events reveal? Maybe Caleb had it right when he commented on the water bottle and mocked, "Are you trying to get in touch with your feminine side?"

It was a reminder that there is currently no intimacy in my life. Despite my literary diligence, a woman is still the desired end. So focused have I been trying to make the men's club at Tadich, living here with Cortez, Johnny and Caleb and working diligently on my poem that there might just as well be a bubble around me distracting me from any feelings for the fairer sex.

Today, two of them—one angry and one sad—broke through my defenses. Were they sirens calling me out? They certainly got my attention. But a positive emotion from each would have been the more seductive tact.

Shayla Reeve, standing on the stairs leading to the bar with an empty wineglass in her hand, struck me as the most salient image of the night. How humiliating that it required a public outburst like tonight's to say the things she needed to say. It humiliated me, too, and everyone else around her.

I knew all about overachieving women like Shayla Reeve. She was like my mother, Jane Taylor Meckler, a small-town girl who made her career lobbying on behalf of schoolchildren at the Minnesota State Capitol. Shayla and my mom were just like Elizabeth Warren, like Ruth Bader Ginsburg, like Hillary Clinton. Each was the daughter of a housewife who transcended their mother's narrow roles and competing with men for power, salary and influence, made their mark on the world. The road they plowed would be followed by the generations of young women coming after them.

Who was that girl on the train? Young, pretty, vulnerable, she didn't seem to have the stamina to achieve Shayla's success. Hers was a more traditional, softer view of womanhood.

I shouldn't have corded her. I knew it was wrong. But I was so angry at Shayla that I just wanted out of her grip. By opening myself up to that pretty brunette, I knew what was in store: a romantic spell placing me on the moony-moony road of reverie, longing for her in quiet moments, soliloquies addressed to her when I felt misunderstood, late-night sexual fantasies featuring the two of us entwined with me inside her. The urge to put her on a pedestal to justify my infatuation will, most likely, be followed by an inevitable feeling of loss and frustration that I'm wasting my time in fantasy.

Glancing at the pink water bottle wedged into the webbing of my backpack, I pledged to find her and return it. And yet here at my desk, with the THC and alcohol kicking in, dazzled by prism light, with the tribal beat of Ibiza Sonica whose energetic giddy-up, giddy-up, giddy-up measures lifting me, I realized that I couldn't actually remember her face, only the color and shape of her aura.

I spent the first hour writing about those women. Since it had been a few days since I last journaled, I had a lot of other things to catch up on. Here's a selection of some of them.

"Oh, the great irony, the fabulous DC monuments inspiring our best angels versus the shallow politicos in charge."

"How quickly gnostic insight passes through the mind. Write it down fast or risk losing it. They're like minnows that flash and swim through the psychic net cast to secure them. Then they're off to the watery depth with their secrets, never to be seen or heard from again."

"I finally made it to the National Museum of African American History and Culture. It documented Black virtue. That seemed to be the message. How wonderful for them that, at long last, they can tell their own story without redneck White folks telling them they're wrong. They have their own space now. Secure in their identity and history, perhaps more of them can reach for the mainstream and enrich it with their presence."

"Settle down, bro'. Only the channel matters. Write all your insights down here. What's rendered at this desk is more important than a dozen bad shifts at Tadich Grill."

Forsaking the sober world with help from Johnny Walker Red and green California cannabis (the Christmas colors of my literary work), this well-rehearsed ritual gets sloppier as the clock ticks on.

It was nearing the end of the evening. I cranked out ten journal pages. Every insight I could think of from the day was recorded. Then I heard Caleb come home. I didn't want to walk downstairs.

But there was still more to say. I looked at my glass. Except for a few cubes, it was empty. The scotch bottle was half-full. I poured out two fingers' worth into a glass. Then I spied the pink bottle. I just needed a little bit of water to cut the potion. I reached for it and poured it in my glass. I let it swish around a little bit so it married with the ice and the scotch.

> This nocturnal catharsis
> Never fails to satisfy.
> Go late, go deep
> Go drunk, go stoned
> Will it heighten awareness?
> Tomorrow's sober eyes will see.

With my Aquarian jug empty, the process of refilling it begins anew at sunrise when I am free to intuit new situations, emotions and feelings, confident that the previous perceptions were logged in permanent ink. It was how my imagination and my intellect synchronized. I went on for twenty more minutes and two more pages. Then I was done.

It was all written down now and sublimated into literary form. Cleansed and refreshed, I let go of all of it. Here was the result I hoped for most: that Shayla Reeve would let it go, not complain to Ron Robbins about my service at table 54 and that I'd get to see that woman on the train again.

I put down my pen and closed my journal. I turned off my lamp, took off my headphones and was ready for bed. There was a disturbance downstairs. Johnny and Cortez returned; the girls were with them. Someone bumped into something, and it crashed to the floor. There was lots of drunken laughter.

"Don't worry about it. It's Caleb's. We'll buy him another," I heard Cortez say. I was reminded that his bed beneath my bedroom had squeaky springs.

I walked back to the study to grab my cell phone and my headphones. But before I returned to bed, one last thought occurred to me. I wrote it down. "The only entity I want to pursue has the initials F. S. H."

I crawled into bed, put on my headphones and fell asleep.

CHAPTER 6

My cell phone rang and woke me at 11:00 a.m. When I reached for it, I saw it was from Ron Robbins. I was scheduled to work the dinner shift at 5:00 p.m. I was hungover and debated whether to answer it or let it slip into voicemail. But I clicked the button in time and uttered a cautious, "Hello."

"Sam, it's Ron. We have a water main break at the restaurant. Water is pouring down from the ceiling. The whole place is flooded. We're not going to open for business today or tomorrow. Actually, I'm not sure when we'll reopen."

"How did that happen?"

"Not sure. All I know is that it's a mess."

"Do you want me to come in and help you clean it up?" I asked.

"Thanks, but no. We've hired a professional outfit to come in and get it done. You have some time off. Enjoy it."

"Thanks, boss. Good luck with the flood."

"Here's another thing. A messenger from Shayla Reeve's office stopped in this morning and delivered a letter. It's addressed to you."

"It didn't take her long, did it?"

"No."

"Am I in trouble?"

"Not sure. She has a lot of influence in this town, so I'm concerned. Maybe you should come in and read the letter."

"Oh shit," I said.

"I'll be here all day."

"Okay, I'll be there in a little while."

I got out of bed and walked to my study to examine the contents of last night's channel. The truth of my late-night confessions is always judged by the sober morning light. With the sun rising, I looked at the nocturnal notes a second time to judge which pages were revealing and which pages were ridiculous. In re-examining the scotch and the Sour Diesel-inspired thoughts, I found both.

I pondered what passed through me. Here was the first thing that caught my eye.

> Men require renewal.
> America requires the same.
> Zero in on that heroic quest
> And get us back into the game.

Of course, the last page was almost illegible. I must have been really loaded because those letters were without right-angle lines or round curves. It was a sloppy kvell, a cheerleading rant about how good things were and a mushy gratitude to the spiritual forces guiding me. Being drunk and stoned is not necessarily a good formula for literary composition. In fact, the end was kind of sappy.

After a shower and a bowl of cereal, I walked through my Capitol Hill neighborhood and down to Tadich, which was over two miles away. The brick-lined sidewalks were sometimes pushed up by tree roots. You had to watch your step lest you trip over a raised brick edge and fall on your face.

Lawn signs highlighting the words of Martin Luther King were seen in the small front yards of the endless row houses. "Let no man bring you down so low as to hate him."

Free book boxes with glass doors secured by a hook and eye were all over the community. I suppose it was an indication that nobody values books anymore, so giving them away is the best way to purge your library. I chose a route that passed by three. There was a great one near the corner of North Carolina and 9th Street SE. It must have been supplied by a scholar because its content frequently found its way to my desk.

Today, as I passed, I found a book entitled, "Homer the Theologian." I loved reading about the Greek poet. Here was a book about my favorite part of his work: the relationship between men and the gods. His rendering of man's relationship to divinity was more exciting than anything the Muslims, Christians and Jews had in their theology. I put the tome in my backpack.

With the sun at my back, I walked past the Supreme Court and the Capitol Building. At the bottom of Capitol Hill, the National Gallery of Art, the National Archives, and the Canadian Embassy lined the wide boulevard of Pennsylvania Avenue on my way to Tadich. When I got there, the barroom floor was covered in two inches of water, and the ceiling above was wet and falling down. A crew from ServiceMaster was on the job sucking up the water and installing dehumidifiers to get the moisture out of the restaurant.

It smelled pretty bad and led me to believe that maybe a sewer line broke from the Carlyle Group floors above us. Whatever trouble Reeve might stir up now was nothing compared to this mess. Perhaps her bad energy even contributed to it.

I examined the letter in front of Robbins. If she was threatening me or the restaurant, he should know. When I tore it open, two one-hundred-dollar bills fell to the ground.

Inside was a short note of apology. She requested that I meet her tomorrow afternoon at the Capitol Grill at 3:00 p.m. "Well, that's a relief."

"What's the two hundred for?" Ron asked.

"Beats me. Her boyfriend left a generous tip, it doesn't feel right accepting it," I said.

"As a waiter, you never question a tip, good or bad," Ron said.

"It's not about the money. Her behavior was awful, and I'm not letting her off the hook so easily. I'm giving it back."

"So, you're going to meet her?" Ron asked.

"I guess. How do you handle a woman like that?"

"You don't. She handles you. Given what I've heard about her over the years, you'll be lucky to get away with your balls attached."

"How long has she been a TV big shot in town?"

"A long time, and she knows everybody. Be careful. If you get on her bad side, it won't be good for any of us."

The next afternoon, I walked through the doors of the Capitol Grill. I told the hostess whom I was meeting, and she led me to a table in the corner of the dining room. Reeve was sitting with Phillip Talbot. Both turned their heads at the same time.

"Okay, Phillip, we're done here. Thank you for coming."

"Am I dismissed already?" He just finished his lamb chops. Three of her six oysters were uneaten before her. "I wondered why you didn't order lunch and kept looking at your watch."

"If you'll excuse us, Samuel and I have things to discuss."

Talbot picked up some papers from the table and gave me an angry look. "I'm not the enemy here, Shayla, and he's not the answer."

He walked out the door. Shayla signaled the waiter. She asked him to remove the dirty dishes. Once clear, I sat down beside her.

"I'm glad you could make it," she said.

I pulled out the two hundred-dollar bills. "Your friend gave me a generous tip. I don't feel comfortable taking this as well."

"It's not about the other night. It's about Sunday night, the twenty-second. I have a gala for the National Symphony Orchestra at the National Portrait Gallery. I'm on their board, and I need a date. As you can well imagine, Phil Talbot is no longer an option. That two hundred dollars is what I'll pay you to escort me."

"I usually work Sunday nights."

"No, you don't. The restaurant is closed on Sunday. Even I know that. If you come, I'll throw in another hundred. It's that important to me."

"Why me?"

"You're a waiter. You know how to act. I know that I can be a bitch on wheels. You handled me like a pro and even protected me that night."

"I was afraid of getting fired."

"I just heard about the restaurant shutting down. You'll need the money, so don't deny it," she said, handing me a menu. "Order a steak, then we'll go and fit you for a tuxedo."

I ordered a New York Strip; she did, too. We ate. "How long have you been working at Tadich Grill?"

"I've been working lunches there for months. The night we met was my first dinner shift."

"Do you like it?"

"I'm kind of the rookie compared to the other staff. But I like that part because I'm learning the ropes from some real old pros."

"Despite its controversies and bad plumbing, it's not a bad place to eat."

"What controversies are you talking about?"

She laughed. "They never told you?"

"Tell me what?"

"The place is jinxed."

"How so?"

"Three of their original waiters are dead. A fourth almost died in a car crash and can't wait tables anymore. And Gerald was one of the best in town," she said. "The HVAC system is a mess. The heat never works in the winter, and the air-conditioning never works in the summer. I hate that it's so hot inside. I think that's why Phillip insisted I meet him there."

Suddenly, I realized she was right. I was so intent on making the team that such consideration went right under my radar. Bursting pipes, she explained, were just some of the many problems they've had.

"Ever wonder why the place is the roost of Republicans, but you rarely see a Democrat in there?"

"As a matter of fact, I have," I said.

"You'd think that because it's a San Francisco restaurant in Nancy Pelosi's own congressional district that they'd swarm there, but they don't. Democrats can't be seen there."

"I thought it was because of its proximity to the Trump Hotel."

"No, that's not it."

"What's the real story?"

"The Buich family, who owns the San Francisco location, has been accused of being racist. It was in all the papers when Tadich opened. Didn't you see it?"

"I must have missed it."

"Years ago, when their daughter Terry was in her twenties, she ran off with an older Black man who was still married at the time and came with him to DC. The family disowned her, and they still haven't reconciled. Turns out Terry had some harsh things to say about the family."

"Whom did she marry?"

"Gene Upshaw."

"The lineman for the Raiders?"

"Not only that, he was also the head of the NFL Players Association. He died of pancreatic cancer a few years ago."

"So that's why we only get Republicans?"

"That's why."

"No one told me."

"Why would they?"

"But we have Black employees, and the manager, Ron Robbins, is the most liberal guy I know."

"That's not the perception."

"Did your network run the story?"

"Of course, after the Washington Post printed it, we had no choice."

"But it's not true," I said.

"Maybe, but the restaurant never offered a credible response to the press. The news cycle kept talking about it, and the Buich family never tried to change the narrative."

"That doesn't seem fair."

"In DC, perception is everything," she said. "If I were you, I'd take the date. You might need the money very soon."

A car picked us up after lunch. We went to an L Street haberdashery. She introduced me to a tailor named Manny. He fit me for a tuxedo and shoes. He put them in a plastic bag and then her car drove me home. "My car will pick you up at six forty-five Sunday night. Please be ready, and if you have the time, get a haircut."

Sunday night, a black limousine picked me up on time. The fellas watched from the window as I walked down the steps to the car. Shayla was in the back seat, and she looked beautiful. Her low-cut dress showed her cleavage but hid the bruise on her shoulder. The dress matched the color of her eyes. Her long blond hair was tied up in a bun.

When the limo got to the National Portrait Gallery, we had to wait in line with other cars inching their way to the entrance. When a doorman opened her door, she was greeted by a gaggle of photographers, who snapped her picture. I got out on the other side.

When we were side by side walking up the stairs and about to enter the ball, she whispered, "Listen, because of who I am, there's going to be a lot of gossip about you. As a favor to me, please drink responsibly and don't embarrass me."

The place was packed with the Washington, DC, illuminati. Jeff Bezos was there, as well as Michelle Obama and Senator Lamar Alexander. I even recognized a few of my customers. But dressed in a black tuxedo instead of a white waiter's jacket, no one recognized me. While Shayla went off to socialize, I found my way to the bar and ordered a scotch.

One man I did recognize was a short White guy named Dan Jones. He was a banquet captain dressed in a white jacket with purple trim and the logo of the catering company stitched upon it. We once worked together at the steakhouse Smith and Wollensky. A Boston native, we shook hands and talked as he stood beside the bar supervising the event.

"What are you doing here with all this pond scum?" Dan asked.

"I'm playing male escort tonight."

"Who's the bitch?"

"Shayla Reeve."

He gave me a sly grin. "You're moving up in the world, Sammy."

We spent several minutes together and then I said, "I have a vape pen in my pocket. Want to take a few hits?"

"Sure. Follow me."

We walked down a hallway where no one was and took a few tokes each. Since there was no odor from the smoke, we were pretty nonchalant even when two guests from the party passed by. It relaxed me, and I actually took a greater stock of the whole affair.

When we went back inside, Dan attended to a few banquet matters as I surveyed the crowd. When he returned, there was a shit-eating grin on his face. Then Shayla walked to me. There was a grimace on her face.

"Would it kill you to mingle a little? Leave the hired help alone and pretend that you belong here," she said and then added, "Why are you smiling?"

"I don't know. It all seems kind of comical."

"My livelihood depends on it, so earn your money."

"Wait a minute," said Dan, offended that she treated me disrespectfully. He momentarily glanced at me and, in a softer voice, said, "Is this the bimbo?"

When I nodded my head, he took two steps into Shayla's personal space. "Let me explain something to you, lady. This is no ordinary gigolo. This Samuel Taylor Meckler, waiter emeritus, scholar extraordinaire and a man held in high esteem by his peers. Not only that, he could strap you down, stick it inside you and make you cum three times without breaking a sweat. Show some respect."

Startled by his aggressiveness, Shayla turned and walked away. I looked at Dan, and we both started giggling. "Thanks, man," I said.

"Sammy, it's going to take more than scotch and weed to make those foul breasts seem erotic."

Shayla walked to the farthest part of the room and greeted a small group of women. I tried not to fraternize with the hired help even though I found them more interesting. On my way back from the bathroom, I ran into another waiter. He was passing out Crab Rangoon on a silver tray. We struck up a conversation. I told him I worked at Tadich and asked him how he liked doing banquets with this catering service. "I like it," he said. "They're always looking for talent, even if it's only part-time. The majority of the wait staff here are dolts. You might want to apply."

When the cocktail hour was up, we all sat down to a dinner of filet mignon, mashed potatoes and asparagus. When you consider it was served for four hundred people, it was a pretty good meal.

Most of the guests were older than me. Many were big shots in some capacity, including two members of the president's cabinet at the table beside ours. I made small talk with them all. No one asked me what I did for a living. That was probably lucky for Shayla, lest I let it slip that I was the waiter she abused last week at Tadich Grill.

Then, as chair of the symphony's board of directors, Shayla got up and made a speech. She was funny, self-deprecating and noble. I had to admit, the public side of her persona was way more interesting than the private person whom I knew to be a termagant.

She spoke without notes for about fifteen minutes, and when she stepped down, she received a thunderous standing ovation. I, too, stood and clapped. When she returned to the table, I pulled out her chair and started to congratulate her but backed off when she was swarmed by well-wishers.

Around 10:00 p.m., I recognized a man I knew. His name was Brian Lambert. He was the Librarian of Congress. I didn't give a damn about the politicians, plutocrats, media celebrities or the musicians in attendance. They had nothing to offer me. But Lambert did.

He was a Vermont native who began his career as an English professor at Bennington College. He'd been in charge of the Library of Congress for many years.

I walked right up to him, introduced myself and shook his hand. When I told him I was a friend and protégé of the Minnesota poet and politician Russ Nelson, he was impressed.

"I attended a reading of his several years ago at the Folger Shakespeare Library," Lambert said. "He made an excellent showing."

"I was sitting in the front row that night."

"How do you know Nelson?"

"I'm a former Twin Cities reporter. I've done two newspaper stories about him. When he contracted cancer, I also became kind of a part-time caregiver, which mainly consisted of supplying him with marijuana so when the effects of his chemotherapy overwhelmed him, he was better able to cope."

Just then, Shayla walked up beside me. I stuck out my palm and put it in her direction to make sure she didn't interrupt.

"He also paid me to write about periods of his life like his childhood, his college days, his time in the Minnesota State Senate, then in the US Senate, his two gubernatorial terms and most interesting, his poetry and how it all evolved. I'd do long interviews with a tape recorder, transcribe them and then write feature stories for the benefit of his family and his legend."

"What are you doing in DC?" he asked.

"I'm here working on a literary project. It's actually a long poem, and because of that, my Library of Congress library card is one of my prized possessions."

"Why's that?"

"I like to read old books of poetry criticism. My wheelhouse seems to be from 1880 to 1914. When an author praises a writer I've never heard of, I go to the LOC, look up the guy and have his old books delivered to my desk there. If he appeals to me, I order his work from Amazon or one of the other used bookstore sites online."

"I've always loved that time period," he said.

"Me too. It reflects America in a more innocent time. It was before twentieth-century events like World War I, World War II, the Holocaust, Hiroshima, the Cold War and, of course, it's also before the advent of radio, television and the digital age. They just seem to write a cleaner, more literary prose, which I find instructive to my own work."

"Tell me about your poem."

"It's called 'A Firm State of Heart.' It's an attempt to find an idealistic way forward through this messy muddle America finds itself in."

"How are you going to do that?"

"Not sure. I know it's important to use great poems as templates for my work, but Homer and Virgil focus too much on war. That's a terrible thing in the twenty-first century, especially with globalization. Milton's 'Paradise Lost' focuses on scripture and that's no role model either since we live in a time of multiculturalism. Wordsworth writes really well about nature but in an era of climate change, he doesn't address current issues either."

"What is it you actually want to comment upon?" he asked.

"Culture and how it's evolving in the digital age."

"Maybe you should come to my office," he said. "There are a few librarians I can introduce you to. They might be able to help."

"Do you have a card?"

He reached into his wallet and handed it to me.

"Thanks, Brian," I said. "I'll call you this week."

"Are you still in touch with Nelson?"

"Of course."

"Then send him my regards."

"I will," I said.

Shayla listened attentively. I think she was surprised to find that I knew more than the Tadich menu. I turned. "Let me introduce you to Shayla Reeve. Shayla, this is Brian Lambert."

"I know who he is," she said. They knew each other by reputation and seemed genuinely happy to meet. "Nice to meet you, Brian."

Just then, a photographer walked by. "Shayla," he called.

She turned and, seeing him raise the camera to his eye, grabbed hold of my arm and shot him a big smile. He snapped three pictures.

"Who's your date?" he asked.

"The poet, Samuel Meckler," she answered.

"Thanks, Shayla," he said and walked away.

With her speech done, a photo taken and sufficient mingling with the crowd, her goals for the evening were met. "Samuel, I'm exhausted. Please take me home."

"Certainly."

Once back in the limousine, she let out a giant sigh of relief. "Oh god, these events just exhaust me."

"Really? You seem like a natural."

"A natural? No, not at all. It's a lot of work for me."

There wasn't any talk as the car took us away from the Portrait Gallery and back up to Capitol Hill. I figured I'd give her the space to decompress.

What is it that inspires people like her to be out in the spotlight? At one time, in a cynical mood, I thought it was all vanity. But she had talent, too, and that was more significant. But the price she paid for her time out front seemed steep.

When the limo pulled up to her condo, I got out and opened her door. "Charles, take the rest of the night off. I'll send Samuel home in an Uber."

"Yes, ma'am, good night."

"Come up for a drink. I'll give you the rest of your money."

"It's been a long night," I said. "I only live a mile away. I think I'll just walk home. Send the money to the restaurant."

"Come on, just one drink. I've been a teetotaler all evening. I don't want to drink alone."

Her condo was a fifth-floor penthouse in a Pennsylvania Avenue Southeast building that previously had been a hardware store. It burned six years ago and was recently rebuilt with housing above it. It was a spacious three-bedroom unit with floor-to-ceiling windows in the living room. They looked west with an unobstructed view of the Library of Congress, the Supreme Court and the US Capitol.

There were two oil paintings above the living room couch placed side by side. Both featured attractive women in alluring attire painted by the same artist. The sofa and chairs were black leather; there were several wooden antique pieces and bookcases. Most of the books were nonfiction—memoirs and celebrity books about Washington, DC. There was a wall of photos with her beside such notables as George W. Bush, Michelle Obama, Marion Barry, Steve Jobs and Bill Gates.

Shayla turned on the big-screen TV and watched her own station review her performance at the gala. It was the last story of the broadcast. They caught all the nuances of it, and she seemed pleased by their report. I think that was why she was in such a hurry to get home. When I rolled my eyes at her narcissism, she said, "You don't like me, do you?"

"What's to like?" And it felt good to say it.

"The bar is right there," she said. "Pour yourself a drink. Make me a Basil Hayden on the rocks. I'll be right out."

She went to her bedroom and changed. When she emerged, her makeup was off; her hair was in a ponytail. She wore yoga pants and a large bulky T-shirt. We sat on a couch outside on her fifth-floor balcony. Storm clouds were moving in from the west, slowly blotting out the stars.

"Listen, I know I can be a pain in the ass," she said. "It comes with the territory. But you were great tonight. Thanks."

"You know dozens of men. Why didn't you ask one of them?"

"Most of them don't like sharing the spotlight with a woman."

"Oh, so being that I am a waiter, you just figured you could bully me like that night at the restaurant?"

"No, I liked you because you weren't afraid of my temper tantrums. That's why I asked you along as my date."

"Okay."

"I need people around me who can stand my blasts."

"Maybe you just need a whipping boy."

"Maybe you should just shut up. I'm not a waiter. I play in the big leagues. What I do is pressure-filled and important."

My face must have expressed some gesture of disdain. She noticed. "The evening is over. Why are you so resentful?"

"Because you have fame in a city that craves fame. You have money in a district full of plutocrats. You're a role model and a trusted voice in tens of thousands of living rooms every night, and yet you're miserable. It makes no sense to me."

"Don't be ridiculous. This is a man's world, and I've had to fight like hell for my piece of it. And I got it, all of it."

"Then you should shoulder the stress of it better."

"I shoulder the stress just fine, thank you."

"A lot of waiters in this town would disagree."

This conversation wasn't going anywhere good. I just shut up and took a long gulp of my drink, waiting for the right moment to rush out the door. The skies were pissing down rain. It was going to be a twenty-minute walk home in the deluge. She must have an umbrella I could borrow. But hell, then I'd have to return it. Maybe it was best to just get wet. What the hell? These weren't even my clothes. Now I was chomping at the bit. My brain started churning out ideas and insights that were perfect for my journal. I wanted to get them written down on paper before they flitted out of my mind and into the ether.

To get a head start on the channeling part, I reached inside my tuxedo pocket and pulled out my cannabis pen. Part of me was hoping that she would be offended, kick me out and I could be on my way.

I took a long drag and blew out a cloud of smoke. To my surprise, she reached for it. She examined it closely. "How do you do this?"

"Press the button till it turns blue and then sip it." She took a long drag and blew out a cloud of smoke.

"Hmm, not bad," she said. Then she took another one and then another one before handing it back to me. I watched. For the first time, the muscles in her face relax. A dreamy look came to her face. Finally, she broke the silence.

"God, I need a vacation. I'm spending the Fourth of July on Cape Cod. Where will you be?"

"Working, I suppose. I don't really like that holiday."

"Don't like the Fourth of July? Why the hell not?"

"The rocket's red glare, the bombs bursting in air."

"I never heard a man say that before."

"One evening when I was a kid, I was sitting with my father watching TV. The Iraq War started and we were watching the bombardment of Baghdad. They called it "Operation Shock and Awe." For me, it was like the Fourth of July fireworks. I even cheered at the giant explosions. My dad stepped in my shit."

"What did he say?"

"Don't you dare cheer for that! Thousands of people are dying, and all they've worked for is now in rubble."

"What did your father do for a living?"

"He's an administrator at the Veterans Hospital in Minneapolis. He said that in the next few years, thousands of men were going to be admitted to that facility, and he would be in charge of their physical and emotional health. It infuriated him that the war they committed themselves to was based on a lie about weapons of mass destruction. And he was right. Within the next few years, thousands came to the hospital. Some of them eventually committed suicide. Those were the lucky ones. Others became drug addicts, alcoholics and homeless, much to the detriment of their wives and children."

"I see," she said.

"He demanded intellectual honesty and emotional health from his children."

"Your father sounds like a man of integrity."

"He is. In the 1970s, he was drafted into the army and sent to Vietnam. He hated it and encouraged me to be an adventurer instead of a warrior."

"What's the difference?"

"One kills men, the other fucks women."

"Are you good at fucking women?"

"Very good."

"And why is that?"

"Because of the delight I take in it."

I never fucked someone famous before. I wondered how the energy and power she exuded in her career might translate between the sheets. Perhaps some grand secret to success might be revealed to me in the passion of her embrace. Then again, maybe not.

"If I was a man, I'd choose the adventurer too."

"It's a clear choice," I said. "Violence is boring. In so many movies today, you see the protagonist caught in a tense situation. Most times, he blasts his way out of his predicament with guns instead of taking responsibility for his own actions."

"Are you currently fucking anybody?" she asked.

"At present, no. Are you?"

"No."

That seemed like an important exchange. She changed the subject.

"What did you study in college?"

"I have an English degree from the University of Minnesota. Before moving here a few years ago, I was a newspaper reporter."

"Why did you give it up?"

"Why would I want to write about another man's ideals when I could write about my own?"

"You could make your mark in this city."

"My scholarship is more important to me than a career."

"Why can't you do both."

"Because it's going to take me years to articulate what I want to achieve."

"Which is?"

"A new model of American idealism."

She laughed. "Nobody is thinking like you."

"I know and it gets lonely sometimes."

"Yes, I know all about that," she said.

"You're one of the most celebrated women I've ever met. What do you know about loneliness?"

"Don't let all the attention fool you. I always thought that if I achieved success, the trauma of my early years would autocorrect. It doesn't work like that. I still go home at night alone and have to live with my regrets and my anxiety."

"Maybe you should be in therapy."

"What makes you think I'm not?"

"What's the origin of it all?"

She started to speak but then held back. "You're a former reporter, right? And I don't know you very well, right?"

"You mean you don't trust me enough to confess."

"Right."

"That's probably smart. I might get a reporter's rush and write an essay for the *Huffington Post* entitled 'My Night as Shayla Reeve's Bitch.'"

"Come on. It wasn't that bad."

When I didn't answer, she stood and grabbed my glass. "Let me refresh your beverage." She poured me my second, a strong one, too, and then one for herself.

"Tell me about Phillip. Is he your lawyer, your husband or your agent?"

"Once upon a time, he was all three. We're in the middle of divorce proceedings, and it gets ugly, as you saw for yourself."

"Yes, it does get ugly, doesn't it?"

"Well, the divorce is pretty much settled since we've split our assets. My contract with the network is up this fall. He's negotiating a new one. But it turns out I'm being courted by several cable news networks, too."

"That's exciting."

"I'm not sure how interested they really are. To tell you the truth, I'm in a rut, personally and professionally. I need new energy and new inspiration. That's a part of the evening that we haven't spoken about. I feel that you might be able to help."

"A woman worn down, looking for refreshment?" I asked.

"I used to be cool. Now I'm middle-aged. I've lost my élan."

"Maybe I can help you find it."

"Why, because you feel sorry for me?"

"Yes."

"Well, at least you're honest."

"It's not about being honest. It's about having a firm grasp of the obvious."

"There's a chance I might go national. But Phillip's taking his own sweet time about it. I'm not sure what the deal is, but the proceedings are slow and drawn out. It gets on my nerves."

"That could be a step up."

"Maybe, but they have reservations," she said. "They're looking for a fresh face."

"Are you too old?"

"That's a lousy question to ask a woman."

"You brought it up."

"Yes, maybe. When I was your age, I was young and ambitious. I was going to take the world by storm. Now that I've achieved it, I don't know what to do with myself."

I finished my drink in one long gulp as she finished her sentence. I needed to get out of there. There was a tension in the air, perhaps the result of the barometric pressure of the thunderstorm. The hair on my arms was standing up, and I was feeling anxious.

"Listen, it's been a long day," I said. "I drank a lot at the gala and here too. I'm stoned and I just want to go home."

"Wait," she said. She stood up and pulled the rest of my money from her pocket. "Are you okay?"

"I'm fine." I stood up to leave. "By the way, can you lend me an umbrella?"

She reached into a kitchen drawer and pulled out a white one with the Channel 4 logo on it. I started for the door. My hand was on the knob when I saw a lightning flash reflect against the door followed quickly by a thunder crack. The lights momentarily dimmed, and I felt a shudder up my back. The strike must have been right above the building. The crack was deafening, and the flash illuminated the room. Against the wall beside me, I saw the shadow of Shayla Reeve crumble to the ground. When I turned and looked back, she was face-first on the carpet.

I ran to her and put my hands under her neck to make sure she hadn't bruised her face. She bumped her head on the side of the coffee table. There was a bruise but no blood. I picked up her feet and let the blood rush to her head.

She awoke to find my hands wrapped around her ankles. She was mortified that something like this should happen, perhaps even conscious that my alleged *Huffington Post* story just got juicier. She rose to her feet and tried to pretend nothing happened.

"I guess I fainted," she said.

"Are you okay?"

"Not sure. Stay just a few minutes longer, just until I collect myself. Pour yourself another drink. Pour me one, too."

"Are you sure that's a good idea?"

"Yes."

Protected by a roof above us, we returned to the balcony, fascinated by the thunder and lightning in the sky. The lightning strike shattered a tree on the boulevard of Pennsylvania Avenue. Another lightning strike touched the dome of the Library of Congress. She slurred the first word of her sentence when she went to speak. Perhaps the stress of the evening, the pot, the whiskey and the bump on the head were showing their effects.

"I'm not feeling very well," she said. "I need to lie down."

"You might have a concussion."

"I did a newscast about that very issue last year. I'm scared. Do me a favor. Spend the night. This way, if anything happens, you can call an ambulance."

"I'll just curl up on this couch and sleep outside here."

"No, you can sleep in my bed. Just keep your underwear on and keep your hands to yourself."

Inside her bedroom, I stripped to my underwear. She kept her T-shirt and yoga pants on.

"Let me see your tattoo." It was on my upper arm on the left side. "Coexist" was what it said, using the religious symbols from a variety of religious traditions for the spelling. The T was the cross, the C was the crescent moon of Islam, the O was the Tao and the X was the Star of David.

"I saw that on a bumper sticker once," she said.

"I like it better on my arm."

She pulled the covers back and fluffed the pillows. "Don't sleep on your back," she said. "I don't want to be awake all night with your snoring."

I rolled over on my side. Not more than a minute later, her arms were around me; we were like spoons.

I fell into a deep sleep.

CHAPTER 7

I awoke the next morning alone in Shayla's bed. She was in the kitchen making breakfast. The table was set, and I could smell the food cooking, which consisted of a cheese and vegetable omelet that we shared, bacon, and juice.

"How are you feeling this morning?" I asked.

"Great, I haven't shared a bed with anyone since Phillip left eight months ago."

"I was referring to the bump on your head."

"It's just a little bump. I'm fine."

"You scared the hell out of me last night. I didn't know if it was the weed, the bourbon, the lightning or the thunder that caused you to faint. But I felt responsible."

"I'm not sure what happened either. Though I admit that it's been years since I got high."

"I'm just glad you didn't bruise your face. It might have cost you a week's worth of work."

"Relax, Samuel, I'm not a waiter. I have a contract and I get paid regardless. Phillip made sure of that. The coffee's ready. Do you take cream?"

"I'll take it black, thanks."

She brought the pot over and poured it into my mug. "Nice pour. If the network doesn't renew your contract, perhaps I can get you a job at Tadich."

"Don't be smug. I put myself through grad school working as a cocktail waitress. I could probably still run circles around you."

"I doubt it."

"Listen, I have a proposition for you. I need your friendship. You are young and ridiculously idealistic, while I've become a middle-aged bore."

"What would that entail?"

"To start with, I need you to write a Wikipedia bio for me."

"How many words are you thinking about?"

"Probably about seven hundred."

"That's easy enough. I've published over a hundred feature articles. We could crank that out in an afternoon."

"Oh no, I can't be involved. You'd have to do it on your own. I'd want it to be objective."

"Then forget about it," I said. "I'm not interested in an in-depth investigative report. To do that, I'd have to include your drama at Tadich Grill and you passing out last night. Besides, you've done good work in the community. That's the only thing that matters. I'll only do it if we work together."

"Aren't you worried about your journalistic integrity being compromised?"

"Shayla, what passes for journalism these days is an embarrassment. Some right-wing clown says something ridiculous, and every media outlet in the nation falls over themselves to cover it. It's all about controversy, not community, and that's stupid. If I don't feel passion for a story, it's no fun to write," I said. "I'm not going to judge you. Just tell your story as it happened. That's the only way I'll do it."

"Well, that would be better for me."

"What's in it for me?"

"I am welcomed in the best salons in Washington. You will be too."

"I already work in one of the best salons in DC. It's where the action is. I get paid to be there and paid well. Under your plan, I have to hang out for free. It's better the way it is now."

"Yes, but my way, you get to sit at the table. Your way, you have to run around and work hard."

"And how would you introduce me? As your protégé, your lover, your boy toy, your gigolo?"

"We can figure that out later."

"You're not going to become a succubus who drains my best energy for her own immoral purposes, are you?"

"Does that scare you?" she asked.

"Yes."

"When it comes to working with competitive men, I have a terrible reputation. But you're different. I've always had as much respect for personality as for accomplishment."

"You don't respect men. That's not a very attractive trait."

"When you work in my profession, toxic masculinity is a constant problem," she said.

"I've got no public persona and have nothing to lose. But what about you? Aren't you concerned about the gossip?"

"I'd roll you out after the contract is signed."

"This whole proposition sounds like a bore."

"Don't be silly. I'm talking about the National Republican Capitol Hill Club, the Cosmos Club, the National Press Club, the British Embassy and the White House, just to name a few. You would be my escort, and you'd get to know people who might advance your career."

"I'm an introvert."

"I've seen you in the dining room. You're charming."

"But hanging out with a bunch of stiffs isn't any kind of reward."

"But consider how it might inspire your poem."

"No offense, but I'd prefer a blow job."

"Well, you can just forget about that. A sexual relationship will have to be earned, and it will only be actualized over a long period of time."

"Thanks, but no thanks," I said.

She cleared the plates and the silverware and loaded them in the dishwasher. Then she sat back down. She paused for a moment and then spoke.

"I saw the way you handled the situation at Tadich. The way you protected me from those women was magnificent. I took you for just another lazy millennial. I didn't realize you were inspired. I'm interested in your world because mine is stale and dissolving," she said. "I wonder if we might be able to help each other. What I am missing is inspiration. What you are missing is cash."

"I have enough money, thanks."

"Samuel, Tadich is going to be closed for at least a week, maybe more. I spoke to someone at a city inspector's office. You don't have enough money."

"I'll manage."

"I wonder then if we might have a meeting of the minds."

"What do you mean?"

"I didn't get to where I am with just a pretty face. I am a good reporter, too. Please know that."

"I never doubted it."

"What is it that inspires you to write poetry?"

"It's the best medium we have for exploring emerging issues and making them real," I said. "We live in a digital age that's accelerating beyond our comprehension. Poetry slows you down. It asks you to appreciate its rhythms, its pauses and its meaning. Appreciating it demands the same deliberate concentration and thought as what the writer himself put into it. In a digital age dedicated to speed and sensation, that's significant."

"But why put all your energy into poetry?"

"It's a calling."

She suggested that I use the tape recorder on my cell phone to record all we were saying.

"What's the most difficult part of writing a long poem?"

"Grasping the component parts of the genre and trying to fit your personal impressions into the narrative in an interesting way."

"What did you say the name of your poem is?"

"A Firm State of Heart."

"How did you come up with that title?"

"It came to me in a dream."

"Do a lot of your literary ideas originate in dreams?"

"Yes."

"What does the poem's title refer to?"

"An emotional state where compassion and the urges of the heart prevail. Anything's better than the current mood propagated by cynical, small-minded talking heads."

"Is there a story to the poem?"

"Yes, I watched a movie with my father long ago starring Jimmy Stewart, *Mr. Smith Goes to Washington*. It's based on that."

"If I remember correctly, it's about a young man who comes to Washington and finds his idealism tested by the power politics of the city."

"That's a good synopsis of my poem."

"How did you get on this path?"

"Governor Russ Nelson of Minnesota tricked me into it. When he was going through chemotherapy, I used to get him high on marijuana to help with the symptoms. Whenever he was stoned, he'd wax poetic about poetry. In the process, he got me high on the democratic ideal of it. He made it look so noble, so American, and so much fun that I couldn't resist. I'd look at that old man's life and think to myself, 'Yes, I'm havin' what he's havin'.'"

"Does your father support your literary pursuits?"

"I'm the youngest of three kids. His daughter is a doctor. His oldest son is a lawyer. It gave me permission to be bohemian."

"Do you really think you can change American society with a poem?"

"It might not change America, but it might change me."

Her face contorted with a supercilious expression.

"It must sound weird to you," I said.

"It does. I mean, seriously, poetry is an adolescent medium reserved for gangster rappers, children and milquetoast college professors."

"It stands apart from most media," I said. "Thus, it carries a certain virginity to it."

"But it's of no real importance."

"Maybe to someone like you. But to me, it's everything."

"How do you become a poet with something to say?"

"Nobody teaches you that. You have to follow your own trail, plumb the depth of your soul and bring back something that's useful to others."

"But no one reads poetry anymore. You'll have no audience," she said.

"Maybe I'll steal yours."

"Good luck with that, Samuel. People recognize the names of poets and even pay lip service to their work. But few ever read them and fewer still understand them."

"Right now, that's not my concern."

"Tell me more about your poem."

"It's in its infant stages, but I have high hopes for what it might become. I'm looking to make it a long poem like Hart Crane's 'The Bridge,' Percy Bysshe Shelley's 'Prometheus Unbound,' and Walt Whitman's 'Leaves of Grass.' It's an attempt to render the American nation fit for the coming globalized, high-tech, multicultural world that's forcing itself upon the body politic."

"What are you going to do to make it fresh?"

"Create a worldview that transcends religion and nationalism with a new age theology."

"The Bible warns men not to long for that which lies beyond their reach," she said. "Do you honestly think you can do it?"

"Yes, all I need is one thing."

"What's that?"

"A long life. It's going to take me years to figure it out."

"Have you ever considered that maybe Crane, Shelley and Whitman are just more talented than you are, and you'll never come close to them?"

"I'm not conceding anything to anybody. They may be masters of technique and have that over me, but I excel all of them in consciousness. All I need is a few more decades to grow and molt and take ownership of my advantages."

"And what advantages are you talking about?"

"Good health care, a computer, a variety of bookstores and online libraries, the Library of Congress, spell check, the belief in multiculturalism, Jersey, Minnesota, Judaism, Catholicism, marijuana, jet travel, the internet, television. Compared to my grasp of the world, they're primitive. I'm going to reinvent the heroic formula for a digital age."

"Your goal sounds like a lonely one."

"I know, but I've put myself on this path and I can't stop. Plus, it's very satisfying. That beats everything because it makes me happy."

"But poetry has nothing to do with the language habits of most Americans," she said. "Do you ever fear that it's a fool's errand?"

"Do you think I'm a fool?"

"No."

"I realize that being a poet in a digital age is odd. But I have this faith that with concentration and study, I can work through each literary roadblock. I get a better handle on the material every day, and as such, I'm better able to organize it into a coherent, comprehensive narrative."

"How do you do that?"

"By articulating a sense of emotional health that transcends the rhetoric, the moral outrage and the fear that's everywhere. At the risk of offending, you are one of the villains I'm fighting against."

"Me? What are you talking about?"

"I've seen your news show. It's about murder, sexual abuse and tragedy. It almost seems as if you purposely prime your audience with horror stories so they can feel relief when the good news comes."

"What good news are you talking about?"

"A blue bear hugging toilet tissue."

"Oh, you mean the commercials."

"It seems like manipulation, but of course, it does pay for this fancy condo. For you, I suppose, it's a good deal."

"TV is a business. It's not a morality play," she said. "TV is fast and dramatic because each on-air minute influences the buying habits of the American consumer."

"It's the incessant bombardment of disconnected TV images and the lack of a credible context that gets me," I said.

"As a broadcaster, I deal with what's real."

"I'm sure it seems that way to you," I said. "But real ideas are intuited in the mind first, then felt in the gut, then reinforced by events until they crystalize into an emerging issue. Anyway, that's the way it all evolves with me."

"How do the words come to you?"

"Spontaneously, and most times by their own leave. Often, my best reception comes when I am drinking scotch and getting high. My housemate Caleb says that because of that fact, they should be disqualified. But I feel compelled to write them down, lest they fly off into cyberspace, never to be recognized again."

"If I was to read your poem, what would I get out of it?"

"A better understanding of cultural processes with all its twists and turns, its dialectical progressions, its vicissitudes, its confusions, its tragedy and all the ways that life is reflected in it."

"How will you know when it's done?"

"When I'll run out of things to say."

She was a careful listener. I was excited to answer her cogent questions. Some of what I told her was heard by my own ears for the first time. And yet they were spontaneous and true. She pulled stuff out of me that I wasn't even conscious of. During our back-and-forth, I discovered the best part of my literary self. We went on like this for the next hour.

I was reminded of plants underneath Lake Harriet in Minneapolis. No one ever considers them because they're out of sight. Then, one day in July, they emerge from the depths and reach for the sunlight above the waterline. That's how Shayla Reeve made me feel at her table.

It was me who decided to end it. I think she might have allowed it to go on for the rest of the morning. But now my mind was brimming with so many new ideas that I was longing for my desk. Plus, I had it all recorded on my phone. When I told her I had to go, she repeated her line from an hour ago. "A meeting of the minds."

I realized her value. My male ego, fired with passion, leapt at the opportunity to speak to her full lips, blue eyes, pretty face and patient glance. How gracefully the bad bitch at table 54 morphed into a three-dimensional character, someone I actually liked because, through her, I got to discover more of myself.

When I arrived home, the boys were eating breakfast.

They applauded when I came through the door.

"How was the gala with Shayla?" asked Johnny.

"We argued, insulted each other and discussed poetry."

And I said it with an ironic air to cast doubt in their minds. They didn't want to believe me. Instead, they were hoping for something lurid. Their imaginations wanted to think that we had sex.

"We saw you last night on TV," Caleb said. "Channel Four did a small segment about it, and in one frame, they showed you sitting next to her at the banquet table."

Cortez stared at my feet until I noticed. "What are you looking at?" I asked.

"Wanted to see if *Cinderfella* returned with both his shoes."

Looking down, I said, "They better be there. They're rented."

CHAPTER 8

W hen DC anal retentiveness overwhelms me with its traditions, mores, pecking order and rules intended to impose order and stifle the imagination, the irrational wells up inside me. To accommodate those deep swells, I resort to ritual.

Certainly, the most important one takes place at my desk late at night where I detail my travail. But those feelings are the culmination of quiet moments intuited during my daytime hours. One of the sacred sites where I collect them is at Congressional Cemetery.

Unknown to tourists and most Washingtonians, it's located in the very eastern part of the city near the Anacostia River. It's a quiet residential part of the city, quickly becoming gentrified. Since Tadich was closed and there was still plenty of afternoon sun left to the day, I walked alone to that thirty-five-acre site.

On blue summer days, I enjoy walking its shady lanes beside green grass, under giant trees, inhaling the scent of summer flowers, listening to birdsongs and buzzing bees.

As I pushed through the iron gate of the fenced-in necropolis, a labradoodle puppy with brown curly hair rushed to greet me. His owner was an older woman with a big smile. The young pup jumped around me with glee when I got down on one knee to pet him. Dogs are unleashed in the cemetery, and while most ignore the solitary stranger in their midst, often you'd get to pet a friendly hound happy to be running loose.

The cemetery is a quiet, reflective place filled with the literature of past lives. Here, written in stone, the dead often get the last word. A dozen yards inside the gate is a marble bench. Written upon it is a quote from Edward Streeter (1891–1976): "A cemetery is not a gloomy place that speaks of death but a vigorous entity that vibrates with life."

Karl D. Maxwell has a bench with these words: "I'm rejoicing with my savior where no tear will dim the eye." Not far away, Leona Atkins Halberstein wrote, "A wonderful bird is the pelican."

They were three of a dozen benches paid for by families of the dead where mortals and spirits were invited to sit together and reflect.

Established in 1807, it's filled with the bodies of the lesser-known founding fathers. In the early years of the republic, it was considered an honor to be buried here. It has over a hundred dead congressmen and senators.

John Quincy Adams, the sixth US president from 1825 to 1829, has a stone. He must have had a tight crew during his presidency because he and the majority of his cabinet were recognized with cenotaphs, which are small monuments to individuals who are buried somewhere else.

They included former vice president John C. Calhoun. A congressional office building is named after the South Carolina congressman right on Capitol Hill. Next to him is Henry Clay, a Kentucky congressman who was called "the Great Compromiser." His work postponed the Civil War by a decade. William Wirt was attorney general of the United States from 1817 to 1829. Samuel Southard was a former governor of New Jersey and president pro tempore of the Senate.

There's also a plaque commemorating the life of John Smilie, who left his Pennsylvania farm to fight in the Revolutionary War.

Later, as a member of the Pennsylvania legislature, the abolitionist was instrumental in passing the state's antislavery law, which made slave smuggling a crime with the penalty of death. He served in the US Congress for eight terms until he died in 1812.

Major General Uriah Tracy was a Revolutionary War general and later a US senator from Connecticut. He was the first member of Congress to be buried here in 1807.

Studying tombstones takes my mind away from its predicaments. Here, every life is complete. The dates of their birth and death tell their stories. Wm. H. Weatherall Jr. lived from August 1917 to December 1918. "Baby Bill," as he's referred to on his stone, lived just over a year. Considering his date of death, I wondered if it was the result of the Spanish flu of 1918. That worldwide pandemic killed fifty million people.

The multiculturalism of American history is represented here, too. Pushmataha, the Choctaw Indian chief who fought with General Andrew Jackson against the British during the Battle of New Orleans in the War of 1812, is here. So is Taza, son of the Chiricahua Apache war chief Cochise. DC was the nation's first sanctuary city. Thirty thousand runaway slaves migrated here around the Civil War. The Howard family, a large enclave of African Americans, are buried here. Howard University, founded in 1867, is named after one of their clan members.

There are memorials commemorating the lives of gay Americans, too. Several longtime same-sex partners lay side by side. John Matlovich, a Vietnam veteran, died at the age of forty-five. He has a large headstone. Inscribed upon it are these words:

> When I was in the military
> They gave me a medal for killing two men
> And a discharge for loving one.

There's also a section for beloved pets. There's a stone for Ava and Max. Another for Neva, "best dog daughter." Sophie Pie was a seventeen-year-old cat when she died. On a more infamous note, former DC mayor Marion Barry and FBI director J. Edgar Hoover have graves here, too.

What pleased me most about the cemetery was how the vibe differed from what transpired just two miles west at the US Capitol Building where…

> Lobbyists are on the make
> Legislators are on the take
> News, relentless and unforgiving
> Is staged nonsense and
> Commentators drown in cynicism

I did my best thinking at the grave of "The March King," John Phillip Souza. He was the leader of the United States Marine Corps Band from 1880 to 1892. There's a broad cement bench at the head of his grave with two finely sculpted arms on its flank, perfect for an elbow.

Souza wrote music so snappy that the entire nation all marched together. I found in him an egalitarian role model. Even today, his music transcends the divisive political nonsense tearing at America's social fabric.

Sometimes, I'd pull out my smartphone, plug in my headphones, go to *YouTube,* and play some of Souza's big hits, like "The Stars and Stripes Forever." Its piccolo solo is fabulous. Does that sound corny? That's okay; I'm from Minnesota. We produce as much corn as Nebraska.

This is a place of oratory where rhetoric has no place. I confess freely here. Sometimes, in the silence of this summer scene, I sing out my odes to self, soul and sun.

> The American milieu
> Is a pity to be a part of.
> Conflict and clamor
> Moral outrage and accusation

Uttered by the stiff, straightened backs
Of the self-righteous.
None of them have any idea
How desperately we need
A community newspaper.

Mostly, I read at the Souza site. The silence of the page streamlined perfectly with the silence of the surrounding dead. Lately, I've been reading books about American poets. My current favorites were Jersey boys: Walt Whitman, William Carlos Williams, and Allan Ginsberg. Today, I was reading Stephen Tapscott's book *American Beauty: William Carlos Williams and the Modernist Whitman.*

I loved the intimacy of the page. It fits in with the boneyard mentality. Steeping yourself with too much breaking news is like being sucked down into the whirling pool of Charybdis. To counteract it, I make sure that I read a healthy diet of books written by men not of this era.

Whenever my conception of "A Firm State of Heart" hit a wall, when moving forward felt thwarted, this was where I went to filter out the noise of time and plumb the depth of my literary ken.

I heard my smartphone beep. It was a text from Russ Nelson back in Saint Paul. "Just heard from an old pal, my commissioner of health from way back when. He says this virus from China is going to overwhelm everything. Said it'll kill an old geezer like me if I'm not careful. Don't mean to be an alarmist, but I canceled my book tour. The East Coast is going to get it bad. DC will be the command center. Be a good reporter."

I was disappointed that he postponed his visit since I considered him my most valuable coach. The day before I left Minnesota for DC, he had words of advice.

"I'm worried about America," Nelson said. "I fear that we're a nation in decline. Since the decline of a nation is preceded by the decline of language, go to DC, young poet, and find a way to revive the language and hence the republic."

That was why my Tadich shifts were so important to me. It strapped me to the emotional engine of the DC body politic. I didn't have to chase stories or politicians; they came right in and sat at my tables. I got to see firsthand what big men were supposed to look like, talk like and act like. I was looking forward to sharing all my impressions with Nelson. Now, it would have to wait.

After an hour and a half, I began losing concentration. The sun started going down. I walked home to find the boys glued to the TV.

"Sit down," Cortez said. "We're about to watch your girlfriend at work."

Shayla wore a blue dress that matched her eyes. She was serious while reading the news. Her banter with the other broadcasters on the set was charming. Although a few momentary expressions on her face reminded me of her shadowy side.

"How are her breasts?" Johnny asked.

"Nice, but they might be fake."

"She has lovely hands," said Caleb.

"They held me all night."

CHAPTER 9

After a week, Tadich reopened. I prepared for my second dinner shift by studying the dinner menu the night before to remind myself of what was on it.

My first month at Tadich was the most exciting. The presidential inaugural parade of 2017 was right out front along Pennsylvania Avenue. As a result, a cadre of Secret Service agents was stationed at the door screening everyone who came into Tadich that day with an electronic wand to make sure no guns were smuggled inside.

The place was packed with customers wearing "Make America Great Again" attire on hats, T-shirts and pins. The TVs were all tuned to Fox News.

When a live TV clip showed President Barack Obama mounting the stairs of a helicopter that would fly him away and end his second term, he turned and waved goodbye for the last time. That was when the Tadich crowd mocked him with a spontaneous song. The lyrics of the old tune, which everybody knew, were from a band called Steam. They all sang, "Nah, nah, nah, nah, nah, nah, nah, nah, hey, hey, goodbye."

I worked six hours straight that afternoon in a packed house. Just when I thought my shift might be done, the host asked me to set up a party of nine in my station. Twenty minutes later, Senator Ted Cruz of Texas, with his wife, staff, and friends, sat down. He was dressed in a pair of jeans and a blue Oxford shirt.

How many times have I cringed at the terrible things Cruz uttered on television? Last week, I heard railing about something I believed in. He acted purposely offensive and disrespectful, a cartoon character mouthing demagogic blather.

Cruz would have been the spotlight kid at the Liberty Ball or the Freedom Ball, one of the many such celebrations on this inaugural night. But the new president publicly insulted his wife and his father during the campaign. Cruz wanted no part of his celebration. Instead, he sat in my section.

His party rang up a dinner tab of $700. He was as gracious as the dead at the pearly gates. He called me by name. He shook my hand at the end of the meal and said thank you. He tipped me $150. I was amused because he treated me better than the majority of his Senate colleagues. What this experience taught me is that how a man acts in restaurants and how he acts in front of the TV cameras is not the same.

The very next day, hundreds of thousands of people, mostly women, walked down the very same Pennsylvania Avenue path for the 2017 Women's March. They wore their pink pussy hats and tried to outdo the hoopla of the Republican Party faithful the day before. The Tadich TVs were tuned to *MSNBC*. Each time the new president appeared, the packed house booed.

While it was true that working at Tadich required one to sift through lots of bullshit, it was also exciting because what happened there captured the historical moment. It manifested right before my eyes, and I wanted to be a valiant witness of this American era. The events of those two days now seem like ancient history. But symbolically, they illustrated the political division fuming in America. My friends were curious about which group tipped better. In truth, it was about the same.

This morning, the *Washington Post* published a newspaper story about the gala. Included was a picture of Shayla on my arm.

The caption read, "WRC anchor Shayla Reeve with poet Samuel Meckler." Suddenly, I was famous.

That evening, at the pre-shift meeting, Ron Robbins said, "Congratulations are in order for our young Samuel. We can all take a lesson on how well he handled himself in the grip of a terrible situation."

"I hope you got laid," said Leon.

"Dave Lovette crossed her one night at The Palm and ended up getting fired for it," Harold exclaimed. "How did you end up as her sweetheart?"

I straightened my back and put on a poker face. "Good looks and charm," I said, which made it funny. At least it dismissed the rumor that I was some sort of dining-room jinx. Robbins promised to make it up to me during this shift. He was true to his word. I had a great station. The first three tables in the door went to my station.

The first one was a three-top. Two older men and a woman sat down at table 37. After taking their order, we began to chat. Many of my customers are visiting from out of town, and this group was from Minnesota.

When I found out, I started to laugh. That's because I seemed to be a magnet for visitors from the Land of Lakes. In my tenure there, it had happened so often that it became a Tadich dining-room joke.

"Minnesota? Oh, jah, sure. I hear it's a real nice place to raise your kids up," I said with a fake Scandinavian accent to cover my Jersey brogue.

They nodded slightly, suspicious that I was making fun of them. But I wasn't.

"Want to know how I know that?"

"Sure," said the woman.

"I'm a graduate of South High in Minneapolis and the University of Minnesota."

Suddenly, it was old home week. One was a Minnesota state representative, one was the city manager of White Bear Lake and the other its mayor.

They knew my mother from the state capitol and had nice things to say about her. I grabbed my smartphone and took a picture of them holding their wineglasses in the air. Making sure I spelled their names right in the accompanying text, I sent it home.

My mother replied immediately. She reminded the state representative of a successful education bill they helped pass last year. It affirmed their visit to DC. Everybody had fun. Their bill was $195. They left a $55-dollar tip. That kind of synchronicity is a component part of a great restaurant shift.

I had a conversation with a tall Native American kid who came in with his family. They were in DC to receive the Silver Star medal from Secretary of Defense James Mattis for his late father, who was killed in Afghanistan. His body had recently been recovered from the Taliban.

"Did you take pictures?" I asked.

"Of course," he answered and pulled out his cell phone.

The whole table was caught on camera with Mattis and an array of generals.

He pulled a small box out of his pocket. Upon opening, I saw the medallion. It was attached to a red, white and blue ribbon. The Silver Star medal was actually at the center of a gold star that made up most of it. "We're Apache, a warrior tribe. Many of our men join the armed forces. But this honor is more for my family than for my father," he said.

When they went to leave, I was surprised. "Damn, bro', you're a lot bigger standing up. How tall are you?"

"About six feet seven," he said.

"I always wanted to be taller," I confessed.

"Well, it's not all gravy," he said. "It has its disadvantages."

"Like what?"

"Sitting on airplanes is tough. Seats are so cramped that I end up chewing on my knees for most of the flight. Plus, when I'm with my friends at noisy bars, I miss out on a lot of conversation because the discussion is going on a whole foot underneath me."

"Damn, I never thought of that."

I was waiting for two martinis at the bar when Gimbutus appeared. "The poet Samuel Meckler? I had no idea," he said. "Listen, Samuel, I'd like you to meet me and a small group of summer interns one day next week. That I have an American poet coming to meet them will get them excited. I want you to talk about your impressions of Washington, politics and poetry."

"That sounds like fun."

"And let me tell you, I have two interns, young beauties in their early twenties who might be right up your alley," he said. "Of course, dating someone like Shayla Reeves might put you out of their league."

"What day are you thinking of?"

"Sunday evening, say seven p.m. at the Lithuanian embassy on 16th Street."

"Okay, thanks. I'll be there."

We shook hands, and he walked out the door with two men who looked like bodyguards.

"You know that guy?" asked Steve, the bartender.

"Not really, just an acquaintance. Actually, he's from the Lithuanian embassy."

"I remember him. He was sitting at my bar a while back, drunk as a skunk and shooting off his mouth. He was offering hundred-dollar bets that Trump would be elected president. And he was willing to bet anyone."

"Did you bet him?"

"No, somehow it seemed like a sucker's bet. But several of my regulars did. When the election results were in and he won the bet, they never returned to my bar for fear of having to pay up. If I were you, I'd be careful around him."

"What could he possibly want from me?"

"I don't know."

Tonight's clientele was the usual group of mid-level managers working for the federal government. Here, at the end of a stressful day, they came to actualize their love of politics and their love of feasting while sorting out collectively their place in the day's political drama.

Playing squire to those swains was never a problem for me. In doing so, I got to study the people in charge. I paid close attention to the dignity, speech and movement of these hard-headed men and women. I took what anecdotal scraps they left behind and worked it into my own personal point of view.

In a way, I felt sorry for them. In doing their job, they contended with a flurry of dull imperatives that curtailed their imagination and narrowed their access to a larger vision of life. At least I was doing something productive with my time: I was feeding them dinner. I was never quite sure what most of them actually did for a living. I even worked out a schematic documenting the travail so many inept political hacks suffer.

Ambition, Intent, Arrival, Hard Work,
Hubris, Ate', Scandal,
Shame, Exile, Oblivion.

When it comes to customers, every waiter has his own wheelhouse with whom he feels most comfortable. Give me a party from New York or New Jersey and I am happy. I was born and raised in that area. People from Massachusetts and Connecticut? I share their political liberalism. African Americans? I love them, and if their tips are any indication, they love me too. People from Minnesota? Right up my alley. My mother was from a big Irish Catholic family, and her relatives are all over the state. Somehow, I could always find a meaningful connection with folks from back home.

But seat me an older White guy from the Deep South and I tense up. They come from a culture that seems backward to me. Their politics are not my politics. I always hate to stereotype, but by my reckoning, many of them are rednecks. I always felt a little stiff in their presence, lest I reveal the fact that I was from the People's Republic of Minneapolis and have it reflect poorly on my tip.

That's my issue, I suppose. Since we live in a multicultural world that I embrace diligently as an American and as a waiter, I always try to transcend it. I've devised little skits to break the ice in order to make both me and my customers feel comfortable.

A sixty-year-old man and his blond wife were the last table seated in my station. When he told me where they were from, I said, "Oh, Alabama? Say, why do they call it the Yellowhammer State?"

It's a legitimate question. No self-respecting Alabamian ever missed it. A teacher probably drilled it into them in second grade. "It's the state bird," he answered with a smile. "We like to shoot them every time the Alabama Crimson Tide wins a football game. That's why there's currently so few."

It was a good answer and for the rest of the meal, we were friends.

There's a true sense of democracy in the dining room. Here, everybody's money is created equal regardless of race, religion, sexual orientation and economic class. You never know which of your tables are going to be big hitters. Sometimes, individuals surprise the hell out of you. A solicitous attitude can bring out the best in people. In return, there'd be a good tip, a word of praise to the manager on their way out and a nice review on Yelp.

Whenever I read the ancient classics, one thing that always struck me was how feasts and celebrations took on a religious ardor. It was as if celebrating the good things in life was a moral obligation as if the joy of life had to be recognized and affirmed. That was always on my mind when I put on my apron and attended these folks.

In Greek mythology, Ganymede is the Mount Olympus cupbearer to Zeus. I've made him my patron saint. Each and every one of us prays to his own individual god. On the dining-room floor, Ganymede is mine. He helps me stay fast, focused and friendly. I always thank him for a good tip and a satisfying shift.

When patrons fill the dining room, and a restaurant rush engulfs me with more tables and tasks than time, I whisper a prayer for Ganymede to stand beside me and help me work my way out of it. His aid comes in many forms.

When I hit the send button on the service station computer, which informs the kitchen to get busy, he makes sure I've rung in the correct menu items for the correct table at the correct seat number. He keeps my mind clear of fear so that the pressure of the moment doesn't steal my composure. He helps keep the tray of drinks I am carrying stay horizontal.

Uncertainty accompanies every restaurant shift because the whole of it is beyond your control. You never know how much money you are going to make, who you might meet or what drama awaits you with the people you work with or the customers in your section. That's why luck is so important.

So is timing. One hopes that the order you've just rung in is not behind a dozen other tickets that your fellow waiters have rung in before you. That the hostess doesn't triple-seat you. That the bartender is free to make your drinks and is not too engaged with his own customers. Your income depends on it.

One quality of a good waiter is that his moral strength prevails, and he doesn't freak out, get angry or fuck up. Grace under fire. If you can't shoulder the stress, you're not a professional waiter.

Though it was only my second night shift, I was killing it and the night's tips were adding up. Since it was my first income in a week, the money was already burning a hole in my pocket. My confidence soared. Just as I was about to claim a big win, I let my guard down, filled my head with dreams of long continuance and got full of myself.

There was a ten-top in Khalid's section from the FBI. When their entrees were ready, I helped Khalid deliver them to his guests. An award stood in the middle of the table. An older woman was the guest of honor. She had been awarded the trophy for developing a program of community-oriented policing that brought down crime in ten different cities.

When told her story, I congratulated her and laughed when I said, "Great, maybe now you guys can do something about Donald Trump."

Their smiling faces went dour. The guest of honor turned her head to the left and then to the right to see if anyone else in the dining room heard me. The president had just fired FBI director James Comey. The friction between the White House and the FBI was pitched. Just by listening to my comment, I compromised them. I recognized my mistake right away. "Oh my God," I said. "I'm very sorry." Embarrassed by my stupid attack, I backed away.

One of them walked to the host stand and complained to Robbins. His voice was loud enough to be heard ten yards away. "Is that kid crazy? Do you know how much trouble we might have gotten into if the wrong ears were listening? Two at our table are political appointees. Half of Trump's cabinet lives right across the street. I suggest you muzzle that waiter."

Ron found me at the coffee machine. "Listen, Mr. Meyers was pissed off by your comment," he said. "If you want to work here, you have to keep your opinions to yourself. He's booked two big parties next month, and I don't want him pulling out because of you. Do you understand?"

"Yes, Ron. I'm sorry. It won't happen again."

I worked two Tadich Grill night shifts and both of them were marred. Since my political attitude was also a problem at home with Caleb, I vowed to keep my mouth shut and my opinions to myself. From now on, all criticism was reserved for my journal.

I was the first waiter cut at 9:30 p.m. I was out the door with three hundred dollars in my pocket. But I realized I still had a lot to learn.

CHAPTER 10

The monthly feast at the Fourth Estate was on the fourth Sunday of each month. Johnny's energy put it in motion.

His restaurateur parents instilled a love for the culinary arts in him. Cooking was in his blood. He loved playing host, with me as his erstwhile wingman. Such dinners were usually followed by a sporting event on television.

The plan was a big meal at 6:30 p.m. followed by a Sunday night preseason football game in the living room at 8:30 p.m. Tonight, the hometown favorites, the Washington Commanders, were playing my Minnesota Vikings.

The evening's banquet took all day to cater. Johnny and I woke up early and shopped the vendors at Eastern Market. It was an old-school enclosed market located just a few blocks away. It was one of two local communities I loved. Congressional Cemetery was a community of the dead; Eastern Market was a community of the living. They also had a weekend flea market outside the building that drew tens of thousands.

We walked around the variety of vendors and picked out the best meat, seafood and vegetables available. At the liquor store, we bought two big bottles of booze with handles or what in Minnesota we call "homewreckers."

The night's menu consisted of pan-fried Chinese wontons filled with cream cheese served with a spicy Thai sauce, a Caesar salad made from scratch, and shrimp risotto served with French baguettes and butter. The entrée was a twelve-pound roast beef. Johnny coated it with kosher salt and coarse black pepper before placing it in a big pan. It cooked for several hours at a low temperature and came with four asparagus spears each. For dessert, he planned crème brûlée.

While Johnny sautéed the shrimp for the risotto dish, I got to work on the Caesar salad dressing. It was his father's own recipe from Zuma's Italian Paradise and a dressing I'd loved since I was a kid. I pulled out the blender, and beside it laid out the ingredients: egg, olive oil, lemon juice, garlic, anchovies, Worcestershire sauce, black pepper and parmesan cheese.

"Remember, if it's too thick, add more lemon juice," said Johnny. "If it's too thin, add more parmesan."

"Got it," I said. With that, we both went to work—he at the stove, me beside him at the kitchen counter.

When we were kids, we liked to hang out at the restaurant. We'd arrive after school. The waitresses were pretty, and the bartenders were cool. I suppose it was where I got my love of the restaurant business since it felt like a family where I was always welcome.

Johnny channeled his dad when cooking. Gino died of a heart attack while working behind the cooking line one night at his restaurant. He was his dad's best friend. The two of them loved working together on Saturday nights, beginning when Johnny was ten. A large part of Johnny died when they put Gino in the ground. In cooking these meals, Johnny went into a trance, acting as if his dad was right beside him. It was a pantomime of their Saturday night shifts together. I felt that this was the real purpose of these meals.

"Caleb's bringing a date," Johnny said.

"Who is it?"

"Vickie the bartender."

"Really?"

"That's what he said."

"I wonder what his Evangelical folks back home would say if they knew he was dating a bartender," I said.

"She's finishing her master's degree, so she won't have to tend bar too much longer."

"Well, at least she's cool," I said. "I'm glad he's not bringing one of those uptight biddies from his church."

"Yeah, but we're still going to have to be on our best behavior. Don't talk smack about him while she's around."

"That's going to take a lot of self-control," I said. "Caleb can't shit unless he takes off all his clothes in the bathroom. Should I tell her?"

"Better not," Johnny said.

Caleb and Vickie seemed like a mismatch to me. She was more broad-minded and licentious than he was. At the end of a bar shift, she was sometimes as loaded as her barstool customers with whom she sometimes went home with. But she held her load, always a recommendation for a bartender.

And yet, out of all of us, Caleb was probably the best husband material. He was devoted to God, religion, family and country. If that was what Vickie was looking for, he was a good choice.

"You can invite Shayla if you want," Johnny said.

"I don't think so. By her standards, you guys aren't even housebroken. For that matter, I don't think I am either."

"Oh, it's like that?"

"Yeah, she's kind of a snob."

"Bro', you're a working man and a poet. Why are you messing with her?"

"I guess I'm flattered by her attention."

"What does she want from you?"

"I don't know," I said.

"Don't let her head-trip you."

"What about the women you and Cortez hooked up with the other night? Are they coming?"

"Tasha and Sookie? Yeah, they'll be here. Tasha is with me. Sookie is with Cortez. You'll be the only one of us without a date."

"That's okay," I said.

"Kind of sorry I invited her. I mean, we had great sex the other night, but who knows, she could be a crackhead or an unwed mother with four kids."

"With a body like that? I don't think so," I said.

"Diego is coming."

"Good, I'll hang out with him."

"He promised to bring marijuana, something for each course."

"How many courses will there be?"

"Five. The appetizer course, the salad course, the risotto course, the main course of beef and asparagus, and then dessert."

After making the dressing, which met with Johnny's approval, I shredded romaine lettuce for eight and set the dining room table. A bright red cloth covered the battered wooden tabletop. I set and polished the silverware and glasses, folded linen napkins and gathered up eight chairs from around the house, including my own desk chair from the attic.

Most of the table settings were from the dollar store, but the water and wineglasses were top shelf, stolen from different restaurants around town.

Vickie, wearing black spandex pants that showed off her ass and a loose-fitted pink blouse, and Diego, dressed in a white button-down shirt, arrived at 6:00 p.m. Tasha and Sookie were late.

"They're on Black time. You never know when they'll arrive," said Cortez.

"Call them up and find out," said Johnny. "Dinner is being served at 6:30 with or without them. I'll be damned if I let the beef overcook."

They showed up fifteen minutes later. Sookie, there for Cortez, was a big girl. But there was a wonderful roundness to her.

She had long braids and a pretty smile. She had a big bottom lip that hung down almost against her chin. Her response to Cortez was aloof when she walked in the door. But when she said, "I think I may have forgotten an earring in your bedroom," with an unmistakable lascivious look, Cortez answered, "Well, let's go look for it."

Tasha was tall and thin. She wore a wig the first time I saw her. It was gone now. Instead, she wore a Washington Nationals baseball cap. When she removed it, I saw that she had short, straight hair colored orange.

The bone structure of her face had amazing definition. It seemed as if her skin had been stretched over its high cheekbones and a strong chin. Her profile reminded me of an African warrior princess.

As she entered the kitchen, Johnny and I noticed how her long legs were set close together. She walked with a definite rhythm, which resulted in a noticeable wiggle.

Tasha's white teeth shone brightly against her dusky complexion. She wore glasses, too, so at first glance, you'd have to take into account her intellect instead of her beauty. He gave her a polite hug but was a little standoffish because the courses were nearly ready, and Johnny didn't want to burn any of it. Lost in his father's presence, he was polite but reserved.

She didn't ask for anything more. They were both playing it cool. There was a stoic look on her face as if his lack of attention was a test she was patiently going to pass. When she left the kitchen so Johnny could cook, she sat on the couch and studied her cell phone with an introvert's calm.

Now, another might have interpreted Johnny's aloofness as disregard. But he was taking a traditional Jersey attitude toward women. It consisted of doing the responsible male thing and playing hard to get. There would be a time for the goo-goo eyes, but not before he showed her that responsibility came first.

We sat down to eat. Johnny's first course was cream cheese wontons. Everybody got four. We served it with a glass of pinot noir from one of the three bottles that Vickie brought.

Diego's first course was a sativa strain, Blue Dream, rolled in a white paper joint. He passed it around the table. Each of us took a hit. Vickie did not.

"Sorry," Vickie said, looking at Diego. "I don't know why, but sativa strains make me anxious. I think I'll pass." Next to her sat Caleb; he passed on it, too.

"Hey, Diego, I heard you used to work at one of the most expensive restaurants in town," said Caleb. "Why did you give it up to become a drug dealer."

"Marijuana is not a drug," said Diego. "It's a plant. Don't compare it to cocaine or opioids."

"It's the perfect counterirritant to the digital age," I said.

"Yes, but why become a criminal?" Caleb asked. "Don't you realize that as an immigrant, you can be deported and never allowed to return to America?"

"Hate to disappoint you, but I am a US citizen, have been for over fifteen years," said Diego.

"So why would a US citizen resort to selling illegal substances?"

"Because the truth is that when it comes right down to it, nothing is as virtuous as marijuana," said Diego. "I like the way it makes me feel and the way it makes me think. It reveals a spirituality in me that's way deeper than your religion."

"What do you know about my religion?" Caleb said.

"Lots," said Diego. "Or don't you remember how you lectured me about it for twenty minutes last week?"

"I did no such thing," said Caleb.

"No offense, Caleb, but you did," said Vickie. "It was at the bar and I listened to it, too."

"Do you stand on street corners and sell nickel bags to Black folk?" Cortez asked.

"No, I sell it at trap houses."

"What's a trap house?" I asked.

"They're pop-ups where vendors like me gather to sell our products. The location usually changes every day."

"What about the police?" Caleb asked.

"We have to hide from them," Diego said. "While it's legal in the district to possess marijuana and consume it, selling it is still illegal."

"I can't believe you gave up an honest job for that," Caleb said. "Pot is like the apple in the Garden of Eden."

"Christ, Caleb, you act as if he's violating one of the Ten Commandments," said Johnny. "The reason you can possess it and smoke it but can't sell it is because DC laws have to be approved by a bunch of redneck Republican congressmen from Texas who make up the House Committee on Oversight and Government Reform. They're imposing their narrowmindedness on the rest of us."

"Hey, watch it, Johnny," Caleb shouted. "Those are my people. They're afraid DC will become a den of iniquity like Amsterdam if they allow its sale."

"Yes, but do you realize how much money the city is losing in tax dollars because of that silly rule?" Cortez asked.

"That's okay with me," Diego said. "If they legalize it, the only people who will make money are big corporations. The city will institute all these requirements like pesticide tests, mold tests and TCH level tests that only big operators can afford to do. They'll put little guys like me out of business. It's what happened in California. Marijuana has always been a black market, underground kind of product, and I like it that way."

"Sounds dangerous," Sookie said.

"Yes, you have to watch out for cops and robbers," Diego said. "Ghetto thugs try to rob you at the end of the night to steal your weed and money. Cops try to arrest you. But lately, something funny has been happening. The cops will raid a trap house and arrest everybody. But then, when they go to court, the judges dismiss the case, and then we're back at it the next day."

"Why is that?" Sookie asked.

"The courts no longer want to prosecute marijuana cases in DC."

"Sounds like a weird job," said Cortez.

"Maybe, but it's a moneymaker. I am my own boss, set my own hours and am making more money than I ever have before."

"That's interesting," I said.

"Sam, you'd be great at it."

"Thanks, but I already have a job."

"How do you find where these places are?" Johnny asked.

"It's all done with smartphone apps," Diego said. "There's Instagram, which tells where the location is. Google Maps helps you find your way there. Many vendors take Ubers so they don't get stopped by the cops. I even take Venmo for guys short on cash."

"Damn, it's nice to know that the counterculture is alive and well in the nation's capital," I said.

"Given your beat, Johnny, it might be a good story for you," Diego said.

"Damn, I might pitch it to CNN," Cortez said.

"Nobody would want to go on camera since many of the vendors have straight jobs during the day. But a newspaper story might work," said Diego.

Johnny agreed. "I'll talk about it with my editors."

"On any given night, there're at least a dozen trap houses up and running around town," Diego said.

"I've been to one up on Georgia Avenue," added Tasha. "They're cool. It's great to have so many different kinds of weed available to you. I mean, you can buy flower, cartridges, shatter, moon rocks, gummies, cookies, brownies and a half-dozen products I've never tried before."

The Caesar salad was served next with two warm baguettes and butter. The dressing had just the right amount of garlic; the croutons were store-bought. Diego brought out a joint of Gusher Punch, which was a hybrid—50 percent sativa and 50 percent indica. The joint was passed around the table. Vickie took a hit and handed it to Caleb. Not wanting to be left behind by his date, he took a hit, too.

"How's your poem coming, Sam?" Vickie asked.

"It's going well. But it's going to take at least another two years," I answered. "It seems to reveal itself at its own pace."

"Perhaps it's not really the poem you're looking for," said Tascha. "Maybe it's a woman."

"Yes," said Vickie, "how come you don't have a date tonight?"

"Because I'm holding a candle for someone special. No one else will do."

"Who is she?" Sookie asked.

"Don't know her name," I said. "I saw her once on Metro, and I've been looking for her ever since."

"That's kind of romantic," said Vickie. "What do you know about her?"

"She lives somewhere around Eastern Market. She has a brown complexion and a pretty face."

"Is she a sista?" asked Tasha.

"I think she's mixed."

"My grandmother used to say that Americans are the prettiest people in the world because of all the mixed marriages," said Johnny. "It smooths out the harsher ethnic facial features."

"What else do you know about her?" Tasha asked.

"She has a tattoo, a green heart on her left wrist."

"Oh my god, I've seen her at my bar," said Vickie.

"Really?" I asked.

"Sometimes I see as many as a hundred people a day at the Veil," Vickie said. "And it's funny, I seem to recognize people more by their tattoos than by their faces. If I remember correctly, she's got long, dark, wavy hair and a great figure. She came in with a girl named Angela, one of my regulars. I don't know Angela's last name but I might be able to find out. Would you like me to do some investigative work for you?"

"Absolutely," I said.

"Wow, you must really have a thing for that gal," said Caleb. "I haven't seen you this excited since you found that old book on Virgil."

"I guess I am," I said.

"Who is Virgil?" asked Tasha.

"An ancient Roman poet," answered Caleb.

"That doesn't sound very exciting," she said.

"It is to him," said Caleb, rolling his eyes.

"I'll snoop around, too," added Tasha. "Maybe we can hook you guys up."

"Thanks."

The risotto course came next. Johnny scooped it piping hot into small bowls in the kitchen. Each serving had three large shrimps. I served. Diego brought out a vape pen of the OG Kush. "Here, Vickie. This is an indica. I think you'll like it."

Vickie took it from his hand and took a big hit. "That's good," she said.

Then she handed it to Caleb. He hesitated. "I'm okay with getting a little stoned, but I don't want to go crazy," he said.

Cortez said, "Go on, boy. Take another hit."

With all eyes upon him, he did. He then blew out a giant cloud of smoke. It caused him to cough and cough some more. When he finally stopped coughing, he managed a small breath and said, "Smooooth."

Everybody laughed.

"So, Vickie, how's school going?" asked Cortez.

"I'm almost done. In four months, I'll have a master's degree, and I'll be able to put out my shingle as a therapist."

I laughed. "How is that going to be different from being a bartender?"

"There'll be less alcohol and less stress. But the call for stories will be the same."

"What's it like being a therapist in Washington?" asked Sookie.

"People living here are more driven and have a broader worldview than the rest of the country. But they are also wounded. I get the idea that many of them came to DC to compensate for some childhood injury. It's like they seek power to compensate for some neurotic symptom that they'd rather not deal with until it starts interfering with their careers and their relationships. Then they come to people like me."

"What makes a person want to be a therapist?" Johnny asked.

"I've spent several years with my own therapy. I think I get it and want to help others find their way, too."

"You've been in therapy?" Caleb inquired with an air of disbelief.

"Yes, do you have a problem with that?" Vickie replied.

"No, I just always thought therapy was for crazy people."

"*Crazy* is a vague term that explains nothing," Vickie said. "I'm the daughter of two abusive alcoholics. What I learned in therapy was that their dysfunctional behavior was not about me."

Sookie said, "When my daddy drank, he turned into someone else. We used to walk on eggshells around the house. It was awful."

"I know," said Vickie. "Abuse runs in families. I'm going to make sure the Jensen family abuse stops with me."

I cleared the table of plates while Johnny prepared the main course. He had a meat thermometer in the roast. When it hit medium rare, he pulled it from the oven. All its blood went to the center of the roast. He let it rest a bit to replenish itself while stacking the dinner plates inside the oven to keep them warm.

The main course took longer. We were in the kitchen for a good twenty minutes preparing it. He sliced the roast into thick pieces, slapped it down on a plate and added four pieces of asparagus. Of course, Cortez liked his meat well done. After slicing off a piece and plating it, Johnny threw it into the microwave before bringing it out. When everyone was served, Johnny and I sat down and began eating with the rest.

"Can you believe what that dumbass of a president did this week?" Tasha said.

Tasha was Johnny's date, and it fell to him to tell her. "Don't be breaking the house rules now, girl. At the Fourth Estate, we don't discuss the president."

"Why not?" she asked.

"It makes us argue," Johnny said. "Me and Sam hate the man. Cortez and Caleb like him. A house divided cannot stand, said Abraham Lincoln. Over time, we reached a pact never to mention his name. It just makes living together easier."

I thought to express my own opinion on the subject. Personally, I thought the president was a corrupt liar. Keeping my mouth shut about it took all my self-control. But I just got reprimanded at work for a stray comment, so I was careful not to engage Caleb or Cortez about it for fear of ruining Johnny's dinner party.

"What do you and Tasha do for a living?" Diego asked.

"We're nurses at George Washington University Hospital," Sookie said. "I work in the emergency room. Tasha is in the maternity ward."

"Have you two been friends very long?" Vickie asked.

"We're cousins," said Tasha. "We've known each other since we were kids. We went to Eastern High School together and nursing school together, too."

"That makes you each other's institutional memory," I said.

"Yes, I suppose that's true," Tasha said.

"Cortez, were you and Caleb friends before you moved in here, or did you become friends after you became roommates?" Sookie asked.

"We met in the army while serving in Afghanistan. We were both in the 29th Infantry, "the Blue and Gray Division." We were friends there and stayed in touch. Since I'm from DC, this is home. When Caleb got a job with the Christian Broadcasting Network, we moved in here with Johnny."

"My momma watches that station every day," said Tasha. "She's a big fan of Jesus."

"God bless her," said Caleb.

"Did you guys see combat?" Vickie asked.

"Yeah, we saw some shit," Cortez said. "Saw some of our friends die, too."

"I got shot by a sniper from three hundred feet away while standing in back of a truck," Caleb said. "It knocked me right to the ground. Fortunately, a Kevlar vest stopped the bullet. Cortez was driving. When he saw me fly off the top of the vehicle, he slammed on the brakes, jumped out of the car, and pulled me inside while they were shooting at us. I was shaking like a leaf. He was the one who told me I was okay."

Cortez enjoyed the story of his war heroism and beamed. Sookie said, "Thank you for your service." Sitting next to Cortez at the table, I saw her hand on his thigh.

"That's what patriots do," Caleb said. "America needed our courage, and we answered the call."

"Please don't talk to me about patriotism," Vickie said. "It has a very dark underbelly, which is narcissistic, arrogant, emotionally unhealthy, chauvinistic and totally lacking in empathy. It's not inclusive and always comes at someone else's expense, be it Mexicans, Muslims, liberals, Blacks, Jews or gays who aren't allowed to participate in it."

"Well, that's not true," Caleb said.

"Oh yes, it is," said Vickie, holding her ground. She watched as Caleb's facial expression softened.

"I once was a Christian soldier, Vickie. Now, I just want to be a Christian."

"Did you suffer from PTSD?" Tasha asked.

"Yes, it was only my faith in Jesus Christ that helped me get over it," Caleb said. "I had this fabulous parson back home in Tennessee who took me under his wing and helped me heal. At his encouragement, I got this tattoo in Hebrew around my wrist. It says, 'Jesus Christ is my Lord and Savior.' Reverend Grist is a remarkable man. Once in a while, he'd be giving a sermon and get so overcome that he'd start speaking in tongues as if he were possessed by the Holy Ghost himself. It was amazing."

"Give me a break." I moaned. "If he was really remarkable, he'd speak English in a clearly channeled voice from spirit, not the gibberish you describe."

"Damn, Sam, sometimes you say things with such innocence," said Caleb. "But when you do, I usually hate everything you have to say."

"That's about you, bro', not me."

"You being a religious half-breed, I don't think you have a real bead on the importance of religion in a man's life," Caleb said.

"Are you mixed?" Tasha asked.

"Yes, my mother's Catholic, and my father's Jewish."

"Sam doesn't believe in original sin," Caleb said.

"Which religion do you like better?" asked Tasha.

"Judaism," I said.

"Really? Why?"

"My Jewish roots run deeper. I was part of my father's Jewish family in New Jersey in my early years, and I took to it. Then my family moved to Minnesota when I was thirteen, and we became part of my mother's Catholic family."

"I understand that," said Vickie, "but which group do you actually like better?"

"The Jews," I said. "They don't suffer from as much shame and guilt as the Catholics. They're more self-actualized, and their women are better in bed."

"Compared to Evangelicals, they're both second-rate," said Caleb.

I decided not to engage him on the topic because my literary inclinations were working to transcend religion entirely.

I cleared the table. Back in the kitchen, Johnny grabbed eight crème brûlée out of the refrigerator. He got a small blowtorch out of the kitchen closet and began burning the sugar on top till it took a sheen of light brown. I served.

"Damn, it looks like shatter," Diego said.

"What's shatter?" Johnny asked.

"It's a marijuana distillate that looks like the top of your desert. Very powerful stuff when smoked," Diego said. For this course, he brought out a pack of marijuana-laced gummy bears.

Then the meal was over. Our little feast was a success.

"I'd like to make a toast to our host, Johnny 'Chubby Lovin' Zuma," Cortez said. There was applause.

"My man," said Diego.

"Nice job, Johnny," I said.

"I haven't eaten this good in a long time," Tasha said.

"Oh, honey, the eating's not even started," said Johnny with a smirk.

Tasha laughed.

Since we shopped, cooked and served, the rest of them, managed by Cortez, cleaned up, loaded the dishwasher and scrubbed the pots while Johnny and I sat in the backyard and drank a scotch.

"Gino would have been proud of you tonight," I said.

"Yeah, I really miss my dad. I think I do this to honor all he taught me."

"Well, it was a great meal."

"It's funny. He never wanted me to go into the restaurant business. He thought it a job for immigrants, not real Americans."

"He instilled a love of it in me," I said. "For that, I'll always be grateful."

When the cleanup was done, Tasha joined us in the backyard. Johnny stood, grabbed her and planted a great, big, welcomed kiss on her lips. At his request, they decided to take a walk around the block before the football game started.

The gummies kicked in; Washington kicked off to begin the game. We all gathered in the living room to watch it on the big-screen TV.

I alone was rooting for the Vikings; the rest were rooting for the home team—Diego, Vickie, Cortez, Johnny, Tasha and Sookie. Caleb loved the Tennessee Titans. Since he had no dog in the fight and being unaccustomed to the cannabis products, he fell asleep on the couch along with Tasha. Halftime came; the score was tied at 14.

"Looks like your date has passed out," I said to Johnny.

"That's okay. Let her sleep," he said. "When the game is over, she'll rally."

Vickie said, "Caleb tells me you have a pagan altar in your attic. Is that true?"

"Sure. Would you like to see it?"

"Yes."

I led her upstairs to my study, carrying my chair back to its desk. She examined the little Buddhist and Native American figurines, totem animals along with small gnomes, dragons, feathers, tortoise shells and gemstones on its shelf.

"This is a great room. How lucky to have your own study to work in."

"After working a busy shift at the restaurant, I like to come up here and repair," I said. "You're in the hospitality business, so you know how that goes."

"I absolutely do."

"Here, sit down in the chair. I want to show you something." I pulled the chair out for her, and she sat down in front of my six quartz crystals. I turned on my desk light. "Check out the prism light in each of them."

"They're beautiful."

"I like to sit here, smoke and drink and get my divine on with reading and journaling."

"Are those your journals?"

"Yes."

"Wow, you have a whole shelf of them."

"It's my therapy, a written record of my neurosis. After I write it down, I'm able to release it all and move on. In some ways, it's even better than therapy because it leaves a written trail of the whole process. I return to it time and time again to trace my own healing."

"And you have a bedroom up here, too?"

I led her to it. She looked around the room. Then she faced me and touched my hand.

"What are you going to do if you can't find that woman?"

"Find someone else."

"What exactly are you looking for?"

We were both loaded. The world seemed to stand still as I gazed into her eyes. I might have said, "Someone exactly like you." But a voice from the bottom of the attic stairs interrupted. It was Caleb.

"Vickie, are you up there?"

"Yes, she is, Caleb," I said. "Come on up."

CHAPTER 11

When I set out for the Lithuanian embassy, it was with a lighthearted step. I saw this as an opportunity to connect my literary DNA to my paternal Lithuanian grandfather and the old-world culture that molded him.

My grandfather was a positive presence in my early years. That I was named after his father gave me a special place in his heart. He believed as deeply in America as the ancient Hebrew prophets believed in Israel. He instilled that idealism in me.

I remember our trips together, by train, just the two of us, into the city. When Jersey folks say "the city," they mean New York City and no other because, for many of them, it's the center of the universe.

My grandfather would say, "Come, we'll go spazieren," his Yiddish word for walking. He'd take me up and down Fifth Avenue, then we'd board the subway and go all over town. We'd lose ourselves for hours in used bookstores like Gotham Books and the Strand Bookstore. He searched their shelves for old-world European texts that refreshed his faded memories while I sat on the floor and read books about sports heroes, American presidents and jet airplanes.

We'd kibbutz with some of the personalities hanging out in Times Square. There was also the obligatory meal at one of NYC's famous Jewish delis. I preferred cheese blintzes and potato knishes.

My grandfather liked borscht and cow tongue. Sometimes, old-timers from his old neighborhood of Vilnius met us. There in conversation, sometimes in broken English, other times in Yiddish, he would show me off as if I were a prodigy and let them pinch my cheek.

But his death and my family's move to Minnesota took all aspects of that culture away from me. I was reminded of a book written by Israel Joshua Singer, Nobel Prize winner Isaac Bashevis Singer's smarter, older brother. His memoir of Jewish life in Eastern Europe was entitled *Of a World That Is No More*. Tonight's soiree held promise that the lost world I wondered about might be rekindled by the people I was set to meet.

Plus, there was one more thing. To be summoned to speak as a poet, not as a reporter and not as a waiter, was symbolically a giant leap forward.

Gimbutus said his interns wanted to press me for my opinions on everything. It was flattering because, as a quiet scholar unaccustomed to attention, the prospect of expressing my ideals and having them questioned, perhaps challenged, might help me grow as a poet and a man. For me, they were inseparable.

I realized that I was never going to be a Washington, DC, big shot. I was not built for the Mandarin, bureaucratic, team player, company-man role. Instead, I craved the luxuriance of the poetic trance. Transcending local norms and writing about them in a clear, meaningful way was my mission. This enthusiasm put speed in my step as I hoofed it up the 16th Street bluff after riding Metro to McPherson Square.

I rang the doorbell of the large white stone building. Gimbutus met me at the door and welcomed me to the Lithuanian embassy. He led me to a room with a large mahogany table surrounded by a dozen chairs. There was a large red, green and yellow Lithuanian flag pinned to the wall. It was painted the same yellow color as on the flag. The window frames were red.

There were five young men my age in attendance. When we spoke at the bar, he suggested women would attend, too. He must have changed his mind. I was introduced to them all. All were master's candidates from Vytautas Magnus University in Lithuania and were currently in DC as interns. I recognized Lukas, a man I met at Tadich and liked. We shook hands and exchanged greetings. He was a short, stocky man with jet-black hair, a pug nose and thick lips. He had a warm smile and a good heart.

The two seats at the head of the table were for me and Gimbutus, who was head of cultural affairs at the embassy. Two men, older embassy staff, stood behind us and watched. They were dour-looking men with gray mustaches who did not shake hands. A bottle of Samogon, a Lithuanian vodka, was on a tray with glasses surrounding the bottle.

"Here we have real Lithuanian vodka, a true representation of the strong drink from our country," Gimbutus said.

He filled the glasses himself and passed them out. "To Lithuania," he toasted. We all shot down the vodka and slapped the glasses down on the table.

"Let me tell you who we have here," said Gimbutus. "This is Samuel Meckler, an American poet and a descendant of a real Jewish Litvak. I met Samuel at a DC restaurant when he was our waiter. I found him an insightful source of information and opinion. Samuel engages the DC apparatchik on a daily basis. As such, he has a distinct point of view. I am hoping he will share it with you in order to broaden your understanding of America."

Gimbutus asked me to begin by telling the group about my grandfather, Chaim Meckler. I told them how he lived in Vilnius while studying to be a rabbi. When the Nazis marched into Lithuania, he escaped to the forest and became one of the Vilnius partisans.

Two years later, he took a bullet in the leg and could no longer run. He signed on as a sailor with a fake passport, found passage to

Sweden and escaped the Holocaust. But not before two medals for courage were awarded to him from the Kremlin, which he coveted till the day he died.

As a refugee, he found his way to America and settled in New York City. He gave up his rabbinical studies and opened up a hat factory on the Lower East Side of Manhattan. He married my grandmother, Idel, and started a family.

"Perhaps it will be best if we leave these young people alone to hash out their own truths," Gimbutus said to the two older staffers. "But perhaps before we go, one more shot of vodka."

He doled out a dose in each of our glasses with a steady hand as he walked around the table. We drank a toast to friendship, and then the three older men walked out the door. Now, I was looking forward to some good conversation.

"What are you guys studying in school?" I asked.

Two of them spoke at once and gave their answer in Lithuanian, which, of course, I didn't understand. Then, a third interjected, "Communication and psychology."

I grew suspicious when I saw two of them signal each other and change seats. Of the five men, two sat on opposite sides of the table and took notes. The three others faced me and did all the talking. One was Lukas, another was named Alexander, and the third, Vlad.

While I hoped that this meeting of millennial minds might reach for comity, I was jolted from that notion when I heard the tall blond kid, Vlad, say to one of the others, "Why are we wasting our time with this stupid American waiter?" It was said just loud for me to hear. If he had any tact, he'd have said it in Lithuanian. But no, he wanted me aware of the contempt he felt for me. "What's the matter? He can't get a real job?"

I wasn't sure what to do. With Gimbutus gone from the room, I recognized that I might be facing an inquisition. But in the course of a shift, waiters deal with all sorts of individuals, nasty and nice. I was not intimidated. Of the three men assigned to interview me, one played good cop, Lukas; one played bad cop, Darius; and the third, Vlad, played asshole.

"Why are Americans so fat?" asked Vlad, who was tall and thin. "I look at them, and I'm repulsed."

"It's the fast-food diet," I said. "It's advertised relentlessly in TV commercials. It's filled with sugar, preservatives and carbs. That's what's causing it all."

"Are Americans so stupid that they don't realize that?" asked Darius.

"I guess not," I said.

"It must be from the endless hours they waste in front of their televisions," Darius said. "Entertainment, entertainment, entertainment. They wallow so deep in their fictional nonsense that they no longer think for themselves. Americans accuse Eastern Europeans of being brainwashed, but Americans are much worse."

I happened to agree with him and mounted no defense. "Mr. Gimbutus once mentioned the term *self-censure* as a trait rampant among East European intellectuals," I said. "What's that all about?"

"We're often pressured by men in higher positions than ours to stay within boundaries," said Lukas. "In America, they might call it, 'Don't rock the boat.' Should we stray from the accepted government line, severe reprimands might follow."

"But in the digital age, we have so much opportunity to share photographs, messages, news and ideas via the internet," I said. "I'm surprised that the gatekeepers still have so much control in your country."

"Our leaders are more interested in stability than they are in truth," Lukas said.

"I get that," I said.

"What do you think about the international Zionist conspiracy of plutocrats who put their jackboots on the necks of so many people worldwide?" Darius asked.

"I don't know about that," I said.

"Look at this guy. He's just another nearsighted American who can't face the truth of his religion's imperialism," Vlad said. "That, to me, is a form of cowardice."

Wait a minute! Who is this dog-ass bitch named Vlad? Hey, fuck you, man, I thought. *I got a good mind to take this shot glass in hand, hurl it across the room and bean the motherfucker.*

"Why are Americans so obsessed with guns?" asked Darius. "I read where thirty-six thousand Americans are killed each year from gun violence."

"I think you can trace it to the Wild West mentality of America in the old days. Back then, it was a lawless frontier. Guns were the only defense you had against outlaws and hostile Indians. Now, it's part of American mythology. But the majority of those gun deaths are actually caused by suicides."

"Are American men that insecure about themselves?" Lukas asked.

"Perhaps."

"This president of yours with his red hat followers reminds me of the fascists who invaded our country in 1939 and liquidated your people," said Lukas. "What do you think of him?"

Damn, I thought, *I can't talk about the guy in my own home or at work. Why should I rage against him to foreigners?* "You could waste a big part of your day obsessing about that guy," I said.

Vlad started to snicker. "Your president is an idiot, elected by a bunch of American idiots. President Putin was head of Russian intelligence for years. That's why it was so easy for him to manipulate your elections, your shallow American president and all his stupid followers."

I got the feeling Gimbutus "hung me out to dry." I thought that expression summed up my predicament best. Outnumbered five to one, perhaps his idea was to get me drunk and let his young Turks have at it in an effort to boost their confidence. They came well-prepared and well-rehearsed. While the three spokesmen proceeded with their interrogation about the American shadow, two others,

Alexander and Dovydas, played secretary and took scrupulous notes as if Gimbutus was going to test them on the material.

"What do you think about the American penal system? Your country has more prisoners per capita than any nation in the world," said Lukas.

"Much of it is the result of racism," I said. "In America, the cards are stacked against people of color. They go to the worst schools, live in the poorest neighborhoods and work at the lowest-paying jobs. Some poor Whites like it that way, thinking that no matter how low they are, at least Black people are below them. I think that gives them a certain satisfaction. Racial discrimination against people of color in America is getting better, but there's still a long way to go before they reach equality."

"What do you make of the current American political scene?" Lukas asked.

"I'm appalled by it," I said. "America's political debate is harassed by online agent provocateurs who fail to distinguish truth from lies, rhetoric from oratory, right from wrong, corruption from the law, racism from righteousness."

"We are interested in the concept of political correctness," said Darius. "Isn't it true that the Democrats hide the ugly fact that many of their constituency are criminals, prone to laziness, dysfunction, and antisocial behavior, which as a political party they can never confront or admit?"

"That's an awful generalization," I said, "and it's not true. Back when I was a reporter in Minnesota, I once did a story on John Hainsworth. He was an older Black man who was the former head of the Minnesota National Association for the Advancement of Colored People, or what they call the NAACP. He wrote a book about his life. He told me a story that I'll always remember.

"His group lobbied the Minnesota legislature to make lynching illegal after a mob in Duluth hung three Blacks from a traveling circus because they allegedly got too familiar with a White woman in 1921. It resulted in the first anti-lynching law passed by a state in America. A few years after that, the same NAACP successfully lobbied the *Saint Paul Pioneer Press* newspaper to capitalize the letter *N* in *Negro* when they wrote the word in their paper. Later, they got KSTP radio to stop using the word *nigger* on the air."

"What's the point of your story?" Lukas asked.

"That psychological steps come before political steps," I said. "It's the little things like stopping the N-word on the radio, capitalizing the word *Negro* in the papers and outlawing mob rule. Each instance was a baby step, allowing people of color to overcome the racism of White people."

"Are you trying to tell us that these poor colored wretches we see sleeping on the street and begging us for money are equal to White people?" Vlad asked.

"DC has a lot of rich Black people with big jobs. You just haven't noticed them."

"Tell us about the poetry you write," Darius said. "What kind of politics do you defend?"

"I prefer to leave politics out of my poetry. I see no reason to enter into the pissing contest that's currently dividing America."

"That's ridiculous," said Vlad. "All poetry is political. And in your country's case, it serves the cause of rapacious greed."

"I'm more interested in the cultural processes that drive politics and the common humanity that all of us share," I said.

"That's laughable," Vlad said sarcastically.

"I wouldn't presume to throw the blood spilled by Putin on your doorpost," I said. "The sins of our fathers are not yet the sins of their millennial sons. We have the ability to change the world. But you seem more than happy to put on a Russian Army uniform and pick up an AK-47 so as to continue the malicious intent."

Vlad made a hand gesture that dismissed everything I said as nonsense. "You're ridiculous," he said. "Poetic vision is always politically charged. If it's not, it's shit!"

The tone of their questions reminded me that, like American culture, cynicism and political polarization were a worldwide phenomenon. They zeroed in on the negative aspects of America. While their questions were legitimate, I grew bored with playing American apologist.

It was disappointing that these guys, who might one day be my friends, were confrontational instead of open-minded. One day, our generation will take charge. The idea of perpetuating the same stale truths of our elders wasn't going to solve anything. While their questions were relevant, they weren't looking for truth; they were looking to reinforce negative stereotypes. I squirmed in my seat, and as I did, I was reminded of the vape pen tucked tightly in the front pocket of my pants. I got the idea that perhaps it might free these guys from the terrestrial tyranny of vodka and bombast.

"Gentlemen, put down your pens. Let's really talk," I said. "I am a poet. I'm trying to rise above all this nonsense. Here, this is the best counterirritant to a corrupt age," I said. Reaching into my pocket, out came the vape pen. It was all charged up, too. I put it to my lips, inhaled and blew out a cloud. "Here, you guys should try some of this. And don't be afraid. It is legal in DC."

"Just what I expected," Vlad said. "You cannot justify your country, so you resort to drugs and alcohol to numb yourself to it."

"We talked earlier about self-censorship, Vlad," I said. "This is how I push back. You should try it. It might lift you above your cynicism. Of course, I understand your reluctance. You're probably so accustomed to kissing authoritarian ass that the idea of searching for a firm state of heart is terrifying."

He reacted as if I had challenged his manhood. He was the first one to try it. It went around the table twice, and everybody took part. It didn't take more than a few minutes for the psychoactive ingredients to kick in. The realpolitik blotting their brains was blown aside by a gnostic gust. We realigned ourselves. Now, the tone and tenure of the conversation shifted. My stream of consciousness plowed the road.

"If you want to understand America, don't get caught up with the details. Follow the process," I said. "The American Founding Fathers set up an enlightened system of government that later generations have been trying to actualize for two and a half centuries. It's like they created a blueprint and challenged each generation to push its idealism a bit further."

"America sucks right now?" Dovydas asked, having laid down his pen. "Do you agree?"

"Maybe," I said, "but change happens very quickly in America. Tomorrow might begin a golden age."

"What is it that makes America great?" Lukas asked. "Is it the weapons, the farmland, the money?"

"For me, it's the Bill of Rights. It basically says that a majority of dolts, even if democratically elected, cannot limit my freedom of speech, assembly, religion or my pursuit of happiness. As a poet, I find that most important."

"Are you critical of American leadership?" Darius asked.

"Yes," I answered. "It's time for baby boomer Americans to step down and let individuals of our generation take over."

I was amazed at how good their English was and how much they understood, especially now that the Sour Diesel vape pen had opened us all up. Even Vlad lost his edge. Suddenly, we were laughing and having fun. We even did another shot of vodka.

Then they wanted DC dating tips and where to go to meet girls. I told them to go right up 16th Street to Columbia Road and make a left. "There's a great street life in the Adams-Morgan neighborhood, especially on weekends," I said. "The Shaw neighborhood is also hip. However, getting smartphone apps like Tinder or OkCupid is a faster way to meet girls."

The pen was making another turn around the table. I took a big hit and blew out a big cloud. At the same moment, one of the dour, mustached men returned. "What is this?" he screamed.

"Hey, bro', not to worry, it's legal in DC," I said.

"This is not DC. This is Lithuania."

"This is a meeting of millennial minds," I said. "You should leave us be."

He started in with a Lithuanian rant, browbeating his interns for their waywardness. Dovydas burst into laughter but was quickly stared down. Then, turning to me, he said, "I am afraid, Mr. Meckler, it's time for you to leave."

I stood up, put my pen in my pocket, and said, "Fellas, I work at Tadich Grill on Pennsylvania Avenue. Come by and see me so we can continue this conversation."

No one said goodbye. Back on the street with my head down, walking down 16th Street as the sun began to set, I realized how loaded I was. Thinking about what just happened, I said to myself, "Samuel, you're one naïve motherfucker."

I boarded an orange line train at McPherson Square for home. Suddenly, I got lonely. For some reason, and it was spontaneous, I stepped off the train one stop early. At Eastern Market station, I sat down on the platform bench between the two tracks. I pulled the pink water bottle out of my backpack and put it on the bench beside me. I was in a lovelorn emotional state that cut me deep. It must have been the vodka. I searched the crowd coming off the train and walking to the exit.

> Love, make her appear.
> Fill me with her presence
> That she might
> Command my devotion.
> Help me transcend
> Loneliness and illusion,
> With dreams
> Of contentment,
> Of wholeness
> And release.

It dawned on me that in my vodka-induced state, she might pass by without me recognizing her. No, I'd recognize her anywhere. If not with my eyes, then with my heart. Seven trains came and went. I scoured the faces of each woman who passed, looking and longing for that elusive object of beauty I once saw depart at this very place. She did not appear.

"This is pathetic," I said to myself. On my phone, I googled "love and foolishness." A host of articles appeared on my screen. I didn't realize it was such a hot topic. But none of the content resonated with me. I must be a different kind of love fool.

That revelation jolted me out of my loveless swell. Holding on to her pink water bottle as if it were some sacred link was rendering me ridiculous. She probably replaced the water bottle the very next day.

Perhaps it was the urge to be at my desk writing about tonight that caused me to give up. Disappointed, I reached for the bottle beside me and held it tight. Perhaps I should just throw it in the trash and be done with it. It was only a ten-foot toss to the garbage can. With a good arc, I could nail it. I faked a free throw but did not release my grip. Instead, I returned the bottle to my backpack. I might find her one day. But it wasn't going to be tonight. I boarded an eastbound train for Potomac Avenue.

CHAPTER 12

When I returned home, Cortez was watching a war movie in the living room.

"How did it go with the Russians?" he asked.

"They're not Russians. They're Lithuanians from an independent state that just happens to be a little too close to Russia."

"Okay, so how did it go with the Lithuanians?"

"It was weird. They welcomed me because my grandfather was one of them back in the day. There was lots of vodka. Then the old men left and it was just me and five millennials. They started peppering me with questions about the current political scene. They wanted to know about African Americans whom they fear, the president whom they mock, our oppressive penal system, the absurdity of political correctness and other stuff."

"You got strong opinions. Maybe Gimbutus thought you might provide them with an alternative point of view," Cortez said.

"Those guys don't think for themselves and don't even realize it might be a problem."

"They come from a different culture."

"And two of them were taking notes the whole time."

"Maybe they were just looking for meme material," Cortez said.

"It was like speaking to a bunch of *National Enquirer* reporters."

"What did you do?"

"I took out a vape pen and got them all high."

"Inside the embassy?"

"Why not? It's legal, and the vape pen has no smell."

"Oh, you are my hero," Cortez said.

"That's when the conversation got really interesting. We started talking about the big picture and how it's all being distorted."

"What do you think they got out of it?"

"Something essential, like how to pick up American girls and where to go for the hunt."

"That's something their old men can't help them with. I'll bet you were a big hit."

"I think next time we have a big dinner, we should invite them."

"That's okay with me," Cortez said.

"Speaking of dinner, how'd things go with Sookie?" I asked.

"Why do you want to know how I'm doing with Sookie?"

"I'm just lonely," I said. "I guess I'm living vicariously through you."

"We're having fun."

"They say a man can only grow through intimacy," I said. "You know how it goes, you fuck, you cum, and after all that intimacy, all sorts of confessions come out. You grow a little emotionally, intellectually and sexually. That's a good thing. You got that now. I don't."

"A woman can be a lot of work, too," he said. "They always want to be in charge."

"True, I've seen some of the head-trippers you've gone out with."

"Enjoy your solitude while you can. It won't last forever."

"You're right."

Then my phone rang. I saw who was calling. "Oh shit," I said.

"Is it the whale?"

"It's Shayla," I said. "Why do you call her that?"

"Because she's a big fish in this town," he said. "Don't just sit there. Answer it."

"Hello?"

"Just checking to make sure you're still available tomorrow night to help me rewrite my Wikipedia page and online profile," she said.

"Yes," I said. "I've been waiting for your call. What time?"

"I can meet you right after my broadcast. Shall we say eight p.m. at my place? I'll even feed you dinner."

"Okay. I'll bring a small tape recorder. I'll transcribe the conversation and write something up. Then we can go over it next week and shore it up."

"I'm still uncomfortable about being involved in the story."

"I thought we settled this," I said. "I wrote for community newspapers, Shayla. We didn't write about the dirt, only the flower. No reporter can capture the depth and drama of your passage. I am not going to cheapen it with a phony facade of objectivity. So, there it is. Take it or leave it."

"I understand. Thank you. See you then."

When I hung up the phone, Cortez raised his eyebrows and smiled. "Damn, bro', if I had her on my arm, I'd be in front of a CNN camera in no time."

"Fine, she's all yours."

"Sam, I don't think you realize what a woman like that can do for you."

"She's never going to do my restaurant side work or write my poem."

"Still, having her as a lover—"

"Bro', don't use that word. It isn't love, I promise."

"Sammy, tell it to someone who'll believe you."

"Shayla lacks tenderness, Cortez. I look at Sookie and damn, that girl got some tenderness."

"Oh yeah, she's down with pleasing her man."

"I think Shayla's going through some kind of midlife crisis," I said. "She's got a lot of work to do on herself, and I think she's clinging to a younger version of herself through me."

"You can't dismiss all her issues with that one excuse."

"The midlife crisis is not a pejorative term. It's real, and she's not the first person to suffer from it."

Just then, Caleb walked in the door. He had a bag in hand.

"Did you go shopping?" Cortez asked.

"Yes, I bought a present for Vickie," he said.

"Let's see," Cortez said.

He pulled a small box out of the bag and opened it up. It was a small gold cross on a gold chain. "Damn, Caleb, when you're courting a girl, you address the body, not the spirit," Cortez said.

"Do you think she'll like it?" he asked.

I shrugged my shoulders.

Cortez said, "I guess we'll find out soon enough. When are you going to give it to her?"

"Tomorrow at the bar."

I went upstairs and checked out Shayla's online profile. On the WRC website, there was a picture of her taken ten years ago. The written part of it seemed more like the description of a debutante than a serious DC broadcaster. She was the daughter of a prominent attorney and a San Diego socialite. It spoke of her big blue eyes, her blond hair, and big white teeth. There was very little about the work she did for the network or the journalism prizes she'd won over the years.

Accustomed as I was to writing Highland Villager feature articles, I knew I could do better than that nonsense. I wrote out a list of questions for tomorrow night.

The next evening, before we were to meet, I turned to her Channel 4 broadcast. Cortez sat beside me. I watched her on the tube again for a better understanding of her on-air work. Drive-by shootings, car crashes and a sexual predator story highlighted her presentation. The broadcast ended with a heartwarming story of a ten-year-old's successful recovery of his lost dog.

Her broadcast was a plethora of horrible stories punctuated by TV commercials that had nothing in common with the news content. It reminded me of a Dadaist poem written to intentionally confuse.

"She's the queen of lousy content," I said.

"That's what people want to see," Cortez said. "It's all about the ratings and the money shows can charge for a minute of commercial time. On some, it's more than you make in a year."

"Damn, I'm going to have to hold my nose while I write this."

CHAPTER 13

I lived about a mile from Shayla. It was a nice evening, so I decided to walk. Dusk is my favorite time of day. The temperature cools, your responsibilities are complete and people are out on the street enjoying the end of the day. But because I've worked nights at so many different restaurants over the years, it was a time of day I rarely got to enjoy. Tonight, there was an orange glaze to the horizon as the sun set that I studied while walking west to her condo.

When I arrived, I checked my phone for the time and realized that I left it at home. The machine in my pants was actually the small tape recorder I used for my *Highland Villager* stories. I mistakenly thought it was my phone. It forced me to realize that I was more nervous about this meeting than I cared to admit.

She answered the door all hot and sweaty. "You're early," she said. Her hair was pulled back in a ponytail, and she was dressed in spandex. As I walked into her condo, a door to a large room was open. A high-ticket Peloton exercise bike had a TV screen, and the man narrating her spin session was on hold. She turned it off. There were racks of clothes on hangers covering two entire walls. There must have been nearly two hundred dresses.

"I never wear the same dress twice in one season."

"Why not?"

"My viewers would notice, especially the women."

"I never would."

"True, but you're a guy. Guys are oblivious to such details. Since they are all expensive, I have to maintain my figure to make sure I fit into them all. Pour yourself a drink. I'll just be a few minutes." She excused herself and went to shower.

I sat down outside on her fifth-floor balcony as the sun set directly behind the Capitol dome. It shone through the dome's windows from behind. I considered the possible metaphors. Was it symbolic of the sun setting on the American empire or the light of God seeking to illuminate the members of the legislative branch? Regarding both points of view, I figured a considerable amount of copy could be written about each.

She returned in her yoga pants and a tight T-shirt. In the oven at a low temp, Chinese food was warming in white boxes. Plates and chopsticks were on the table. She removed dinner from the oven. It consisted of Szechuan beef and cashew chicken. There was white rice, too. We started eating.

This was our fourth meeting and we were beginning to get used to the idea of one another without being defensive.

"Did you read what they had online about me?"

"Yes."

"What did you think?"

"You come off like a bimbo."

"That's a mean thing to say."

"You asked, I told you. You need to cut yourself loose from the sycophants."

"Well, what can we do about it?"

"Update it. If you're looking to make yourself more relevant to a millennial audience, you have to change."

"How am I supposed to do that? You saw my crowd. They're all smug and self-satisfied," she said. "Sometimes, I just feel so stifled around them."

"You need to cultivate a new you."

I pulled out the tape recorder and put it on the table. "Okay, let's get started. I'll interview you and then I'll transcribe the conversation at home and write a feature article that does honor to the twenty years of you showing up to work on time."

"Fine, let's get started."

I started with the basics. She was the oldest of three girls from La Jolla, California. She grew up in a big Tudor house with a live-in maid and rich parents. Her lawyer dad also owned a stock brokerage house; her mom didn't work but was active in San Diego-area society. She was active in the Junior League, the League of Women Voters and served on the board of a local hospital.

In her senior year of high school, Shayla was class president, a varsity cheerleader and editor of the yearbook. She went east for college. Her undergraduate degree was from Wellesley College. Her master's degree was from the Columbia School of Journalism. She started at Channel 4 in 2002.

In her early days as a reporter, she got to choose her own stories. It gave access to everybody in town. Soon, she was as popular as the individuals she reported upon. Three years later, WRC promoted her to news anchor, a position she still holds today.

The photos on the wall testified to her presence among the high and the mighty. How comfortable she looked standing beside them all as if she were a natural part of the elite aristocracy that runs the Washington agenda.

"Sometimes I look back over the past twenty years and scratch my head, thinking whatever possessed me to make the choices I made."

"What's the answer to that question?" I asked.

"I don't know," she said. "When I arrived in DC, it seemed like all the doors opened for me. I was riding a whirlwind and the city seemed to be at my feet. I charmed and was charmed. I seduced and was seduced. I had success in a city where success really meant something. I had money, fame, and the satisfaction of doing good work. And I loved it. It opened me up in so many ways. But as the years passed, it became a burden, not to mention emotionally exhausting. I think that's why I married Phillip. I needed a respite from it all."

"Any regrets?" I asked.

"A few. I would have liked to have been a mother. But now it's too late."

I now had the highlights of her life. I was on my second drink and I probed a bit deeper. "How did you meet your husband?"

"At a dinner party. He was young and dashing and full of idealism, a young student at Georgetown University Law School with dreams about changing the world."

"That's not the impression he gave at the restaurant."

"He finished law school deep in debt. He went corporate. Over time, he lost all his ideals."

"Is he still representing you with the network?"

"Yes, but my contract is not up for another three months and no one seems in a hurry to resolve it. Since all of this is moving at a snail's pace, I sometimes wonder if Phillip's goal is to make me twist in the wind. To tell you the truth, I'm worried that I'm soon going to be out of a job."

"What would you do then?"

"It's too terrifying to think about."

"Do you think that's his intention?"

"No, I don't think so."

"How long have you lived here?"

"Three months. He got the Georgetown townhouse. We split the value of it and I bought this. And it's all mine. It's great to have my own space. Being that it's up here on the Hill, I'm as far away from him as I can possibly be while still living in the district."

"Has your divorce made the papers yet?"

"No, not yet."

"Will it have any impact on your career?"

"After I sign a deal, no."

She waxed poetic about Greg Archer, a high school basketball sensation to whom she gave up her virginity in her junior year of high school. "He was a year older than me and I let him go all the way on his 18th birthday."

"Whatever happened to him?"

"He got a basketball scholarship to Ohio State and was the starting guard his junior and senior year."

"Was he White or Black?"

"White, of course."

"What's he doing now?"

"He's the director of athletics for the state of Ohio."

She confessed to a lack of sex since splitting from her husband and buying this condo.

"Why?"

"Because Phillip and I travel in the same social circles and I don't want that part of my life to be open to gossip."

"Are they all as stiff as he is?" I inquired.

"They were all great people when we were in our twenties. But then we all got older, got chained to a career, some started families and got weighed down with responsibilities. I don't even like myself when I'm around them. You saw the worst of it at your restaurant that night."

"You were awful."

"Want to hear what's worse? I knew how awful I was. But I just couldn't stop."

"Is Shayla Reeve your birth name?"

She paused for a moment and bit her lip as if she were hesitant to confess.

"No, it's Shayna Revetsky," she said. "But I'd like to keep that out of the article."

"Are you Jewish?"

"Yes."

"If I remember my grandmother's Yiddish correctly, Shayna means 'pretty,' doesn't it?"

"Yes."

"You certainly lived up to your name."

"Thanks. That's the first nice thing you've said to me since we've met."

"You're welcome."

"Why did you get into broadcast journalism?"

"I was a cheerleader in high school and I liked being in the spotlight. As I got older, I realized I didn't have to cheer for men. I could compete in their world as an equal. I suppose I was a bit of a gossip in high school, too. I still like to be in the know. Working as a newscaster just came naturally to me."

"What is it about the job that you like?" I asked.

"Certainly, the money. But I also like being an insider, able to share news with my audience."

We went on for another thirty minutes. Because she wanted me to write only a short feature story for Wikipedia, I had enough material.

"Okay, I think I got it," I said. "I'll transcribe the conversation onto my computer and write something up. It should be ready next week."

"I'm eager to see how it looks on paper," she said.

"You're still sexy on camera, Shayla, but that's no longer enough."

"What do you mean?"

"When I was living in the Twin Cities, I was always embarrassed that I was writing for community papers instead of one of the daily newspapers in Saint Paul or Minneapolis. But over time, I saw how the digital age was destroying the community with all sorts of nonsense. That's your way forward, Shayla. Community values and a defense of bridges, not walls."

"I'll give it some thought."

"This will be fun to write. If there's anything we left out or doesn't sound right, we can correct it."

"Did you bring the vape pen?"

"After last time, I didn't think it was a good idea."

"I've never passed out like that before in my life. I hope you didn't think less of me because of it."

"What do you care what I think?"

"Unfortunately, you're one of the few honest people I have in my life right now. The rest just patronize me."

"My friends have no problem telling me when I'm full of crap," I said.

"You seemed close to doing just that with me when we met at Tadich."

"But I didn't."

"Why not? I certainly deserved it."

"Ron Robbins would have fired me," I said. "Plus, there was something else. I felt like you were trapped in a situation that you were desperately trying to escape."

"That's a pretty accurate rendition of where I am right now."

"What would your therapist think of me and you together?"

"She's encouraged me, thinks I'm finally finding the courage to step out of my comfort zone. Plus, here's another thing. I've never been able to confess so much of myself to a man the way I'm able to do with you."

There was a pause as I considered her words.

"I'll get us a refill," I said, standing up. I walked to the kitchen to refresh our drinks.

"Waiters have the most beautiful bodies," she said.

"I guess that's from so many steps we walk during a shift."

"What do you think of my body?" she asked.

"I'll let you know when you show it to me."

I poured her a glass of cabernet. For myself, some of her very good single malt scotch. I put her goblet before her and sat back down.

From listening to the stories, I recognized that playing Shayla Reeve was a high-pressure role. Her anxiety sometimes caused her to lash out at those around her, if only to alleviate the stress that ran rampant through her veins. Yes, I understood that.

"Do you have much experience with women?" she asked.

"Yes, and I need to tell you, if we sleep together, you're not going to boss me around."

"For once, I'd love to have someone boss me around."

"You can't own me either," I said.

"Can I borrow you for a while?"

I didn't answer, so she added, "I can give you what you want."

"In bed?"

"How's this, I will give you what you want. You just have to ask."

I looked her in the eye and gave her a chance to retreat. She did not. I stood up, reached out for her hand, led her to her bedroom and closed the door.

"Take off your clothes," I said softly.

In the seconds that followed, they were thrown to her feet. "Where do you hide your sex toys?"

"On the top shelf in my closet," she said.

"Go get them."

Shayla promised to give me what I wanted in bed and she did. We were passionate, naughty too. I pushed her comfort level. I felt this intense need to possess her. She was unrestrained and surrendered to an abandonment that seemed new to her. It was wild, rough and wanton. And it lasted over an hour. Though it was our first time together, we both enjoyed an orgasm. I rolled off her, exhausted and satiated.

Every man likes a good fuck story. For some, it's as epic as we ever get. Yet, it always seems so indelicate and boastful to speak of a sexual encounter. Descriptions of the actual play-by-play and the patient, progressive moves toward mutual climax never do justice to the actual act. It's as if by detailing the transition from pecking to petting to promiscuous pummeling, you were somehow violating a sacred, intimate oath.

I sometimes looked upon it as the equivalent of the Hebrew prohibition against graven images. Keep God sacred and don't degrade him with descriptions. So, I won't go into the sexual details here. I'd rather stress the highlights of our carnal act.

I found delight in her mouth; her breasts; her clitoris, which was delicious; her vagina; her toys; her bright eyes; and her throat, purring sensual sounds of affirmation. The afterglow lit the room. Her bed felt safe as a womb. I was proud of her effort to please me and she was proud of mine. The ensuing release inspired us both.

Looking over her body as she lay next to me, I started to laugh. "Damn, girl, you got some weird-looking feet which is funny since aesthetically, the rest of you is so perfect."

"I know. The second toe is way bigger than the big toe. It keeps growing and I can't make it stop."

"When I was young, we used to refer to that as 'retarded toes.'"

"Well, that's not fair to the disability community."

"It's just a joke. I didn't mean to be politically incorrect."

"Well, it's no joke to me," she said. "Do you know how hard it is for me to buy shoes? They never fit."

"I never considered that."

"I told you about Greg Archer in high school," she said. "How old were you the first time you took someone to bed?"

"Two and a half."

"Two and a half?"

"I stole my older sister's Barbie doll, took off her clothes and brought her to bed. When Lyn found out, she thought the doll had cooties and didn't want her back. I slept with Barbie for years. As a matter of fact, the two of you remind me of each other."

She rapped me gently on the arm.

"Excuse me, I have to use the bathroom," I said. I jumped out of bed and walked to the guest bathroom near the front door of her condo. A few minutes later, I jumped back into bed with her.

"Can I ask you a personal question?"

"Sure," I said.

"Do men use tissue to wipe themselves after they urinate?"

"No, why?"

"A woman would never think of not wiping."

"That's because your plumbing is different."

"I know, but I worry that you might pee on my sheets after a bathroom visit."

"Shayla, I just ejaculated all over them or don't you remember?"

"Of course, I remember, I have a wad of tissue up between my legs as we speak. I just always wondered."

"Did you ever ask Phillip that question?"

"No," she said, "I only thought about it for the first time now."

"There's this old rhyme from Jersey I remember from my youth. 'No matter how much you wiggle or how much you dance, you'll always get those last few drops in your pants.'"

"That's gross."

"Would you like me to put on my underwear?"

"Would you mind?"

"No." I got up, put on my black briefs and rejoined her in bed.

"You never answered my question from earlier this evening."

"Which question is that?" I asked.

"What do you think of my body?"

"Your nose is like the tower of Lebanon, which looks toward Damascus."

She slapped me on the arm. "Are you suggesting that I've had my nose fixed?"

She reached for a photo set on a headboard shelf. "Look here. That's my mother and my sisters. Check out the nose. This is my mother's nose."

I stared at the photo. The four of them were all dressed up as if they were attending someone's wedding. Among her sisters, Shayla was the prettiest one. But in her day, the mom outshined them all.

"That line is from the Bible, *the Song of Solomon,*" I said. "How beautiful is your love, my sister, my bride. How much better is your love than wine and the fragrance of your oils than any spice! Your lips drip nectar, honey. The fragrance of your garments is like the fragrance of Lebanon. Let my beloved come to this garden and eat its choicest fruits."

"How many women have you used that line on before me?" she asked.

I shrugged my shoulders because I didn't want to tell her. "Shayla, you have a beautiful body."

She gave me a sly smile. "Take off your underpants. I want you in my mouth."

She was good, better than the first time. Then she straddled me and prepared to mount what she incited.

"Wait," I said. "Don't forget about the Kleenex."

She reached between her legs and threw the wad onto the carpet. I watched as she moved up and down in a frenzied motion on top of me. My hands held her breasts. We climaxed at the same time. She collapsed upon my chest, exhausted. A minute later, we were both asleep.

When we woke the next morning, good feelings prevailed. She was sitting at the table drinking coffee when I joined her and reading the on-line version of the *Washington Post.*

"What's new and horrible in the world?" I asked.

"The State Department just expelled ten East Europeans for espionage."

"Too bad. They're going to miss the World Series."

"I doubt they follow baseball," she said.

After a quick breakfast of toast and coffee, she volunteered to walk me home. It was a beautiful morning. The sky was pure blue.

The humidity was low, a cool breeze blew and the temperature was in the low seventies.

She wore a pair of big sunglasses and a Washington Nationals baseball cap pulled down over her eyes. No one recognized her. As we walked along, I told her how I was going to write out last night's interview this afternoon.

The morning sun was in our faces as it rose above the Anacostia River. When a black Mercedes, waiting at a red light rolled into the middle of the crosswalk, she yelled at the woman driver. "You're in the crosswalk. Pay attention."

Then turning to me, she said, "They only ever think of themselves."

A block later, a man at a red light threw his cigarette out of his window and onto the ground, still burning.

"Hey, are you out of your mind? That's poison. A smoker and a litterbug? Next time, throw your damn butt where it belongs."

The muffled response from the car was, "Fuck you, lady."

Two blocks later, I saw an old, dark penny heads-up on the sidewalk. I stopped and picked it up. "You're not the only one with street rituals," I said. "This will bring me good luck."

At a construction site, soon to be a five-story apartment building along Pennsylvania Avenue SE, the sidewalk was covered with a wooden roof to protect pedestrians from the builders at work above. A sign affixed to a plywood wall read, "Walk your bike."

When two bike riders went by and came close to hitting us, she yelled at them, "Walk your bike!"

"Ride your walk!" the biker called back.

"Go to hell!" Shayla shouted in response.

"Hey, lighten up, Shayla," I said.

"If I don't correct them, who will? I believe that everybody should have an equal opportunity to a quality life. Sometimes, that quality of life begins with people taking responsibility for their actions. I'm just trying to help bring forth a more competent city order."

"I don't like too much order," I said. "It makes things rigid. I prefer the irrational, spontaneous side. It allows for eruptions from the libido and the unconscious which sometimes become an emerging issue that promotes change."

Shayla disagreed and shook her head. Seeing another "Walk your bike" sign at the other end of the construction site, she stood waiting for the young Arabic man who was about to ride his bike down the narrow passage. Now, not only was she going to holler at him but she also had the sign as a visual prop. She positioned herself for the ambush right beside the sign.

"I'm just going to pretend that I don't know you and walk over here," I said. I went up ahead, not wanting to witness it.

She jumped in his way and pointed to the sign. "Walk your bike!" The startled guy banged into the plywood wall beside him and almost fell off his ten-speed.

He jumped off and started screaming at her. "Are you out of your mind? Stupid cow. You could have killed me!"

She hadn't expected that kind of response. His anger was so pitched I feared he was going to punch her. Putting myself between them, I said, "Sir, please excuse my Aunt Judy. She ran out of her medication last night, and she's just not herself this morning. We're on our way to CVS right now to refill her prescription of Aripiprazole. I apologize. Please forgive her." The sincere look I gave him was enough to make him back off.

"She looks and acts like that silly Shayla woman on the TV news," he said.

"What the hell did you just say?" shouted Shayla. "Are you comparing me to that bitch? She's not half as pretty as me. Maybe the reason you don't obey signs is because you need your eyes examined."

"You need your head examined!" he shot back.

Turning to her, I said, "Aunt Judy, please don't antagonize the man."

"Yeah, well, he shouldn't make provocative statements," she said.

"Sir, let me apologize again. It's not about you." I pointed my finger to my temple and swirled it in circles while raising my eyebrows and nodding in her direction.

He climbed back onto his bike and rode off, cursing her in Arabic as he pedaled.

"Aunt Judy?" she asked.

"It was the first thing I could think of."

"I thought he was going to beat me up. Thanks for coming to my rescue."

"Have you always been a neighborhood bully?" I asked.

"What do you mean? 'See something, say something'—it's an ad all over the Metro system. I'm just trying to make them obedient to the law. Is that wrong?"

"Who knows that much?"

As we turned the corner onto North Carolina Avenue, I noticed two cars were blocking the street in front of the Fourth Estate. Something was going on at the house. It was overrun by cops and plainclothes men. That was when it hit me. "Were any of those expelled East Europeans from that *Post* story you read this morning from Lithuania?"

"Yes, I think so."

"Oh, shit."

"What's that all about?"

"I have an idea. But you better go. Whatever it is, you don't need to be involved."

Before she turned away, I reached into my pocket and pulled out the tape recorder. "You better take this with you. If you don't hear from me in the next hour, call Ron at Tadich Grill. Tell him what you saw and apologize for me for not making my shift today."

At the front gate, I watched as Caleb came out of the house in handcuffs. Seeing me, he flew into a rage. He screamed out.

"Demons are the grossest and most deficient forms in the universe and their prince is Samuel Meckler!" They put him into a black sedan.

On the front steps, I came face-to-face with the FBI. "So, Samuel Meckler, we meet again."

"It's Mr. Meyers, isn't it?"

"Yes."

"What's this all about?"

"Is this your phone?"

"Yes," I said as two men walked by me, each carrying a box filled with my journals. A third came out with my computer.

"We need to take a ride downtown," he said.

A cop stepped up from behind me, grabbed my wrists and put them in handcuffs. They put me into a black panel truck with no windows. Before the door closed behind me, I caught a glimpse of Shayla sitting on a bus stop bench, watching it all unfold. When a Metro bus pulled up, she stood up and walked away.

CHAPTER 14

The van had a bench seat in the back. Hands cuffed behind me, fastened down with a seat belt, I was taken to an undisclosed location. The vehicle went down a ramp at the end of the ride and into the basement of a building. I was escorted by two uniformed officers to a windowless cell with cinder-block walls. They removed the handcuffs. Its door had a small window. There was a bench to sit on and a light overhead with bars protecting the bulb.

I wouldn't say I was scared, but when the door slammed behind me and locked, my throat went dry, my limbs felt leaden and I found myself staring into space.

Slowly, I took possession of myself. Alone in the silence with nothing to read and nothing to write with, I tried to grasp what was going on. It didn't take me long to figure out the cause: Johan Gimbutus. I realized that when the cops interrogated me, I was going to have some explaining to do. I conceived my response as if it were a newspaper story. I needed a strong lead, followed by cogent arguments in my defense and a persuasive close proclaiming my innocence. Of course, it was a half-baked effort since I wasn't exactly sure what I was being accused of.

I was sure it was a result of my visit to the Lithuanian embassy. Was I being used by foreign agents to find deeply embedded dirt on the American soul? Were my opinions going to be used to divide and demean America via the internet? It was the double whammy. Take a tongue-lashing by a bunch of anti-American propagandists and then be accused of aiding and abetting their onslaught.

I had to laugh because given my aloofness from mainstream American values, my intense reading and writing regimes and my search for transcendental truths, I was the perfect choice for the Lithuanians. The denial of the American shadow, wrapped as it was in the venal rhetoric of patriotism, capitalism and God, was an occurrence I was critical of. But was speaking negatively about America to foreigners a crime? Given the morons currently in charge, perhaps it was.

I should have been more suspicious of Gimbutus's motives. But the opportunity to embrace a long-forgotten family history was so compelling that I couldn't resist, even though Steve the bartender warned me.

Since solo time was what I lived for, I didn't mind the solitude of the jail cell. Actually, I'd probably make a pretty good inmate. If only I had a pen, the insights running through my mind could have filled the space on both my arms. I feared I'd soon forget them as time moved on. Somewhere near dusk, two uniformed officers opened the cell door and woke me from a nap. They ushered me into a room where Meyers, sitting behind a desk and another man were waiting.

"Samuel Meckler, I think you're in trouble, son," Meyers said with a degree of satisfaction. "If convicted, you're looking at jail time."

"Ezra Pound spent twelve years locked up in Saint Elizabeth's Hospital over in Southeast DC," I said. "They gave him three square meals a day and time to himself. He wrote five books during that time. I might be able to crank out six."

"You're no Ezra Pound."

"I don't have to be. I'm Samuel Meckler."

"I saw some of your poetry when we were going through your journals," Meyers said. "It's pretty bad."

"I didn't write it for you."

"A pretty young thing like you could be real excitement for all the old chicken hawks behind bars," said the other cop whom I thought I recognized from Tadich. "Your ass could be prime real estate." They both laughed.

"No, it won't."

"Well, we'll see about that, won't we?" he mocked.

"Is this shit scripted or are you two making it up as you go along?" I asked.

"Don't get smart with me, punk. We can lock you away for as long as we want and don't have to notify anybody. Your alleged crimes transcend constitutional rights," the other cop said.

"I'm sorry, I didn't catch your name."

"Why do you want to know?"

"I'd like to know who's insulting me."

"The name is Nick McCurdy."

"I didn't do anything wrong, Mr. McCurdy."

"Oh, really? Son, you're no better than frog spawn in a blind man's ditch," he said.

There was a pen on Meyer's desk. "Can I borrow this a minute?" Not waiting for a reply, I grabbed it and on my wrist, I printed out the words that had been running through my mind all afternoon.

> America, America,
> How did your ranks
> Become rife with such cranks?

When I finished, I returned the pen to the same spot on his desk.

I couldn't help but think of street life back in New Jersey during my early years. It was there that I cultivated a keen eye for bullshit. Hyperbole, exaggeration, intimidation and drama for the purpose of misleading, manipulating and head-tripping provoked little fear in me, just an ironic detachment. A straightforward, honest and forthright approach, the kind most Minnesotans employed, was what I respected in personal interactions. Over the years, I developed a sixth sense, able to differentiate between the two.

"Did you guys expel Johan Gimbutus from the country yesterday?" I asked.

"You're damn right we did," said Meyers. "We want to know about your interactions with him."

"What do you want to know?"

"Did they pay you for the information you provided?"

"No money changed hands," I answered.

"What exactly did they want?"

"From the sound of it, they wanted some insightful material from an outsider," I said. "They thought they could get it from me."

"You've detailed conversations in your journals uttered by senators and congressmen overheard at the restaurant," said McCurdy. "Plus, you've written a lot about your political insights about current events. Did you share it with them?"

"Some of it, but I learned my lesson from you, Mr. Meyers. Keep your political opinions to yourself. The only place they get aired out now is in my journals."

That he played a part in my reticence made an impression on him.

"How did Gimbutus get on your radar screen?" I asked.

"I was at the bar the night he was betting everybody on the results of the 2016 election," Meyers said. "He was drunk and full of some deep, dark secret that he could hardly conceal."

"Did you bet him?"

"Yes."

"Did you pay him the hundred?"

"Yes, that's when we started investigating him. It also put you on our radar screen since he seemed to take a liking to you. How did that come about?"

"My grandfather came from the same town as Gimbutus in Lithuania. Since my grandfather has passed, I liked to hear his stories about the old country."

"Oh yes, and the two metals from the Kremlin?" said McCurdy. "Perhaps you have a family history of being a Russian asset."

"No, that's not true."

"There's one thing I don't understand, though. Why did Gimbutus's aide rant against you when you visited the embassy?" Meyers asked.

"How did he do that?"

"He muttered something derogatory about you to his companion. The African American driver who drove him to Dulles spoke fluent Lithuanian and tipped us off. Why did he do that?"

"The older men got me and five interns loaded on vodka. Then they left us alone. The conversation got so stifling that I got frustrated and broke out a marijuana vape pen. I got them all stoned. That's when we really started talking honestly about the state of the world. Then one of the old men came back in, busted us and ordered me to leave."

"In his statement, your housemate, Caleb Hannemann, talked about your pagan rituals, your lack of patriotism, your drinking, your drug use and your corrupt desire to be primitive," McCurdy said.

"What about it?"

"We have your computer, your cell phone and your journals. We have agents examining them as we speak. If there is anything incriminating in them, you are going to have to find yourself a lawyer."

"How long is that going to take?"

"A few days."

"Am I allowed to make a phone call?"

"No need," Meyers said. "We're letting you go. We have your passport and you're on a no-fly list. You can't leave the country."

"Why would I want to leave?"

"We'd like you to return Friday afternoon at 2 p.m."

"So, I'm free to leave?"

"Yes," said Meyers.

"Where the hell am I?"

"Across the street from Tadich Grill."

"When will I get my cell phone, my computer and my journals back?"

"When we're done with them."

"Should I bring an attorney with me on Friday?"

"We'll contact you beforehand if the occasion arises."

There was nothing more to say. He returned my wallet and my keys. "An officer will escort you to the front door," said Meyers.

"See you, punk," McCurdy said.

It was dark outside when I walked across the street and into the restaurant. I went to apologize to Ron for missing my dinner shift. He was sitting on a barstool. He let out a big sigh when he saw me. "You seem to be a magnet for the absurd."

"It sure seems that way," I replied.

"I'm afraid that I'm going to have to suspend you, Samuel. You didn't call and you didn't show up for your shift. Plus, John Meyers came in for lunch and accused you of some serious stuff. It was my obligation to tell the owners. It was their idea that we keep you off the floor until this is all straightened out."

"Didn't Shayla Reeve call and tell you what happened?"

"No, and it wasn't her obligation."

"I was under arrest."

"I'm sorry, Sam. It's out of my hands. I'm sure you heard about the scandal we had with Gene Upshaw and the Buich family. It nearly ruined us. Half the town thinks we're racist. If it gets out that we're a Russian spy house, too, we'll lose our Republican customers completely. It could bury us for good. We can't have it."

"How long is the suspension for?"

"Until there's some resolution to all this. If it makes the newspapers, that will change everything for the worse. Come in next week and we'll discuss your future here."

I felt humiliated but I tried not to show it. I walked out the door, trying not to make eye contact with any of the other staff members who stared at me as I left the restaurant.

I needed a drink and walked to the Veil. Vickie had a full bar. I grabbed a scotch from her. She was wearing Caleb's gift around her neck. I nursed my drink in silence and tried to make sense of things.

Should I run back to Minneapolis and give up my DC dreams? Should I embrace my grandfather's roots and teach English in Eastern Europe? Should I return to New Jersey and the culture that molded me? How about hit the road, become a vagabond and let fate work its will upon me? I realized it was going to take several more drinks to quell my anxiety.

A big White woman sat down next to me and ordered a shot of tequila. There was nothing remarkable about her except the tattoo on her forearm. I did a double-take since it seemed so brazen. It was a blue ink drawing of a cartoon elephant fucking a donkey from behind. The elephant's trunk held a handgun. I could see it as a joke if that image was worn on a T-shirt but on the woman's arm?

It was one of the most outrageous tattoos I've ever seen. And after my second drink was nearly down, I thought to take a picture of it. I was sure Caleb would get a kick out of it. But then I realized I didn't have my cell phone. "That's a crazy tattoo, even for these times," I said.

"Like it?" she asked.

"Let me take a closer look."

She pulled herself around so I could see. The elephant had the raw look of domination as its wide girth fucked the donkey's ass. The look on the donkey's face was one of humiliation.

The gal's name was Lena. She was from Pennsylvania. She was a big girl with shoulder-length hair and a nice face. "I'm a Republican lobbyist and hate those Socialist Democrats with a passion. When people see that tattoo, they know exactly where I stand and that's good for my business."

"Who do you represent?"

"A few pharmaceutical companies and a gun manufacturer."

"Have you ever been to the Capitol Hill Club?" I asked.

"Sure, I'm a member and frequently take meetings there."

"I used to work there as a banquet waiter."

"Oh, then you know Stan?"

"Sure, he runs the place. You know, it's funny, Republicans have a bad reputation about the way they treat workers. But at the Capitol Hill Club, they treat their staff like gold. They pay well and feed us like kings."

"Of course, that's true. Democrats talk a great game. But waiters always do better in town when Republicans are in control."

"I've heard some old-timers in the restaurant business say the same thing," I said.

"Why don't you buy us both a drink?"

She was sarcastic and dismissive. At that moment, it mirrored my feelings perfectly. Her reckless talk made me feel better than I felt all day. Fuck Gimbutus, Shayla, Tadich, the FBI, Caleb and all the other assholes. I struck my own nihilistic pose. We were getting along swimmingly since my worst impulses were on display and mirrored hers. I ordered another round.

"Hey, I'm over forty. I don't give a shit anymore. I say what I think and do what I want. Political correctness is bullshit."

"You got that right," I said.

She went off on all the Republican talking points—fake news, corruption, double dealings, Hillary Clinton's emails and Obama's failed presidency. I didn't agree. But I was so mad at the world that I joined right in with her. I was high on sarcasm, disrespect and disregard. And with it, thanks to the scotch, I found a natural release from the nonsense of my day.

She bought the next drink and I bought the one after that. I thought I had the chance to take her to bed. Considering my day, I figured soiling myself with her nonsense was par for the course.

Then she got a phone call. Her crew was waiting for her at "Tune Inn," another Capitol Hill bar. She invited me along. Since I didn't have my phone, she ordered the Uber and we took the mile-long trip down Pennsylvania Avenue.

On his dashboard, the Nepali Uber driver had a statue of *Ganesh*, the Hindu god with the elephant's head and the human body. I vaguely remembered the *Ganesh* story. *Shiva*, his father, returns from war and finds his wife in bed with another man. *Shiva* takes his sword, slices off the man's head and throws the head beyond his borders. Only then did *Shiva* find out that he just slew his son. It's kind of a Hindu version of the *Oedipus* story by Sophocles. To fix the problem, *Shiva* cuts off an elephant's head and places it on his son's body. It felt relevant for me since, over the course of the day, my head was cut off, too.

"Yo, man, speaking of elephants, you should see the elephant this big bitch got on her arm," I said to the Uber driver. "The elephant is fucking a donkey in the ass at gunpoint. I can only imagine how she got the idea for such a tattoo. Some violent rape perpetrated against her which she recreated on her own arm."

He said something to me and then I said something back to him. I was wasted and we were both laughing so hard that I didn't even remember our exchange. Arriving, Lena and I walked into "Tune Inn." I ordered a drink at the bar while she huddled with her four friends. I got the impression that they worked for her because they were all my age and they deferred to her when she entered. She was whispering something to them that was out of earshot. The bartender, who called Lena by name when she entered, was in on it too. Two guys stood up and confronted me.

"You have to leave, right now," one of them said.

I was incredulous. "What?"

"Right now," said the second guy. It took me a minute to grasp the situation.

"Why are you smiling?" he demanded.

I thought to say, "Because you and Lena are jerks." But I refrained. Ignoring him, I reached out my hand and said, "It was nice meeting you too tonight, Lena."

She backed away and left me with my hand out. I finished my drink in two swallows and walked out the door.

What just happened? Did I grab her ass and commit some "Me-Too" folly? No, that's not me. It took me a minute to figure it out. Must have been what I said to the Uber driver. Wasn't I the asshole! It was par for the day. I'll probably never see her again anyway. My only concern was that she might complain about the driver on her Uber app.

Actually, the incident was sort of a relief. I'd been treated as if I were guilty all day. If I was going to be treated like that, at least I got to play the part.

CHAPTER 15

When I awoke the next morning, I was alone in the house. With Cortez, Caleb and Johnny all at work, it was as quiet as the Congressional Cemetery. Though I had the whole day to myself, my smart phone and computer were gone. There was no way to communicate with the outside world. Without my journals, there was no way to communicate with my inner world.

I read instead. Alone at my desk, with no commercial interruptions, I absorbed the oratory of a stalwart literary critic named John Burroughs. His book was about Walt Whitman. It offered gnostic insights that soared above the plebian rhetoric of the week. It gave me pause.

> How can I make
> The undiscovered self,
> Personal and universal
> Simultaneously?

The book was a commentary on Whitman's long poem "Leaves of Grass." What Whitman was trying to do in the middle of the 19th century was what I was trying to do in the 21st century—update America's version of democracy.

Books like Burroughs's, written in 1908, were valuable to me. He did not judge Whitman's poem so much as detail what he found delightful in it. Because his insights stood outside the realm of the digital age, it was morally instructive, too, because they heralded the values of idealism.

Reading has always been my enlightened response to DC drama. It was a way to take myself out of my own mind and inculcate it with the ideas of someone smarter than me. My escape into the literary dream often lasted for hours. For once I started reading in my peaceful garret, whole mornings and afternoons passed. Much note taking was done in the notebooks the feds left behind.

> In seeking authentic prophecy
> And a nobler approximation
> Of the best American self,
> I scour literature for clues
> On how to bind the body politic
> Into a tighter community.

By reaffirming liberty, equality and justice for all, ideals written in stone all over the city's grand buildings, I was reconfiguring them for the globalized future. My literary endeavor was seeking the foundations of a new cultural order. Their truths lay in the penumbra of emerging ideas that mainstream society is not ready to assimilate. But it was clear that something new was required, some prescient proposition reinforcing creativity and community. At present, I had only an inkling of how it was supposed to feel. And yet, I was diligently chasing it down.

> Highlight the human meld
> Let us all be free
> Leave out realpolitik
> Speak of divinity.
> Read the psychic signs.
> Trust the cairns
> Everything is telltale
> See, show
> Dissect, deconstruct,

Tear shit up

Then sew it back together.

I stopped when I heard someone enter the house from the front door. "Sam, are you up there?"

It was Johnny returning from a trip to Seattle. He attended a high-tech exhibition. My desk chair scratched the floor as I pulled it away from my desk. I walked downstairs to meet him.

"What the fuck? You don't answer your phone anymore?"

"It was confiscated by the FBI, along with my journals and my computer."

"Damn, Sam. I had to listen to Caleb whine about you for 30 minutes yesterday while I was trying to cover a story. What the hell happened?"

"I met with the Lithuanians at their embassy. A week later, they were all kicked out of the country for spying. The FBI then came after me."

"They were probably hoping to get memes from you," he said. "They're all about sowing confusion and discord on the internet. It's easy for *Facebook* and *Instagram* to banish Eastern European platforms but when they originate from the US, they're harder to detect."

"Well, it seems that I was recruited."

"Why did the FBI confiscate your phone and computer?"

"They wanted to see if I betrayed my country."

"What are you going to do?"

"I'm supposed to meet with them on Friday at 2 p.m.. I suppose my belongings will be returned or I'll be taken into custody."

"Did you write about your time with Lithuanians in your journal?"

"Yes."

"Anything incriminating?"

"Maybe."

"I need a drink," he said. "Let's walk to the Veil. I'll buy you a scotch."

We walked the six blocks to the bar. "How was your trip to Seattle?" I asked.

"Interesting. I got to see a lot of emerging technologies," Johnny said. "There's some amazing shit coming online soon that in four years will be as commonplace as *Uber* and *Twitter.*"

"I've been to Washington State with my parents," I said. "I love the lay of the land out there. It's so green on the west side of the Cascades and so arid on the east side."

"People are freaking out because of that virus from China," he said. "The conference was filled with Chinese. It actually ended a day early over fears about it."

"I haven't read too much about it. But Governor Nelson canceled his trip to DC next month because of it. He called it a killer."

"No one's taking it seriously yet. But we live in a globalized, interconnected age. It's ignorant to think that a virus from China is not going to arrive here too."

Vickie was working behind the bar. She poured us our usual and put them on the bar.

"Are you okay?" she asked.

"Yes."

"Caleb came in last night and told a pretty scary story about what happened at the house. He gave the FBI a statement after they arrested him. Then they let him go. How long did they keep you?"

"Longer."

"Caleb wants you kicked out of the house for what he called your, 'wayward activity,'" Johnny said.

"I knew he was mad," I said. "He screamed at me as they were stuffing him, handcuffed, into the back of a black sedan."

"I'm sorry I missed that. It was probably funny."

"Don't laugh, Johnny," I said. "If you were home, you'd have been right there sitting beside him."

"What's next?" Vickie asked.

"I'm suspended from work for a week for missing my shift. If any of it makes the press, I'm fired. Not sure what I should do."

"If they come after you, you'll need to take control of your story," Johnny said. "Write it out yourself as if it's a feature article. It will allow you to take charge of the narrative instead of letting other reporters exploit you for their own purposes."

"You're right. I'll write out an outline this evening."

"Make it a confession and be brave. And here's another thing," Johnny said. "You need to get a little more Jersey in your attitude and shed that Minnesota 'you betcha' crap."

"You betcha' is how we say hallelujah up north."

"Lose it, bro'."

Diego came in and sat down beside us. "Hey, man, I heard about what happened."

"Did Caleb tell you?"

"No, Leon McFadden. We used to work together and we're still in touch. He said the chances of you getting fired are pretty good."

"I know."

"Hey, listen. My business is booming. If things don't work out at Tadich, come work for me. I'll pay you $150 a night in cash and a bonus if we do well."

"What do I have to do?"

"Sell weed. There's nothing better than selling weed. It's natural because you don't have to explain it to anybody. Everybody gets it. The money's good and you wouldn't have to run around fetching Diet Cokes for tourists. Plus, you'll meet the nicest people in the world."

"Really?"

"How many pot smokers do you hate?"

"I can't think of any," I said.

"Of course. We'll sit behind a table in trap houses and talk about marijuana. What could be more fun than that? There's no stress and you'll promote something you believe in."

"What's the downside?"

"We have to worry about cops and robbers," Diego said. "But each trap house has tight security with guys holding guns against the robbers. The cops are another story. If we get busted, you might have to spend a night in jail."

"How many times have you been arrested?" Johnny asked.

"Just once. It was a piece of cake. Although they did confiscate my weed."

"I have a meeting with the feds Friday," I said. "I'll let you know afterward."

"Come on, man. Give it a try," said Diego. "It's more fun than waiting tables and I need an assistant."

Friday afternoon, I went to the FBI building. I gave my name at the front desk. I was escorted to a second-floor room by a uniformed officer. There, I gave my name and all my stuff was returned. There was no meeting or debriefing. I was free to go. My journals, packed inside two boxes were heavy to carry. I took Metro from Federal Triangle home. I checked both my phone and computer. Both were out of juice.

A package was waiting on the doorstep. It was addressed to me with no return address. I opened it up. My tape recorder was inside. The cassette, the one on which I interviewed Shayla, was gone. There was no note. Up in my garret, I plugged in my phone and computer and waited for them to recharge.

I took stock of my situation. Here I was, playing cupbearer to the mainstays of the establishment. How skillfully I ingratiated myself into their good graces, how pliable, how subservient I acted for the tips they left and the gossip I overheard.

Meanwhile, the Lithuanians played me for a stooge. Should it be proven that I was complicit with a foreign government, Tadich was going to fire me. Shayla ditched me for fear that her new contract could be jeopardized. Who knew if the FBI was done with me? They left me without closure.

When a ping from my cell phone announced that it was recharged and ready, I dialed Shayla. She did not pick up. I decided not to leave a voicemail. Then I called Diego. "What time do I start?"

CHAPTER 16

Confident that my luck would hold up against cops and robbers for the week, I took Diego's offer of work. This adventure would take me away from the straight world of Shayla, Meyers, Robbins and Caleb. If nothing else, I'd return to Tadich with some interesting stories.

Diego lived in Virginia, which had strict laws against marijuana. The fact that Fairfax County had a White police force and Diego was Hispanic made him a target. He kept an office in an efficiency apartment on I Street Southwest where he wouldn't be harassed. I met him there at 5:30 p.m.

"We always want to arrive a little late to these shows," Diego said. "The cops like to burst in at opening time because if they wait till it's filled with customers, they'll need more paddy wagons. Smoking pot is legal in the district, so they'll only have to let the customers go anyway. They're only after us vendors."

And so, for the 6:00 p.m. show, we arrived at 6:15. Diego and I walked in carrying one duffel bag each filled with weed products. He also had a fold-up three-by-four-foot table. The location was a row house far from downtown up the bluff on Georgia Avenue NW above Howard University. It had a large room downstairs empty of furniture. The room's windows were covered with thick curtains. Though the show had only been open for 15 minutes, the air was filled with reefer smoke.

As Diego entered with me, the fucking new guy again, he acknowledged every vendor there with a variety of handshakes and said, "Hey, man, good to see you again."

It reminded me of a National Basketball Association game where a guy going to the free-throw line touches hands with his teammates in a gesture of comradery. Diego introduced me to everyone.

No one used their real name. There was Ali Vegaz, Marley, Fats, E, Black, Star, Young Mo and Dion. Diego didn't seem scared to reveal his name which, of course, wasn't the name on his birth certificate. It was Abraham. I just had my run-in with the law and my disdain was such that Samuel was good enough for me. The vendors were mostly African American; two were Arab; one Latino, Diego; and one White boy, me.

I was introduced to security. Three Black men named J-Dog, A.P. and Zeus stood at the door. In size, they were as big as the defensive front line of the Washington Commanders. To enter the show, each customer had to show an *Instagram* invitation from an individual vendor, allow themselves to be frisked and pay a ten-dollar admission fee.

"Listen, I'm paying you to be cool," Diego whispered. "This is not Tadich Grill, so relax. Talk to people, have fun and keep all negative vibes away."

We set up our table beside four other vendors. Over the table, Diego threw his company banner: Big Ass Buds. The logo was a cartoon. It featured a naked, long-haired hippie chick seen from behind sniffing a giant marijuana plant. And yes, the image featured her big ass and some big buds, too.

Diego sold his marijuana products in small black Ziploc bags. Each contained 3.5 of an ounce or "an eighth," as it was called. Tonight, he featured ten different strains. Each was displayed on the table in clear, plastic jars made especially for marketing weed. The jars came in a variety of colors, brand name *Middleman*. The jars featured a built-in light to highlight the bud and a magnifying glass so you could see its trichrome. With a label maker, he wrote the name of each strain and its percentage of sativa or indica.

Tonight, lined up on plastic tiered display shelves were five indica on the left side and the five sativa on the right of the table. The bottom row was $35 dollars an eighth, the second row was $40 an eighth, and the top row was $50 an eighth. The weed had names like OG Kush, Platinum Bubba, Blue Dream, Sour Diesel, and King Louie. All were imported from California. In all, the pot products we carried in the duffel bags were probably worth ten thousand dollars.

He brought along 18 premeasured bags of each strain. Most of the other vendors had big bags of buds on their table. They weighed out amounts on small scales according to the weight request. They then put them in plastic lunch bags. We handed each customer a premeasured bag which made the transactions seem more professional.

"Why are some more expensive than others?" I asked.

"It's because some are grown outdoors and you just don't have as good a control when you grow outdoors. Then there's the greenhouse variety which is better. Then there's the indoor grown under scientific controls and it's the best there is."

"Remember when we worked together at Smith and Wollensky?" he asked. "They always stressed that their steak was the best because it was dry-aged and prime—not select or choice, it was prime. They measured it by the fat content and the marbling which was why it was the very best. It's like that with pot, too."

"That makes sense," I said.

He organized his table presentation with purpose and precision. "Consistency, Sam, that's the most important thing."

Flanking the tiers of weed jars, he organized all his marijuana vape cartridges in rows. There were three different brands—*Honeycomb, Brass Knuckles, and Kingpen*. Each was lab-tested and developed for the medical marijuana industry in California. On the other side of the jars, he sold moonrocks, which were buds dipped in hash oil and rolled in kef for $50 a gram. When purchased, it was measured on a scale and put into plastic cups. Shatter, a THC distillate which looked like the burned sugar on top of Johnny's crème brûlée, was $45 a gram. It was sold in small premeasured white paper envelopes. There were gummies infused with cannabis from California in commercially designed bags for $30. Pre-rolled joints were sold for $10 each.

Branding was important. These vendors were not ragtag street-corner drug dealers; they were businessmen. Each had their own company name and logo—Smoking Apes, Big Ass Buds, Pakreligious, Budibles, Washington Dabbers and Capitol THC.

The room had a white ceiling. The top of the wall was painted red to waist level. The bottom half was painted blue. There was a big-screen TV on the wall.

Diego introduced me to the master of the house. His name was D.T. He was a tall, thin African American man with a natural smile. I'd say he was in his early 30's. He looked me over and upon hearing that this was my first shift said, "Untuck that shirt, bro'. You need to show some swag if you're going to make it here."

D.T. was also the house disc jockey in charge of the music. He chose the soundtrack: badass gangster rap accompanied by videos on the big screen. It set the tone. Images of women with big breasts and big asses, with spandex pants so tight you could see their camel toes, champagne bottles, stacks of money, fat blunts, sunglasses, rigorous hand gestures, fancy cars, a large gang of friends and their adoring, pretty girlfriends were the foundations of this video culture.

They sang about gangsta' niggas, pussy niggas, sunny niggas, badass niggas, educated niggas and fat niggas. The word was tossed around the room freely. I marveled at how they owned the rights to their own slur. I wouldn't say the word. It was exclusively their own. I must have heard it 50 times in the first hour. In using the word, they bore their souls to one another and embraced their shadow, their culture, their struggle and their exclusion from mainstream White society.

This trap house seemed so mysterious, so dangerous, so avant-garde, so progressive, so decadent, so bizarre, so gnostic that I absorbed every detail of its sight, sound and smell.

It reminded me of a *Star Wars* scene. Han Solo goes into an intergalactic bar filled with dangerous-looking aliens. I tried to stay cool, not stare or blush or reveal the fact that this was my first night.

It struck me right away that I wasn't cool enough to be here. The mores, shibboleths, rituals, handshakes, the slang, the attitude, were beyond me. I just watched carefully as the night went on and took my cues from Diego.

A sudden burst of customers came in at once. They included Asians, Hispanics, Caucasians, Arabs—a multicultural mass. But given the neighborhood, most were African American.

With facial, hand and neck tattoos upon their skin, they weren't competing for congressional office jobs or corporate boardrooms. Instead, they were looking for a flower that would help them rise above their own personal drama.

E, who was an Egyptian with a cleric's beard, was the house trickster. One time, when two Black men were examining Diego's indica selection, he called out, "Hey, Diego, don't tell those guys that your weed's been recalled." For laughs, he stole things off the table of his fellow vendors when they weren't looking. But he always returned it.

Later, he pulled out a large bong and offered everybody a free hit. He had a moonrock burning in the bowl. Marley didn't pass it up. The handsome young man took a large hit and blew out a large cloud of smoke. But there was more smoke in the chamber and he went after it again. The bong had a carburetor. When E pulled his finger away from the small hole, smoke shot right down Marley's lungs. He blew out a second cloud of smoke so large that I got a contact-high even though I was standing ten feet away. Then he started to cough, then his knees buckled and he crumbled to the ground. E's quick hands caught the back of his head before it hit the floor. Everyone gathered around him. "Oh shit," Diego said, "be ready. If he doesn't wake up, we'll have to pack up and get the hell out of here fast before the ambulance and the cops come."

Marley awoke a minute later and was soon sitting up. Embarrassed by what happened, he stood up, trying to pretend nothing was amiss. He returned to the chair behind his table and didn't speak for over an hour. That cat was high.

Since marijuana is illegal in Maryland and Virginia, the two surrounding states, DC is a sanctuary city for potheads. Many of the customers were from there. But we also had customers from as far away as New Jersey, Pennsylvania and West Virginia who drove here to shop, buy weight and resell it back home.

Our first big sale was to three White country boys dressed in ragged jeans and baseball caps. They bought an ounce of weed and four cartridges. Their smiles revealed black teeth.

"Those guys have done way too much crystal meth," Diego said after they left.

"Is that what causes that?"

"Yeah, you don't see it much in the city," he said. "Meth is a rural drug for guys who don't have access to weed."

I listened and watched carefully, handing out the weed Diego requested, which was arranged alphabetically in the ten large plastic Ziplocs inside his duffel bag while Diego's eyes guarded the table from thieves.

A small packet of organic instant coffee accompanied each sale. "The coffee is $50, the weed is a gift," Diego said.

That was all about Initiative 71. The rule, stipulated by the DC city council, said that you could sell coffee or stickers or candy for a price and give the weed away as a gift. Thus, the refrain, "The coffee is $50 and the weed is a gift," though fraudulent, was in keeping with the law. No sale was completed without that disclaimer. It was the first part of the game that I mastered. However, so much violence transpired at trap houses that the cops, coming to the sound of gunshots, didn't abide by that rule.

When I came to DC, I thought the real story was found in the granite-lined halls of government teeming with well-dressed men and women. But this city has a large African American community too. Most White boys like me never knew a thing about their world. The opportunity to steep myself in this undiscovered country just a few miles from the US Capitol intrigued me. Here was a legitimate counterculture. I found it compelling. So, I sat behind Diego's table and I giggled at my good fortune to be part of such a spectacle.

These vendors were the modern-day bootleggers. Compared to the law-abiding civil servants, cogs in a giant governmental wheel, they were way more interesting.

I wanted to know all about them and hear their stories. But I was cautioned by Diego. "Put your reporter's cap away, Sam," he said. "These guys don't know you. They don't want to be telling truths about themselves here. They might suspect you of being a narc and that won't be good for either of us."

But who were these guys? They were providing a dangerous service: selling a semi-legal substance that just a few years ago could land them long prison sentences. Should I look at them as if they were pioneers of a new consciousness bent upon freeing the world from the digital yoke?

Though stifling my enthusiasm, I saw a great story here that perhaps had yet to be written. I'd seen movies about "The Roaring Twenties" of the last century with colorful villains like Al Capone, Legs Diamond, and Bugsy Siegel. They typified the era and seemed glamorous.

Then I started thinking, *What is it that makes one guy's table different from the others? How does a customer distinguish between us all?*

That's when I realized it was a sales job. Since Diego and I were waiters and used to speaking to strangers, we had an advantage because we were good communicators. I got it right away. The trap house was about making friends.

Marijuana was something I knew a lot about. In this setting, even more than I realized. It being illegal, my friends and I never really discussed it out loud because it was a secret. But here, after the initial hour, I found ways to participate.

"This is our sativa side, and this is our indica side," I said to a middle-aged Black man examining our wares.

"What's the difference?"

"Sativa jacks you up. Indica knocks you down."

"Got it," he said.

When the place was temporarily empty of customers, Ali Vegaz, a DC rapper with facial tattoos, rolled a fat blunt, a cigarette rolled in tobacco and filled it with his finest strain, White Runts.

Now, I have to admit a certain prejudice. Rolling great weed in a tobacco wrapper was an African American thing I never liked. For me, it was like mixing Courvoisier and Coke. Why denigrate the spirit with some cheap accompaniment?

And yet, when he handed it to me, wanting to participate, I took a small hit. When I passed it to Diego, he scolded me quietly. "Take more than one hit. You don't want to give him the impression that you think his weed sucks. He might get offended."

"I didn't want to bogart it," I answered.

"Don't worry. We all have more than we can possibly smoke."

So, I took my time and savored it. I took in another lungful before passing it on. I looked in Vegaz's direction, and he nodded in affirmation. "That's top-shelf shit, $70 an eighth," he called to me.

"Thanks, man."

I wanted to be a part of this scene and wise to its ways. But how?

Memories of Daniel Taylor, my maternal grandfather, came to mind. I once accompanied him and my grandmother, my mother and father and my older brother to a beach house they rented on Little Exuma Island in the Bahamas.

My grandfather and I went out for some groceries and decided to explore the island. There was a corner bar beside a remote shanty and old Dan decided he wanted a beer. We walked right into the bar. It was packed. When I realized it was filled with Bahamians and we were the only Whites inside, I was startled. But not old Dan. He bellied right up to the bar and ordered us both a beer. A giant Black man stood beside us and looked at us suspiciously.

"Dan Taylor, Duluth, Minnesota," my grandfather called and he stuck out his hand. "Beautiful island you live on. Yep, really beautiful."

He went to tell him about his horse farm in northern Minnesota. As he continued to speak, a small crowd gathered to listen to his fine Irish storytelling.

Nobody ever fucked with my grandfather. As a man, he was centered, cocksure of his manhood and so willing to praise and acknowledge the manhood of others. As a result, individuals like to stand close to him, perhaps in the hope that some of that libidinal strength would rub off on them. He played the role of elder perfectly. When the beer glass was empty, we shook a half-dozen hands on our way out. That story popped into my head. It was a good example of how one should act in a place like this. I never had my grandfather's command of manhood so I decided to hang back and wait till my energy and theirs found common ground.

The fare at Christ's last supper was no match for what Diego was selling. I loved the reverence with which people approached our table. It was as if we were travel agents able to guide their transcendental forays into the imagination and help them reach their gnostic port of call. That with our help, customers could find an emotional retreat where the content of their lives could be studied high on a spiritual plane. It was as if these pilgrims were asking, "How can I better get in touch with my spirit guides and lead a more meaningful life apart from Washington rhetoric?" They were in search of a lost spiritual chord. It was our job to connect them to it.

A middle-aged Hispanic man looked over our table and said, "Damn, not too long ago, they were sending people to prison for doing what you're doing."

"It's an example of how the world is getting better," I said.

A few minutes later, a young Black tough approached the table and said, "Hey, man, I'm looking for the gas."

Diego pointed him to the sativa side. "I got Sour Diesel and Candyland."

"How much for two-eighths of each?" he asked.

"That's a half ounce. I can do it for one-twenty," said Diego. I reached into the duffel bag and pulled out two bags of each strain.

"The coffee is one-twenty and the weed is a gift," I said.

"I appreciate you, man," he said, forking over the cash.

Ten minutes later, a young woman came and asked for just about the same thing.

"I can do it for a hundred," Diego said. I was surprised at the lower price. When she left, he smiled and said, "Pretty girl discount."

There was lots of downtime when no one stood before our table. In the quiet moments, I reached for my cell phone and, in my notes app, started writing.

> DT cued the song
> An Earth, Wind & Fire classic,
> "I like the way you move."
> She entered the room
> Heard the rhythm
> And moved to its beat.
> She danced to each table
> Examining its wares.
> Oh, the joy of motion
> Big smile, wide eyes.

Her moves were all Eros
Done in delight
Hands thrown straight up
Waving like boughs in the breeze
"I like the way you move."
Diego reached out
Handed her Bubba Kush
She handed him cash
Then danced out the door.
Blessed be the dance.

At 9:45 p.m., I watched Diego tense up. I wasn't sure why. "One reason I need you is that robbers will attack a single vendor walking to his car late at night. But rarely two guys."

"How often does that happen?" I asked.

"More and more. A good friend of ours named Ziggy was walking to his car last week when a van pulled up. Two guys got out and grabbed his bag. He wouldn't let go of it. They shot him eight times."

"That's a hell of a way to die."

"He got lucky. The robbers used a .22 caliber pistol. He survived. But that's an important reason why I need you."

"All right, I get it."

"If someone tries to rob us out on the street, drop the bags, put your hands up, take three steps back. Turn your shoulder in a slight direction to protect your heart and hope we don't get shot."

We started packing up along with the other vendors since the show was ending. Diego called the Uber and gave Big Zeus $10 for escorting us to it when it pulled up.

"I appreciate you, man," Diego said.

"Thanks, Diego. See you again," Zeus said.

We went back to the office and did an inventory. He paid me $150.

"Be here tomorrow at five and we'll try it again," he said.

It was only two miles away from home, so I walked it. When I arrived, it was after midnight. Cortez was watching TV. "How was your night?" I asked.

"Good, I worked till about ten and then went to the Veil for a cocktail before I came home."

"Was Vickie tending bar?"

"Yes, the place was so busy we didn't have a lot of time to talk."

"Was she wearing Caleb's cross?" I asked.

"Oh yes," he said.

"Good."

"When do you think Caleb's going to tell her he's a virgin?" he asked.

"I don't know. Hopefully, it won't be an issue," I answered.

"She's had a lot of experience with men."

"Perhaps she can coach him into sexual greatness."

"With those skinny hips? I don't know, man," Cortez said.

"He's your friend. Maybe you can give him some pointers."

"How was your first night with Diego?" he asked.

"Remarkable. It's like a restaurant job, only you get to do it high."

"Be careful with that Diego. He got some rage. You know that, right?"

"So far, it's not an issue. After all, I'm a great wingman."

"True that."

"We sold fifteen hundred dollars' worth of pot tonight," I said. "Plus, I hung out in the ghetto, chatted up the brothers, and saw a slice of life I've never seen before."

"Do you have any idea how much money is being spent on weed in DC each week? It's in the millions. It's employing a whole group of young Black men who otherwise wouldn't even have a job. That it's all going mainstream just goes to prove that Black people are taking over America."

"Do your people have a prejudice against verbs?" I asked with a grin.

202

"What do you mean?"

"Where the party at? What up? How you be?"

"No, we be cool and just like to economize our speech when we can," said Cortez. "You're a poet. You know about brevity."

"I was just wondering."

"Look at you, young White boy hanging out with the gangsters," he said. "There's money in those buds. But where there's money and young men, there's also guns. Best be on your guard. They might shoot you."

"No, they won't."

"All right, if you say so," Cortez said with a warning tone in his voice.

"I want to take it all in, Cortez. Being paranoid would just shut down the experience. There's a lot to learn there. It's a great opportunity and I want to open myself up to all of it."

"Sounds like something you should be writing about."

"You're right. See you later. I'm going upstairs."

"Oh, by the way. I saw on the news your girlfriend, Shayla Reeve is coming to work at CNN," he said. "She's going to sign a million-dollar, multi-year contract. I might even be working with her."

"Send her my regards."

Up at my desk, I opened my journal and started writing. "I've just broadened my horizons."

It took three hours to write down all I heard and saw.

CHAPTER 17

The next day, we went to the same trap house on Georgia Avenue. They called it "The Cottonmouth Lounge." The same vendors and security staff as yesterday were there. I discovered that they had an upstairs where people could sit on couches and sample what they just bought.

When Diego entered the room, he glad-handed all the vendors. I did the same. It's amazing the different handshakes individuals used to greet one another. And me, not about to be outdone, showed them some old-school Jersey. It consisted of a traditional handshake, followed by a slide grabbing the other guy's thumb, then a lock on his fingertips, followed by a double fist pound to the sternum. The loud thumps gave the greeting an audio component.

Tonight, three additional vendors joined us. We were packed into the room so tight that there was no space between tables. E was next to us on the left side and Marley's table to the right side. To get out from behind your table, you had to crawl underneath; otherwise, you'd knock stuff off your table or your neighbor's table.

I loved this new world. I studied its culture the way I studied the culture of Tadich Grill. Working here was like a restaurant shift, but unlike the restaurant, you actually got to participate and share its fare with customers. The comfort level came easy. There were no self-important members of the bourgeoisie here, no pressure to please. In some ways, this was a better job. No stress, no pretension, no bullshit.

While paying attention to my responsibilities, I studied it all with a sociologist's eye. I noticed subtle trap-house behavior like the way the Black vendors grabbed the collars of their T-shirts and sneezed inside them so they didn't spread their germs. How no one addressed potential customers until they crossed the imaginary line between tables and entered their airspace.

Black men and women seemed less lonely to me than Caucasian men and women. They reached out to each other in a shared language and attitude. There was a lilt to their communal emotion. Theirs was a high-pitched, animated exuberance I rarely saw among Minnesotans. Their love of expression, ear induced; the comradery and the willingness to share it all was what stoked my enthusiasm. It was reinforced with mutual respect. When the respect went missing, though, it provoked anger between thin-skinned customers and vendors. I saw it twice the first night when arguments broke out and security had to intervene. Disrespect a Black man to his face and you're asking for trouble.

There were three basic ways that individuals decided which weed to buy. Some opened the jars and sniffed the buds inside. "If it's good for your nose, it's good for your head," a young man told me. Others with less confidence in their olfactory sense looked through the magnifying lens atop of the weed jar to check out its trichrome and crystals. Others considered the size of the buds. "Size matters," joked a young woman.

I watched a guy with his cell phone light and camera app examine each bud on an expanded camera screen. Never saw that before. After searching all our jars, he settled for an eighth of Platinum Bubba.

"People are picky about their weed," said Diego. "They know where they want their heads to be. You have to respect that."

I certainly had my preference. It was sativa. It opened up all my chakras and stoked my creative energy. For me, an indica was like a drowsy beer high. I didn't like it as much because it diminished my literary light. Why be a couch potato when you could write poetry?

E stopped by with a quartz bong and a moonrock in the bowl. "If you want to be one of us, you've got to be baptized," he said to me. I looked at Diego.

"It's okay with me," he said.

I took the first hit and blew it out. But there was more in the chamber. When I went to suck in the second hit, E opened the carburetor and the smoke flew down into my lungs. I did cough a little bit, but not so much as to embarrass my Jersey sense of manhood whose ethos consisted of, "Hold your load or you're not a real man."

I was stoned a minute later. Diego saw the look on my face and laughed. "Welcome to 'The Cottonmouth Lounge,'" he said. "Relax, you're among friends."

But I didn't want to relax. I wanted to write. Those bong hits opened me up. I longed to be back at my desk. My chakras were open and I started channeling right there. I opened my cell phone app and stared at the blank screen.

"Dude, don't be self-conscious," Diego said. "Nobody's going to fuck with you in here. Look around the room. You got a half-dozen nationalities in here and they've all got one thing in common: they're all in a good mood."

In my notes app. I wrote the following:

Blowtorch
On the pipe's quartz bowl
Fired till it glows orange
Dab tool in hand
E drops in the moonrock
It billows smoke
"Don't watch it burn, man
Toke the fucking thing!"

Soon, ideas for "A Firm State of Heart" came rushing out of me. All my insights were typed onto my phone, soon to be transferred to my journal and then into my poem.

> The unconscious mind
> Is the sole source of Revelation
> Doesn't matter what provokes it
> As long as the barriers
> Between the individual
> And the absolute
> Are diminished.

And when all my insights were recorded, I turned into a chatterbox and wanted to engage everyone. I liked their collective ideal of cool. It was great to talk to customers who stopped by. There was no worry about neglecting other tables in my station. There was only one and they were all coming to me.

The meter of their African American speech captivated me. It sounded like music as opposed to the hard logic of Capitol Hill rhetoric. Here was an emotional tone that might inform my poem. They spoke in a harmonic stream whose aural tone was articulated into a perfect pitch. I loved its meter, the way curse words were inserted in their smooth sentences, its pauses and cadence. Here, I was feted to a big dose of it all in this African American neighborhood of the nation's capital.

I recognized that if I stayed within the boundaries of that speech, I'd be safe because its meter mirrored the mores of the place. It included a song and a dance. This virile community inspired me to a new goal: turn my poetic lines into music.

Black speech, richly redolent in its high pitch and pattern, its rhythm and its rhyme, prolonged the moment and allowed images to linger a bit longer in one's mind because it cast the mental content of ideas in a musical wave. There was a magnetic charm to it all. This was a culture based on a finely tuned ear. The content of their speech included the essence of melody reflecting the motion of dance. Their artful sound went further than reason and penetrated regions that were closed to logic.

The German poet Goethe once wrote that compared to the eye, the ear is a dumb sense. He was wrong. A sensitive ear was responsible for so much more, including athletic ability, dance, joy, lovemaking and a firm heart. Music is the true element of which all poetry sings. It soothes the soul and restores the spirit. It was a condition that DC politicos often lacked and that lack often diminished their intent.

Imagination in the trap house, as exhibited by the Black vendors, who amplified their storylines to reveal the texture of their mood and tone, induced an emotional awareness and a person-to-person connection. Their words were conditioned by the color of their skin, their economic class and the prejudice armed against them. And since it was done in a communal tone, it became a gesture of grace. Their unified rhythmic patterns felt like a tribal response to the deeper feelings, emotional presence and religious inclinations of their culture. I felt more akin to it than I first recognized.

In its highest form, poetry finds its best self in musical speech, a harmony of heart and mind. So, I let my ear preside and tuned in to its prevailing inflection. In this space, I actually breathed differently while seeking a trap house concordance with those I engaged. Their uttered thoughts sounded different from my own and I loved it. It was a ghetto culture, the likes of which my immigrant grandfather might have identified with. I took to it because it offered a deeper and wider understanding of language that would find its way into my poem.

Individuals wore very colorful T-shirts and I commented on several. One guy wore one that read, "Kulture Wars."

"I like your shirt, man," I said.

"It's actually my brand. I market a clothesline with that name."

"I get it," I said. "I'm rooting for our side. I think we're more inclusive, more moral, more courageous, and more gnostic than the other side."

"Yeah, I agree, thanks, man."

There was a chubby, slovenly White kid looking at our table. He painstakingly asked the price of every item. "Okay," he said after some deliberation. "I'm going to smoke a fat blunt, walk around the room and think about it." Fifteen minutes later, he returned and bought six cartridges from Diego for a discounted price of $260.

It was summer and there were scantily clad women. The Black women let it all hang out. It didn't matter their size or shape. They liked tight-fitting spandex. It revealed their cleavage, their ass, their fat, their tattoos and their stretch marks. They were all about the body. Some of them were gorgeous and my age and I liked that part of it, too. My mere presence behind the table gave me credibility. One young woman asked, "What do you have to do to get a job like this?"

"You got to be cool," I answered and assumed that persona.

Steeped in this counterculture, I worked to stay genuine to its vibe, which was egalitarian, unpretentious, and respectful. I didn't dare brag about my work at Tadich Grill, who I knew, what I saw, or what I heard from the likes of Shayla Reeve, US senators, congressmen and cabinet members.

It made me feel phony to place such a high regard on the accomplishments of the individuals I served. Here, nobody gave a damn about the republic. Staying high and happy was the rule of the day. Theirs was not a state of mind; it was a state of being. I felt this space was opening me up to a whole new understanding of DC and my place in it.

The vendors came essentially from two classes of people. They were waiters and others from the restaurant business or they were rappers. And so, a few times during the night, D.T. would go to his computer and bring up some of the rap songs and videos recorded by the vendors in attendance. Ali Vegaz, Young Mo, and Marley all had their time on the big screen.

"Hey, Ali, why is it that so many rappers get shot and killed?" I asked.

"Because they take their poetic gift and they use it to talk shit about people," he said. "That kind of disrespect will always get you in trouble."

While some might say this scene was just rank escapism, the truth was that this whole town was corrupted by lies and incompetence to the extent that I thought perhaps this place was more virtuous than the big-shot dining rooms I worked in.

I watched this guy come in and freeze from the spectacle of the room. He, like me, had never seen such an accumulation of pot products before and I could tell he was overwhelmed.

"It was easier when you were just buying whatever your friend was selling, wasn't it?" I said. "Now you've got to be a connoisseur, an expert, like a wine geek."

"You got that right," he said. He looked over our table. "Which one is the best?"

"There's no such thing as the best, only the best for you," I said. "You need to know what works with your own individual DNA. It reinforces one of my pet peeves. One size does not fit all."

I'd been around pot for a long time, and yet I was surprised how facts sprang from lips spontaneously at the appropriate time.

A pretty girl caught my eye from across the room. She wore blue overalls and had a short gray top underneath it that exposed her midriff. Her long dark hair was naturally curly. I couldn't take my eyes off her.

She chatted with a few vendors and a few customers as she made her way around the room. I couldn't wait for her to get in front of me.

Diego stepped away from the table while I was negotiating my first big sale, an ounce to two men. They wanted four different strains in their ounce. I reached for two bags of each. From the corner of my eye, I saw her walk up to Young Mo's table and buy a bag.

"Oh my god, it's the girl from the train!" I whispered. I saw the heart tattoo. My heart started racing. By the time I counted the $240 price for the ounce, she was out the door. I wanted to chase her down the street and return her water bottle, maybe get her number. But I couldn't leave the table unattended. Plus, I couldn't sneak out. The other tables penned me in. Damn, I missed her again!

She came alone and knew her way around. It was obvious that she'd been here before. I wondered when she might return.

"Giving up Tadich to be a budtender, Samuel? It's probably for the best. As a waiter, you're below average."

I looked up. It was Harold Lamb.

"How much for a half ounce of Bubba Kush?"

"For you? $160," I said.

"That's a rip-off."

Of course, it was a rip-off. But if Diego could give the pretty-girl discount, in his absence, I went for the big-jerk markup.

"That's the price," I said. "Maybe you should check out my man Marley over there. I'm sure he has exactly what you want."

Harold moved to the next table, but before he left, he took one parting shot. "Just to let you know, we don't miss you at Tadich."

CHAPTER 18

Diego was a little frantic when I got to the office on day three. He was running late. The show started at 4:20 and there was still a lot of work to be done. I started filling pre-rolls while he focused on weighing out the individual strains into eighth bags.

When we were finally ready for the Uber, the wait was fifteen minutes. When it arrived, we threw the duffel bags and the table in the trunk. Then, there was DC rush hour traffic to contend with. It wasn't until 5:15 that we arrived. When it came in sight, under his breath, I heard Diego whisper, "Oh, shit."

Four police cars were double-parked out front. On the front steps of the row house, my new friends were in handcuffs. They were about to be herded off to jail.

"Excuse me, driver," Diego said, "I need you to take me back home." He reached into his pocket and handed him two twenty-dollar bills. The driver figured out the problem immediately. He stashed the cash underneath his Washington Wizards cap and drove on by.

Back at the office, Diego said, "We dodged that bullet. No work today, Sam. Sorry, bro, it's an occupational hazard."

"What's going to happen to those guys?" I asked.

"If it's like the past, they'll spend the night in jail, go to court and the judge will dismiss the case. That's what's been going on in

DC. The cops have one attitude about trap houses and the courts have another."

"What happens to all their weed?"

"It's confiscated."

"What do the cops do with it?" I asked.

"I've heard that they sell it to guys who make deliveries around the city."

"That doesn't seem right."

"That's the way it is."

"That would make a great newspaper story."

"Are you going to write it?"

"Maybe," I said.

"Come back tomorrow at 4 p.m. We'll try a different trap house."

The next day, we were inside a small single-family house in Southeast DC near the Minnesota Avenue Metro stop. Seven vendors were cramped inside.

"Do you know anybody here?" I asked.

"Just the promoter. His name is Jesse. We probably won't see some of the others for a while. Most of them got released from jail today. But with their entire stash confiscated, it's going to take some time for them to regroup. Two of them, Fats and Dion, had outstanding warrants and will be locked up a little longer."

"Damn, I'm going to miss those guys," I said.

"You'll see them again."

Business at this place was not as brisk as it was my first two days. During the down moments when no one was here, I thought this might be a good time to read. I had a book in my backpack. It was that book about Walt Whitman. But I felt too self-conscious to read it in the quiet trap house moments. It seemed pretentious. So, instead, I read *The Washington Post, The New York Times, Politico, Huffington Post* and *The Hill* on my phone. I found myself brought back to the sludge that was the American political scene.

My first sale of the evening was an older Hispanic man who bought two *Honeycomb* cartridges.

"I do love these things," he said. "I took one to my daughter's wedding, got a dozen people high and my ex-wife never knew."

A White woman came in wearing short sleeves and shorts. Her tattoos were a menagerie. They featured, on her right arm, a flying saucer from outer space, a tiger in a jungle setting, a raccoon and a cameo of a woman dressed like she was from the Victorian age. On her left arm was a paper airplane, a rose and in block letters, the words, "Dump your boyfriend." She bought two-eighths of Candyland.

Then, this African American kid named Derek came in. He examined our weed.

"This is our sativa side. This is our indica side," I said.

"I pay no attention to that," he said. "I work at a Maryland marijuana dispensary. I don't consider sativa or indica important. We list the terpenes of every package of bud we sell. That's the important thing."

"Why terpenes?"

"Because that's where the real action comes from. Some terpenes are analgesics, others are appetite enhancers, others are sleep aids. That's what you should be promoting to your customers. Find out what they're looking for with reference to the terpenes in each strain and then promote it. It's really about the terpenes."

He really knew his stuff and I interviewed him as if I was writing a feature story. I gleaned new insights regarding the products I was selling. "Thanks, man. You just expanded my world."

Later, when an older Black man walked by, I asked, "How's it going, man?"

"Well, I'm still stumbling forward in life. I got that going for me."

"I sometimes wonder if passing over to the other side is really the greater gift."

"I'm not ready to think about that yet."

"We'll all find out for sure one day," I said.

"That's true," he answered. "In the meantime, what do you have that will help me sleep at night?"

"Try some of this King Louis. It's ninety percent indica. It will knock you down."

Then, I started to notice little things that came with my growing familiarity with the scene. I kept staring at the part in the long hair of African American women. Was it a wig or was it real? It was hard to tell because often their long hair was a wig tied down underneath to their cornrows. You had to look carefully without being obvious. It was just like the way I sometimes looked at White girls trying to discern if their breasts were real or silicone.

Sometimes, Diego and I sat there for 45 minutes between sales. Then there'd be a flash flood of customers and we'd sell $600 dollars-worth in three minutes. It was crazy and unpredictable. There were rules governing this whole process. I just hadn't figured them out yet.

As the night went on, we sold cartridges and some moonrocks. But the sale of weed was slow. The competition was too steep, especially from two Black men at the table across from us. Their names were Sean and CJ. They had their weed in big five-gallon Mason jars. The buds were large and impressive.

Every time a new customer entered the room, CJ called out, "Rapper weed, rapper weed, we got rapper weed." It was his claim that he had the best stuff.

Diego and I are competitive types. Waiters have to be because if you're a slacker, someone else will make the money. We were jealous of them. But the trap house vibe prevented us from expressing it.

The thing that got Diego mad was that they were selling their big buds for $160 per ounce. There was no way he could compete with that price, he said.

Our cheapest ounce price was $200 per ounce. They were lowballing us all evening and making all the sales.

"First of all, they are not allowed to have that much weed on the table," Diego said. "It's against the law. I'm surprised that Jesse is letting them get away with it."

"They're certainly kicking our asses tonight," I said.

"Oh, shit, look who just walked in." I turned to see an older Caucasian man with thick white hair and an athletic build. "That's the Johnny Appleseed of DC trap houses," Diego said.

"Who is he?" I inquired.

"His name is Joe Green, a local businessman. He runs trap houses all over the city. He grows his own pot at his ranch in Sonoma County, California and brings it in by the truckload."

"I've seen him before," I said.

"Maybe you waited on him at Tadich."

"No, it's from somewhere else."

When Jesse, the show's promoter, saw him, he deferred. Green pulled him outside to the front porch.

At about 9:30, two big Black men went to Sean and CJ's table. They started talking about a big sale. They each flashed a big wad of cash and then returned it to their pockets. The duo was looking to buy a pound. Sean and CJ's eyes got big. Diego got madder.

"Damn, by law, the most you're allowed sell to an individual is two ounces," Diego said. But their buds were so big, so fragrant and so cheap that anyone would have wanted more.

Jesse walked up to Diego and whispered in his ear, "You and your White boy need to get the fuck out of here, now."

Diego complied. "Pack it up."

"So early?" I said.

"Yes."

We stuffed the duffel bags with our wares, folded up the table, and called an *Uber*. Standing by the front door, we waited for it to appear out front. CJ and Sean were tonight's stars. Our sales were about $800. The others sold even less. But after a word from Jesse, the other vendors started packing up, too. All the while, the two customers held Sean and CJ's attention with the promise of a big sale.

I watched as the two men sampled their buds. They'd pull out a pipe, insert a bud and smoke it. They waited a few minutes. "I'll take two ounces of that one. Now let's try this one."

The Uber was out front. We walked to it unaccompanied by security. Out on the street, five men were there leaning against the parked cars. Diego stopped, "Hello Joe, how are you, man?"

"I'm good, Diego. Nice to see you," Green said. They shook hands. He didn't introduce me. "You guys need to go right now. The cops are on the way."

But then the old guy looked at me. "How was that book on Virgil I sold you?"

And suddenly I remembered him. The guy owns, "Tomes Greatest Hits," Adams Morgan used book store. "It was good," I answered.

"Just got a new shipment of epic literature last week. You should come in and check them out. You might find something you like."

"Thanks, I will," I said.

We got into the Uber and drove off. "What just happened?" I asked.

"I got a feeling that Ziggy was working for Joe Green and that maybe CJ and Sean were the ones who shot him."

That idea was confirmed when two police cars drove by us in the direction of the trap house, lights flashing and sirens silent.

"Those two should consider themselves lucky," Diego said. "Were it anyone else but Green, they'd have been shot down dead."

Following the event, I walked to the Veil for a nightcap. I saw Vickie. She poured me my usual and presented it with a big smile. "I've got some news for you."

"Did you find out about that girl?" I asked.

"Yes."

"I saw her at the trap house yesterday. She left before I could introduce myself."

"She grew up in Israel. Her mom is from India and her dad is from New York. She lives near Eastern Market and is single."

"What's her name?"

"Dahlia."

"Pretty name."

"Friends call her DD since her last name begins with a D, too. Here's something else. She was in an abusive relationship with an American soldier who did three tours of duty in Iraq. They just broke up."

"I wonder if I saw her the night of her breakup," I said. "She seemed pretty upset."

"Maybe, but she was in the Israeli Army for three years before she came to Washington. She's not a lightweight."

"A Suzie with an Uzi? That's sexy."

Vickie gave me a piece of paper. "This is her email address. I got it from her friend, Angela."

"Did Angela have permission to give it out?"

"No."

"But I told her about you. She promised to tell DD."

At the bar, now with her name in hand, I was still. What should I do? I could email her and ask her out for coffee. But it didn't seem right. I kept running over pickup lines in my head. "I saw you wearing a slinky blue dress one night in July. You're hot." "I found the water bottle you lost three months ago." The longer I thought about my opening lines, the less confident I became.

I know how skittish women are online. First moves are fraught with danger. It's just how dating in the digital age works. Perhaps for the first time ever, literary skills are sexy. I am a good writer and can usually capture their initial interest. But there you are, trying to land a big fish and one wrong sentence in the middle of an email can snap the fishing line. She'll swim away and never contact you again. Often, you never know what triggered it, thus caution is required.

Once back home, I took the paper and copied the email address into my phone. Since she just broke up with her boyfriend, I wondered if I should wait before contacting her. Playing a gal on the rebound before she's ready might risk the whole campaign.

> I stand in search of a lonely girl
> Who'll help me find my way
> Out of this solipsistic realm
> Into the bright of day

The week went by quickly and as instructed, I went to see Ron Robbins. It was just after the lunch rush. I figured he'd have the time to talk. When I walked into his office, I saw the top of my cover letter and résumé sticking out of a file from when I first applied for the job.

"I wondered if you'd show up," he said.

"You said wait a week and it's been a week. Just wondering if I get to file for unemployment."

"No need for that. Meyers came in and said you are off the hook. It never made the papers. I spoke with the owners. We want you back."

"I don't know, Ron. I'm not really feeling the love."

"Please understand that after the beating we took in the press regarding Buich's daughter and her marriage to Gene Upshaw, we couldn't risk another scandal. The jobs of 40 people were hanging in the balance, not to mention a million-dollar investment by the owners."

"I get that. But it still seems—"

"Listen, Sam, let me give you some advice. Sometimes, it's just as bad to take offense as it is to give offense."

I considered his words and began to laugh. "That flies in the face of everything I learned in New Jersey."

"That's true of New York, too."

"What are you offering?" I asked.

"I can give you your schedule back, three lunches and four nights. It's yours if you want it."

"At this point, I'd like three lunches and only that. I'll start at the bottom and work my way up like I did the first time."

"How are you going to support yourself with that schedule? Selling weed?"

"How did you find out about that?"

"Harold told me."

"It's a good job. Plus, there's a woman involved. I'd like to do it a little longer."

"Are you sure that's what you want?"

"Yes, I'm sure."

"All right. You can start next week."

"Thanks."

CHAPTER 19

Then, the pandemic came, and everyone panicked. Governor Nelson was the first person to mention it to me. I didn't take him seriously, thinking he was exaggerating. He wasn't. It was now a crisis America could not escape.

The arrival of COVID-19 reminded me of a Midwest thunderstorm. One first sees it as a thin, dark line on the western horizon. You get an inkling that something is coming. But you don't take it seriously because of the blue sky above you. Its turbulence arrives at a pace that almost seems like slow motion until its thick clouds are overhead and raindrops are teeming down upon you.

When Shayla called my phone, I picked it up and congratulated her on the new job with CNN.

"Who cares about that?" she answered. "The whole world is going to hell in a handbasket."

"True, it all seems sort of surreal."

"Listen, I called to tell you that all the bars and restaurants in the city are closing, indefinitely. The mayor's office is going to announce it tomorrow."

"When?"

"You'll be out of a job in four days," she said. "How are you set for the crisis?"

"Money is tight. But I have some savings and credit cards. I'll probably be able to collect unemployment, too."

"Call me if you get in a financial bind."

"I will."

"When can I see you?" she asked.

"Not sure," I replied. "I might have been exposed to the virus."

"Go into self-quarantine. Promise me that you'll call me in two weeks. Please, Samuel, the whole city is going to shut down. I can't go through this by myself."

"Sorry, I don't think that's going to work. I have three housemates. If one of us gets it, we'll all get it. And to be honest with you, getting the reputation of 'Typhoid Samuel,' the guy who infected Shayla Reeve, is not something I want on my résumé. We just have to wait till this all passes."

"My broadcast is going to be done remotely from my condo. I'm not sure how long I'll be able to take the isolation."

"I understand. But I got suspended from work the day the FBI arrested me. I've been earning money selling weed at DC trap houses ever since. I've come into contact with hundreds of people."

"We've wanted to do a story about trap houses for the past month. Sorry, I didn't know about you working there sooner. Would you be willing to wear a small camera to work so we can do a story on it?"

"No, I'm not."

"Okay, just thought I'd ask."

"Don't hate me for saying this, Shayla, but you might have to go back with Phillip."

"I don't want to," she said.

"I know. But it's only for a while. How long can the virus go on?"

In the time leading up to the shutdown of society, I don't know that I'd have done anything different. I was too preoccupied with my reading, my writing, my jobs, my friends and my diversions to grasp its significance.

And yet, I made it my goal to do what Governor Nelson admonished me to do that afternoon at the cemetery: be a good community newspaper reporter and document all I see.

The COVID-19 virus was spreading around the world. Millions were going to contract it, economies were going to be upended, society as we know it ceased and hundreds of thousands were going to die.

There's an old Chinese curse, "May you live in interesting times." Somehow, that telltale seemed apropos of this pandemic, not only because it started in China but also because the irony of the word, *interesting*.

Yes, it was interesting in an objective sense; maybe that's how they'll refer to it ten years from now. But in truth, it's frightening, especially since no one seemed to have a handle on how it spread or how many people were going to contract it. It was like nothing the world had seen since 1918 when the Spanish flu swept the globe, killing fifty million people.

A poet's trance is one of the most important items in his literary toolbox. It helps him focus his ideas and feelings and assign to them appropriate words. That night at my desk, I wrote the following:

> I grasp for the "pre" words
> *Prescient, presage predict*
> They're concepts that
> Aspire to a divine omniscience
> Able to anticipates the coming horror
> And react accordingly.
> But the man-killing microbe
> With its coronet horns
> Sneaks around undetected.
> Navigating the day
> Becomes like a child's game of tag
> Get touched, get sick.
> Now millions of Americans

Are looking over their shoulders
Asking, "Mr. Corona,
Have you come for me?"

The characteristics, qualities and method of transmission of this nemesis were dimly recognized by science. As summer continued, the idea that thousands would die from the unseen assailant became a stark reality. Social distancing, a term no one ever heard of last month, was the only way to flatten the death curve. Today, the demand to keep six feet apart from your fellow citizens may be what keeps you from being buried six feet under.

For a man who believes in the virtue of globalization and multiculturalism, the COVID-19 virus came as a shock. There were so many dimensions to consider. Except for the fear and chaos engulfing all of us, I had no understanding of how it would alter America. Sorting it out was going to take time and would depend on the damage done. One hundred years ago, events like World War I, the Spanish flu, and the Great Depression promoted two kinds of men: progressives and demagogues. Which would prevail in America?

DC had an advantage over other urban areas worldwide: population density. In the past, no building was allowed to be taller than the Washington Monument. That limitation was amended in parts of the city. But 13 stories is still the height restriction. As a result, the population density of DC was 9,800 people per square mile. In New York City, that number was 27,000; in San Francisco, 18,000.

Just as Shayla said, at the direction of Mayor Muriel Bowser, all Washington, DC, bars, restaurants, museums, and sporting events shuttered, including Tadich. Government workers were instructed to work from home. They even closed the Congressional Cemetery to visitors, although I'm sure not to the incoming dead.

The only businesses not closed were essentials like pharmacies, supermarkets and liquor stores. Because it was part of the underground, trap houses stayed open too.

That afternoon before work, I had a conversation with Diego.

"What's our game plan regarding the coronavirus?"

"The numbers are still low in the district. I think we're safe for a while," he said. "Sam, let's ride this horse till it drops."

"It doesn't seem dangerous yet," I said.

"I'm more worried about this than you are."

The week's suspension at Tadich found me short on cash. I was lucky to have the job with Diego's "Big Ass Buds." Each night, we found pop-ups at different locations to sell weed. The extra money I was able to make would tide me over until my unemployment checks started coming in. But to be honest, while not wanting to succumb to doomsday predictions, another reason to remain was my longing to see Dahlia again before either of us got sick and it was too late. Given the prevailing predicament, I knew she'd be back.

With people furloughed all over the city, selling pot became a mission of mercy. The stress that accompanied this uncertain situation caused a lot of anxiety in both vendors and customers. We were selling more indica than sativa for the first time. Several vendors and customers wore masks and gloves inside the trap house.

I wondered which neighborhoods were safer: the poorer African American neighborhoods where we sold our weed or the affluent White neighborhoods mostly in the northwest quadrant of the city? I decided that the lower-income Black neighborhoods were safer because the residents were, in many cases, marginalized compared to the well-traveled Caucasians. Black folk hung out with their own and as such, had less exposure to that virus sweeping the world.

Working with Diego became stressful since, from the start of the shift to the finish of it, he was on edge. He suffered, by his own admission, from a mild case of obsessive-compulsive disorder. Now that the virus was the sole focus of the news cycle, it ramped up the very anxiety his pot smoking aimed to curb.

Suddenly, my performance was under strict scrutiny. "Sam, don't hold the money pouch so high when you're making change. We can't let anybody see it."

"Stop fist-bumping customers after a sale." I realized that it was no longer business as usual. For the first time, I felt pressure at the job.

A week after the city shut down, Marley was beaten and robbed at gunpoint while walking to his car at the end of his shift. He lost his bankroll and his entire stash. More frightening was that he spent an evening at a hospital where coronavirus patients were on ventilators.

Returning home late from work, I found Johnny, Cortez, and Caleb together waiting for me.

"We need to figure out a house strategy for what's going on," Johnny said. "All of us are still on the payroll, though me and Caleb will be working remotely from home. Cortez still has to show up at the studio. Your trap house exposure has us concerned."

"What's the right thing to do?" I asked.

"I don't know," said Cortez. "How vulnerable are you?"

"Given that we all know next to nothing about this virus, I have no idea."

Caleb stared at me but said nothing. Probably at Johnny's request.

"Given that the district still has under three hundred reported cases and that most of the confirmed cases seem to be highly placed government workers, it seems that we still have time before it becomes a city-wide epidemic," said Johnny.

"Yeah, but Black folk work in grocery stores, go to church on Sunday, ride Metro and buses," Cortez said. "It might not be long till it breaks out in my community."

"What are you thinking?" I asked.

"How are you set for cash?" Johnny asked.

"I have enough money to make rent at the end of the month. After that, I have enough to last a few weeks even if unemployment is denied."

"We discussed it and we can all lend you money if you need it," said Caleb.

"Do you guys want me to quit?"

"Not exactly," said Johnny. "Given that our coming weeks are going to be spent in quarantine, we have a proposition for you. We know that Diego gives you a big discount when you buy weed from him. We'll help cover your rent. In exchange, you spend the rest of your time there taking your wages in weed and supplying all of us with it."

"That's good for me," I said. "I'd rather not just run out on Diego."

Reaching into my shirt pocket, I pulled out a joint I brought home from work, lit it up, and passed it around.

"It's good to have family when you're weathering a crisis," Cortez said.

Caleb handed me a bag. "I was at Goodwill and I bought you a present."

I opened up the bag and found an ice bucket inside. "It will save you steps from walking downstairs to the refrigerator," he said.

"Maybe you should buy me a chamber pot, too. This way, I won't have to walk downstairs to piss either."

"How much do they cost?" he asked.

"Dude, I'm kidding. I can piss out the window."

"Okay," he said.

"Caleb, this seems like some chastisement from God," I said. "What do you think the cosmic significance of it is all about?"

"I don't know," he said. "I haven't seen anything like this since the movie *Independence Day*. I can understand it in an Old Testament context, but in relation to the love and mercy of Christ, I just don't know."

"It's funny, though," I said. "Throughout all this drama, we're still no closer to a proper bead on divinity."

"I think we need to talk about it going forward," he said, "if only to find some meaning to it that we can both agree on."

Turning back to Johnny, I said, "What about Tasha and Sookie? How is our self-quarantine going to affect your relationships with your women? After all, they're both nurses and work at a hospital where there's coronavirus patients."

That question caused them each to pause as they considered both their safety and their loins.

"We need to think about this," said Cortez. "Chances are if one of us gets it here, we'll all get it."

Before the joint was finished, I had a bling on my cell phone. It was a text from Shayla. "If you can, please see my broadcast tonight. You might find it interesting."

We all walked to the TV and turned to her channel. What she referred to did not occur till the end. It was a monologue.

"As many of you might have heard, I was offered a big contract with *CNN* to have my own nightly broadcast. It was a lucrative contract that I couldn't resist, until now. I've decided to stay right here at this post because this station, this town, this community is my home. It's what I truly love and where I belong. So, I'm not going anywhere. I see how many people are suffering as a result of this crisis, especially the waiters, cooks, bartenders, busboys, managers, and hostesses in the city's restaurants and bars. It's a focal point of our city's culture."

"There's a fund out there called the "Restaurant Workers Fund." Here is how it works. You buy a gift certificate from participating places around town. It's good for takeout orders which many places are still honoring. Part of the fund will support hospitality industry workers who've been thrown out of work. I'll be promoting it going forward. In addition, today, I pledged fifty thousand dollars of my own money to the cause. I urge the residents of the District, Maryland, and Virginia to do the same."

"Never saw that coming," I stated.

"Damn, Sam, and you say it ain't love," Cortez said.

The Washington Post did a story on her the next day. It even mentioned her reputation as a dining room terror. I laughed when I read it. Perhaps this was restitution for her awful behavior.

CHAPTER 20

The White girl at our trap-house table had a tattoo on her breastbone. Her V-neck shirt revealed it. "I can't go on, I go on."

She slipped a cartridge up her sleeve from our table. Diego saw her. "Give it back," he shouted. "I saw you steal that cartridge. Give it back or I'll call security."

He didn't have to call security. They heard his accusation. They surrounded her. She became enraged and started screaming at Diego, calling him a liar. Everything stopped in the room. All eyes were upon her. She got so animated that in a fit of rage, she threw her hands in the air and in doing so, the cartridge flew out of her sleeve and fell onto the floor. Security escorted her out the door.

Ten minutes later, a young African American man got into an argument with E. "Disrespect me, motherfucker. I'll let you know just who I am, bitch."

"What the fuck are you talking about? I don't even know you," E replied.

"You'll know me when I kick your fucking ass," he said.

Security surrounded him and told him to leave. But then he started arguing with them, too. But Zeus was too big to fuck with and after screaming out his defense, the guy finally left the room. Stress was showing. Fear and chaos due to COVID-19 was causing people to lose their minds.

Diego and I were hyper-alert to any coronavirus cough in the room. Of course, that was ridiculous, given that everyone was smoking pot and hacking from tremendous hits. Deciding which cough was from smoke and which was from the virus was impossible.

A thin young man entered the trap house. He was about 30 years old and perhaps from India. He whispered to me, "I don't know if I should be paranoid, but I went looking for this address and there are five cop cars outside. A cop looked at me and said, 'What you're looking for is over there,' he said, pointing to this house."

I admit I got a little nervous at that remark. It turned out that there was a shooting across the street. Police were searching for a suspect. Time went by and no cops entered the trap house. Perhaps they understood that letting individuals get high during this epidemic made their jobs easier. Regardless, when the show was over, there was still a cop car out front. We slipped out the back door with the duffel bags, the table and the banner.

As the days went by, we got busier and busier. Each shift was a mad rush we could barely keep up with. There were often six people at our table touching the Middleman jars, handling the cartridges and the other products we sold. Two nights in a row, we sold over $5,000 dollars. Diego tipped me accordingly. I was now making way more money than I ever did at Tadich.

I took my pay from Diego in weed. Since he charged me half of what his customers paid, I soon had a large stash that Cortez, Johnny and Caleb were grateful for. Predictions were that the peak of the coronavirus in DC was not going to occur for ten weeks or more. In the marijuana department, though, we were set. I resumed taking my wages in cash.

I didn't want to overreact but it was now obvious that it was time to stop. In one night, over 250 customers showed up during a trap house shift.

"Diego, I need to step away from the trap house for now."

"Fuck! We dodged cops and robbers!" he responded. "Never thought a virus would shut us down."

But it did. To remain inside those dens was unfair to my housemates. After working there for several weeks, I quit. I think Diego was relieved that it was my idea. He didn't want to throw me out of a job. But the night I quit, so did he. My unemployment check arrived in my bank account the next day.

Now, the Fourth Estate was under lockdown with an uncertain future. We were hostages to an unknown fate. Life as we knew it stopped. The virus death toll rose across America. Despite masks and social distancing, DC was becoming an American hot spot. It all seemed like a giant yank on the American dog chain. And here's what was worse: the president, who was in charge of the American response, was incompetent and lied obsessively about it. That, more than any other part of the predicament, unnerved me.

> New virus means new rules
> Who lives?
> Who dies?
> Who's ruined?
> Who thrives?
> How safe are the people you love?
> How paranoid should you be?
> How does one gracefully dance
> Around this nemesis
> Without letting it pollute you?

Sometimes, in my anxiety, I reached for my cell phone for breaking news, for insight, for comfort. But all the news was bad. Pundits and politicos, stumbling forward through this predicament, were unable to assuage the worried American soul.

Eventually, I figured out that to survive the pandemic emotionally intact, I had to put myself on a news diet. It was making me crazy and the anxiety it caused was making me fat from overeating.

I stopped posting on *Facebook* and *Instagram*. It was all an exercise in futility. Not only that, my posts, trumpeting self-righteous, high-horse opinions, were making me seem full of shit, even to myself. I put all my energy into literary work and by ignoring hapless emerging issues, I calmed down.

Tadich was gone. The trap house was gone. Shayla was gone. The Veil was gone. Only the poem remained. Comfort came solely at my desk. For an introvert like me, self-quarantine was a literary gift. It felt like retirement. Suddenly, without a job or responsibilities, my progress on "A Firm State of Heart" blossomed.

> Happy the man
> And happy alone
> Is he who calls
> His day his own.

Tomorrow, the fates might infect me with fever, but today was mine. And just in case I caught the virus and croaked, I wanted as much of my poem finished as possible. Locked down and in limbo, I created a schedule. Reading, writing, smoking and channeling were the component parts of a good, socially isolated COVID-19 day.

Traveling on Metro seemed risky. Fortunately, everything I needed—groceries, pharmacies and liquor stores—were within walking distance. My new routine included a long walk each day. I managed to get at least 10,000 steps since that was what I'd earn in a typical restaurant shift. On some afternoons, I was able to walk right down the middle of Pennsylvania Avenue because it was empty of cars.

Taking advantage of the empty streets, the public works department repaved roads all over Capitol Hill. They also planted flowers and trees and covered them with manure. As I walked by, the smell filled my nostrils. I was happy to recognize it since I read that the loss of smell was one of the first symptoms of the coronavirus.

The playgrounds and the schools were closed. The newspaper racks were empty. Libraries and bookstores were shuttered. But the neighborhood book boxes were full as people with time on their hands purged their libraries and offered them free to anyone walking by.

Each day, before my afternoon walks, I made sure that my backpack was stocked with alcohol wipes, rubber gloves and a face mask which I wore when entering stores. When walking the streets, I was careful to keep six feet away from other pedestrians.

I hiked to the Lincoln Memorial. The next day I hiked to the canal in Georgetown. The day after that, down the riverwalk along the Anacostia River to the Navy Yard. Then I walked up the Anacostia River to RFK Stadium and Kingman Island. That day was my shortest walk and my wettest, too. The weather application on my phone, the one I relied on, got the forecast wrong. Walking into the house with rain-soaked clothes, I came upon Johnny on his computer at the dining room table.

"Don't you believe in umbrellas?" he said.

"I checked the weather app on my phone before I left. No rain was in the forecast," I said. "It's the second time this week the forecast was wrong."

"That's because there are fewer aircraft flying," Johnny said. "Jets monitor storms along their flight path and send that info back to a computer that weather apps rely on. With fewer flights, there's less information."

"I never would have thought of that," I said.

"How could you? Everything is upended. You can watch the news 24 hours a day and still not get the necessary information."

"I can't watch too much of it. It's too depressing."

"I keep thinking about a professor I had at Rutgers," Johnny said. "Dr. Steiner liked to talk about the guardian of the gene pool. He described it as a detached godhead, the likes of which you might see in ancient religions."

"And what does the guardian of the gene pool do?"

"It fucks with mankind to remind him that he is not the crown of creation."

"I almost wish I would get sick with it already and be done with it. At least I wouldn't be as anxious."

"Not me," Johnny said, "and don't forget Cortez is a diabetic. If he catches it, it might kill him."

As a poet, I'm as interested in myth as I am in fact. A deeper understanding of this pandemic was what I went searching for. I found hints from ancient literature. Biblical authors and the ancient Greek poets wrote about it. Most attributed the epidemics to the wrath of God.

Yahweh sent ten plagues upon Egypt for Pharaoh's refusal to free his Hebrew slaves. In Homer's first book, *The Iliad*, plague breaks out in the Greek camp outside the gates of Troy. "Apollo drove foul pestilence after Agamemnon, their king, dishonored Chryses, priest of Apollo."

In Sophocles' play, *Oedipus Rex*, the king, Oedipus, struggles to find the source of the plague accosting Thebes. Turns out that it's his sins that are responsible for it. The Bible, in the Book of Revelations, 16:17, it's written that the plague is God's way of punishing sinners allied with the Antichrist.

But in Homer's second book, *The Odyssey*, Zeus pushes back. "Humans always blame the Gods for their suffering. And yet they suffer pain beyond their reckoning as a result of their own folly."

During the Peloponnesian War, which pitted Athens against Sparta in the fourth century BC, 75,000 thousand people died in Athens when a plague devastated that city. It killed one of their best men, too—Pericles.

In 1894, scientists isolated the bacterium *Yersinia*. The microbe, transmitted through fleas and rodents, was a major source of plague in Europe. Since then, the matter has been assigned to the realm of science. But that wasn't enough for me. True, there's a science and an etymology to the virus. But the empirical meaning of it was what fascinated me.

It's certainly true that you don't know what you don't know. But as a poet interested in the mythological realm of current events, I kept looking for some intelligent design governing the evil outbreak sweeping the globe. The conventional wisdom was too conventional to satisfy my gnostic curiosity.

I wanted a deeper response, a more cosmic understanding of why it chose to upend the world at this specific time. Should I blame it on the harsh god Yahweh? The devil? Poltergeists? Shiva?

> Hey, COVID,
> Slip me some time
> Wait until
> A Firm State of Heart
> Is complete.
> Until then
> Hang out, be cool.

CHAPTER 21

Cortez called up to my room. "Hey, Sam, come on down, man. There's something you need to see."

"Be right down," I shouted.

I walked downstairs and found him watching the news. There on the screen was a video from a cell phone camera. It showed three policemen holding down an African American man on the sidewalk. One cop had his knee on the man's neck, who was flat on the ground. He was calling out in a muffled voice, "I can't breathe." He uttered it a dozen times.

I recognized the uniforms right away. They were Minneapolis cops. The scene was two miles from where I grew up. "Holy shit. I know that store. It's on Chicago Avenue," I said.

I sat and watched the coverage with Cortez and was embarrassed by what I saw. "That's not the Minneapolis I grew up in," I said.

"Obviously, it is," Cortez said.

In the liberal neighborhood I grew up in, African American moms married Caucasian dads and African American dads married Caucasian moms. Their mixed-race children were accepted as any other. There were gay couples with children. There were transgender children we grew up with whose secrets we kept at school.

I accepted this open attitude as if it were dominant in American culture. But obviously, it wasn't. Most of the Minneapolis police force lived in the suburbs and lawed over communities of color.

The cop's knee, which turned out to be a deadly weapon, came as no surprise to Cortez. "Damn, this shit is never-ending and it just wears you down," Cortez said. "The cops murdered him in front of witnesses. The brothers are going to light up your city like a Roman candle."

He was right. The next few days, in quarantine, we huddled around the TV and watched as rioters burned down the Minneapolis Third Precinct police station, a post office and whole city blocks. Then, it spread into a nationwide protest with similar results in cities all over America.

Cortez's attitude was clear. "No justice, no peace," he said. "White folk should consider themselves lucky. Black people are only calling for equality, not revenge."

The situation was exacerbated by the economic shutdown and the pandemic. Such callous disregard for human life made me angry, too. That anger morphed into depression, especially when Caleb hit me with this barb. "It comes as no surprise to me that this act came from a state that has a governor, two U.S. senators, a mayor and a city council who are all Democrats," he said.

When I moved to Minneapolis as a thirteen-year-old, I recognized the passive-aggressive nature of Minnesota culture. People pretend they're not fucking with you by acting indifferent or giving you the silent treatment. It was a subtle form of head-tripping.

The look on the cop's face—his knee on George Floyd's throat and his hand in his pocket for over nine minutes—is one of indifference, as if nothing was wrong at all. Soon, George Floyd was dead.

There was no defending the event. It was caught by a cell phone camera and it was bad. The triple whammy that was accosting America—Covid-19, recession and George Floyd's death—sparked a literary sense of urgency. My nightly channels consumed more time, more scotch, more weed.

One afternoon, I walked to the White House to check out the demonstrations in Lafayette Park across the street. The White House had a new security barrier surrounding it on all four sides. At last, Trump built his wall. Unfortunately, it was to keep out Americans. A line of National Guardsmen in full riot gear were guarding it. Fortunately, the violence of the previous days had passed.

I listened to a speaker who led the chant "Black Lives Matter" to the racially mixed crowd. The speaker, an African American woman, was from a local chapter of the NAACP. She spoke eloquently. But her remarks were meant for her people and not for White folks like me. She never invited me to get on board.

I liked the sense of community promoted at the demonstration. Individuals were handing out bottles of water, hand sanitizer and masks to any protesters who showed up at the White House without them. It was that generous sentiment I hoped would prevail. Here's another insight I gleaned from it.

> Millennials
> We're being called upon to
> Take responsibility for America.
> It's our turn.

I felt this enormous pressure to be smarter and more sensitive, a conduit for better reception from the astral plane in order to better understand emerging issues. New values and ideals were coming. I wanted to be one of those progressive voices that articulated them.

It was late afternoon when I marched back up Capitol Hill. Most of the walk was with my head down, depressed. Discovering the meaning in all that was happening is a poet's job. But the effort to divine and articulate the dynamics of it all was beyond me.

When I passed an Eastern Market bar, Tunnicliff's Tavern, I realized I hadn't eaten all day. The place was closed except for carryout. I ordered a steak sandwich from the bartender and waited for its preparation outside under its covered patio. Taking out a book, I started to read.

That was when I noticed her. She was waiting for a to-go order, too. She sat right in front of me about six feet away. Today's copy of *The Washington Post* was beside her on the bench. She had the front-page section in her hands. The sports page was beside her. I considered reaching for it. But I laughed when I realized there weren't any professional sporting events going on anywhere in the world.

The newspaper hid her face. When she turned the page and folded it over, I saw a headline facing me. It was an article about the state of Mississippi removing the Confederate symbol from the state's flag. Beside it was another story about the dismantling of the John C. Calhoun statue from its perch above Marion Square in the city of Charleston, South Carolina. The slaver's 12-foot bronze statue lorded over the city for 124 years. The former congressman and vice president promoted slavery in the Antebellum South. People cheered when it finally came down after a day-long effort by the department of public works.

The city of Minneapolis was way ahead of them. In 2018, the city changed the name of its largest lake from Lake Calhoun to *Bde Maka Ska,* which means "White Earth Lake." It's the original name the Ojibway gave it. It received a share of ridicule, mostly because no one could remember the name or pronounce it. But the lake's name was changed to repudiate Calhoun's stand on slavery. It reminded me that despite what Caleb said, Minneapolis is a progressive community to be proud of.

The sight of the two newspaper headlines gave me hope that something good might come from Floyd's death and the destruction of the Minneapolis Lake Street corridor.

I was startled when I recognized the hands holding the newspaper. She was unrecognizable at first, hiding behind a face mask and reading glasses. But when she moved her hands to turn to the next page, I noticed the heart tattoo on her wrist.

I reached for a pen. On the last page of my book, a blank page, I wrote the following:

> In the midst of a plague
> And cities aflame
> I went searching for a poem
> And instead found a woman
> Who might bolster my resolve
> In the face of humiliating circumstances.
> I went looking for a heart
> And found it on her wrist
> Its color, green
> Like my healing.
> In anticipation
> Of this intimate encounter
> I hope to find
> A Firm State of Heart.

I lifted my eyes, pulled down my mask and spoke. "Excuse me, but whenever I see an attractive woman three-times, I sense it might be fate so I always like to introduce myself."

She listened to my words and put down the paper. "Where have you seen me before?"

"On Metro, late one Friday night about three months ago. You were all dressed up in blue except for your eyes, they were red."

"Oh, that night." She shook her head as if trying to break free from its memory.

"The second time was at a trap house up on Georgia Avenue. You bought a bag of weed from Young Mo. You came in and out before I could say hello. And now, the third time, right here."

A pretty woman like her must be subject to a dozen male ploys each week. She studied me and remained silent.

"But there's more," I said. I reached down and unzipped my

backpack. I pulled out her water bottle.

"My mother gave me that," she said. "I've been looking everywhere for it."

"You forgot it on Metro that night."

From another zipper compartment, I pulled out an alcohol wipe and wiped the bottle down as if it were our very own child. She watched me carefully. I handed it to her.

"Hello, my name is Samuel."

When she heard my name, she knew. Vickie greased it.

She pulled down her mask. "Hello, my name is Dahlia."

I reached out my hand. She did, too. We pantomimed the motion of a handshake for fear of infecting each other.

I always hoped I'd see her again. But in my mind's eye, I saw it happening differently than this. Then, the sun came out from behind a cloud. I had a big grin on my face and I started to laugh. It was contagious. I saw her dimples.

"What's so funny?" she asked.

"Oh, just life."

The End

About the Author

Bob Gilbert grew up in Jackson, New Jersey. After finishing his education at American University, he worked in Washington, DC, for a variety of government institutions, including the Department of Housing and Urban Development, the Close-Up Foundation and the Woodrow Wilson International Center for Scholars. In 1984, he moved to Minnesota, where he worked as a newspaper reporter. He also led backpacking trips for the Sierra Club to the mountain ranges of the Far West, raised three children and coached soccer. In 2011, he returned to Washington, DC, and started publishing books. His titles include *Mintwood Place*, *The Shady Elders of Zion* and *Green Goes Forth*. His fourth novel, *A Firm State of Heart*, is his third DC novel. He currently lives on Capitol Hill with his partner, Alexa Posny.

www.ingramcontent.com/pod-product-compliance
Lightning Source LLC
Chambersburg PA
CBHW031057020726
47495CB00007B/1923